Plod on, Sleepless Giant

By M. P. McVey

Columbus, Ohio USA

Plod On, Sleepless Giant by MP McVey

Mount Air Publishing
Columbus, Ohio 43235, USA
www.MountAirPublishing.com

Print Book

ISBN-10: 0986337102

ISBN-13: 978-0-9863371-0-9

eBook

ISBN-13: 978-0-9863371-1-6

CREDITS:

The animal fonts are courtesy of Alan Carr freeware license, created in 1993 http://www.fontspace.com/alan-carr/animals

Cover drawings courtesy of Joe Reisinger. The cover depicts the Columbus skyline, showing the earth' surface below with the Firbolg and Temelephas and the minikin in the background

For my family

Acknowledgements

There are a lot of people that I could never have finished this book without. First off is my mom, Barbara Streets, who read more incarnations of *Plod On, Sleepless Giant* than I would like to admit exist, and my dad, John D. McVey, for his unrelenting support. I definitely need to thank Joe Reisinger for all of his great input and even greater friendship, and Linda Webb Hutchison for both editing my manuscript and for her unparalleled guidance. I'd also like to thank the rest of my friends and family for their endless support. And finally, I would like to thank Bob and Kristi Jendry of Mount Air Publishing for taking a chance on a little book about a sleepless giant.

Prologue

The center of Earth shook and rumbled with the sounds of creaking wood and grinding metal, tumbling through the dark. The din swept through caverns, accompanied by the boom, boom, boom of steady, heavy steps. It would have driven any man crazy, this racket that crept through the darkness, but it was comforting to the one who *had* to listen. It was a noise he had always known, a sound that was born with him. He was the reason for the noise.

For all time he had walked his circle; his large, gray feet beating a pattern into the dirt. Round and round he went, his weight pushing the large, wooden wheel to which he was bound. He groaned from time to time ... long, soulful bellows from his wrinkled trunk.

His ancient head swayed with the thudding beat of his steps, his long immortal ears hanging tiredly at his sides. He would walk until the end of time. He didn't want to, but he was compelled to. It was his purpose ... and without purpose, what would be left?

So he walked.

He could feel their eyes upon him, those that watched him, those that kept him in this existence ... those who gave him purpose. Their stares penetrated the thick hide of his neck, burrowed into his spine and peeked in to his brain, listening in on his every thought. That's how they watched him, how they knew when he was unhappy.

They were in his mind every second of forever, and he came to expect their presence there. After a while he lost track of his Watchers all together, as if they were just another part of him. Life would not have been the same without them.

The Watchers always knew that, sooner or later, the great elephant called Temelephas would work through whatever unhappiness it was that settled in his large heart. After all, he had been walking since the beginning of everything and knew of nothing to which he could compare his sorrow.

Walk, walk, walk, through the darkness he would stomp; his feet pounding his life into the earth. Around he went, his sweaty, tangled hair flowing down around his neck. "Round and round she goes, where she stops … nobody knows."

1

Columbus was a cruel and unrelenting city that winter. Chaotic winds ravaged the tall buildings that had sprung up like giant cornstalks of concrete and glass. The shrill cry of the burrowing wind rang out, deafening those who jockeyed the crowded streets below. Edward Crosby was among that frozen herd, those poor victims of winter's blast. They shivered and rocked from its deep, biting cold, moving slowly about like closely packed cattle.

Edward's floppy, brown hair twirled about in the wintry cyclone; though it made little difference, his hair having always been as well-behaved as a gas fed fire. He was what one would consider *nerdy* in his tall, slim frame. His face was long and adorned with glasses. Dark plastic frames that were determined to slide down his nose, all so he could slide them back up again.

His had a goofy, self-satisfied smile; even then, his heart drumming at a quickened pace. One might wonder the reason for such jovial behavior in a metropolis of bitter wind. His reason was the same as many … love. In three agonizingly long weeks he would marry the love of his life.

With his lips were pursed in a whistle, he stepped sturdily with pride. He seemed to glow with utter joy, feeling no effect from the wicked jabs of Jack Frost. All those miserable nomads, frozen around him, seemed to detest him for his happiness, though he knew their faces could have simply been contorted from the biting, cold wind.

Edward moved skillfully through the horde, weaving through them in an intricate pattern of S curves and end runs. He glanced at his watch absentmindedly, not *truly* worried about being late, but still a slave to the minute hand. He worked for the law firm of Ross & Weinstein, another drone lawyer in a swarm of lawyers that buzzed about the office.

When Edward left for lunch that day, he had left behind a pile of manila folders in the inbox that lived on his desk. It was a very impressive stack when he had left, but Edward was sure that the slight mountain had grown in the last hour. He had been eyeing it all morning long, as if watching a small volcano that grumbled and smoked, beckoning him. He would have to play the part of the sacrificial virgin soon, sadly, throwing himself into its fiery abyss.

He worked in the corporate law section, mostly dealing with mergers, and Edward hoped what waited for him were only routine requests from senior partners to review contracts that had already drafted by other poor souls in law firms across town. Who, though, could really be sure of what lurked deep in those beige depths? He rarely ever reached the basement of that horrendous invention called the inbox.

Maybe some conniving, lazy co-worker had dumped their unwanted workload on him. Leaving it right in that box where it laid in wait, like a venomous snake ready to strike. He was sure there was a personal spot in hell reserved for the inventor of the inbox.

This wasn't what Edward had imagined for his future—back when he was in school, neck deep in law books. It had been seven years of long nights with his nose to the grindstone as the fun of college passed him by. He had always imagined himself as a public defender—like in all those television shows—fighting for justice, one wrongfully accused defendant at a time. He even had his own theme song that got him through all those midnight study sessions, "I Fought the Law and the Law Won." Of course, when he hummed it to himself it was "I fought the law and *I* won."

But now he was thirty-two years old and he had learned that life was less black and white and more nuanced by shades of gray. It was a sad realization, learning that wrongfully accused men were rarer than four leaf clovers, and that the path to justice was only lined with rapists, robbers, and wife-beaters. That was when he went corporate and kissed his childish theme song goodbye.

Corporate law had some perks, though; one being long lunches, affording him more time with his Lily. They always met at the same place, a small family owned diner named Tommy's. Not being gastronomically adventurous, they always ordered the same thing. He always had the Franklinton burger and she the grilled chicken Caesar salad.

It was a respected, neighborhood restaurant, packed with familiar faces, gently chattering the lunch hour away. The food was good and, surprisingly, was outdone by the service. The waitresses would dance with ease between tables and booths; flashing smiles so bright that they were reminiscent of paper lanterns, lit up and floating off and away.

Edward and Lily would sit comfortably amongst it all, chatting quietly as if telling secrets. She would lay her warm eyes upon him; smiling, showering him with adoration. They laughed easily, especially when mushrooms would slide out from his burger and onto his shirt—an accident which was more routine than chance.

That was why Edward smiled, memories of the

lunch he had just left and the woman he kissed passionately in the diner's parking lot. He watched her drive off before beginning his march back to the office—against the wind. His phone rang and shook about in his coat pocket as he thought of Lily; his cold hand swept it up.

"Hello," he said with a knowing smile.

"I miss you," Lily's sweet voice chimed. Edward's smile stretched further across his red face.

"Hey ... I miss you too."

"This could prove to be a problem," she said in a quasi-serious tone.

"What could?"

"Missing you this much. I never thought I could miss anyone as much as I find myself missing you every day."

"That *could* be a problem, especially since we just left each other," he said with a short chuckle. "I guess this means you're stuck with me."

"I hope so," she purred in his ear. "I can't imagine a world without you, without your crooked smile and the way you shriek at the sight of a spider."

"Only the big ones," he reminded her, smiling still.

"Promise you'll never leave me."

"I promise," he said solemnly.

"Say it."

"I *promise* I'll never leave you," slowly stressing each word back to her.

"Oh, fate would be too cruel if it were to separate us," she said in a theatrical tone, recalling all of the skills she had acquired in her high school drama class.

"The world would never be *that* cruel," he said.

Lily and Edward seemed meant to be together. Certainly, in their minds they believed it, and in their hearts that conviction lived, growing like a chrysalis. Some of their family—jaded by love's double edged sword—warned them against such strong devotion. "Hearts can be fickle," they would say. "They are easily swayed."

The two of them never took those warnings to heart. Warnings like those were meant for others—not them. They simply shrugged them off and continued to love one another completely as they planned to do for the rest of their days. Two souls bound together for all time.

They were playful with it, exemplifying the cliché that it was them against the world, marching hand in hand. What an absurd idea, the world making an enemy of anyone! This peaceful rock that turns and rumbles beneath our feet cares not about enemies or friends or even lovers.

They didn't need to worry themselves with the world, however, it meant them no harm. But as it were, the *cosmos* was against them. And the cosmos can be a very powerful enemy.

And the universe kept growing and shifting, as ever changing as it had always been. Stars being born as others flamed out; great dust clouds moving through the ether as black holes devour light like starving beasts on a dark savanna. The cosmos was bubbling over with activity, as it always had over the millennia. Time pressed on and happenings came to pass, mutually as easy and complex as the pollination of a flower.

A chain reaction had begun that would forever change the lives of those two lovers. The universe had come to a crossroads and it was left to decide which road it would take. Perhaps it would drive on through, allow them to continue unscathed, or maybe it would take a turn for better or worse. Right or left, up or down, it made no difference to the cosmos. It all came down to chance.

Joyce had just pulled into the parking lot of a department store—one of the many, identical chains that litter the country. She barked into her phone as she maneuvered the car, her infant son Franklin squirming in his fastened car seat behind her. He struggled and twisted to free himself from the strong straps, but to no avail. His blond mop of a head hung in despair.

"No," Joyce screamed into her lawyer's ear via her cell phone. "He can't do this." Franklin sighed heavily and released a large spit-bubble that exploded and dribbled down his dimpled chin. "I can't believe he would fight me on this. I'm Franklin's mother, he stays with me!"

Joyce leapt from her seat, slamming the door in her wake. She stomped around the car—not straining to hide her fury—like a wildebeest readying to charge a defenseless bullfrog. She yanked the rear door open as she continued to yell, her voice echoing with its unbridled war cry.

Joyce unbuckled Franklin from his car-seat—much to his delight—and turned her back to him. It was for only a second that she had her eyes off of him, *only a second*—she'd later swear. And that was all it took. The window had opened … and life decided to turn.

She gripped her phone, knuckles white, as she continued to scream, all while daydreaming of dashing the little device against the blacktop. Franklin slipped away from her distracted gaze in that moment, and crawled off in that slow, baby-like fashion. The Universe can be funny like that, always offering little twists and turns, just waiting for life to find them.

🐘

She was stark raving mad by the time the police arrived. The parking lot had already become an annoying congregation of looky-loos, all milling about. Some concerned shoppers had actually tried to locate the missing baby, but with no luck. All the comforting words in the world could not quiet the distraught mother, they only drove her further into hysteria.

No one seemed to understand the pain Joyce felt, the guilt that she clung to for turning her back on her own son. *It was only a second,* she had told them all, but she began to doubt it herself. While she had let her fury grow for the coming custody battle, Joyce had let the one thing she loved most slip away from her.

The police would do all they could, but it offered little hope for Joyce. The day was only getting older and time was crucial. Even with the growing group of vigilant strangers aiding in the search, the likelihood of finding Franklin was fading with each passing second. There is nothing comparable to the pain of a mother who has lost her young.

In another realm, separated from Earth by dark matter and vast stretches of space, beyond the visible stars … a conversation was being held. The speakers swam about in a brilliant light as if made of smoke. They spoke softly to one another in low, near harmonic tones.

"How is Temelephas?" Tyriano asked in his ancient, low vibrato. His old, vaguely human figure stood tall, yet frail, over the younger being beside him that watched his mentor intensely. Tyriano's head sprouted feathers where hair would have naturally been found, his being the color of a stormy, ocean sky. They were long and fell about his face as if they were branches from a willow tree.

His face was pale purple in hue—wrinkled from centuries of smiles and frowns—with bright red stones for eyes that even still were sharp. His mouth, always a bit crooked, was surrounded by a similar gray beard of finer feathers. He appeared sleepy these days, getting closer to the verge of the greatest sleep of all.

The younger being had the same red eyes, but his seemed to smolder more. His skin was the same color, but it was smooth like glass and had rosy patches in the cheeks. His head feathers were a bright blue and plumed up, styled in the fashion of the youth of his kind and time.

"He seems fine," the younger one, Dezriak, answered. His voice was crisp and youthful and he tucked his hands behind his back, mimicking his teacher. "He seems a bit lonely, though."

"Well ... aren't we all?" Tyriano asked rhetorically, peering pass the stars. "Aren't we all?" he echoed. He looked through the light years and gazed upon the great elephant, Temelephas who walked in his unending circle with his head hanging low.

His eyes appeared vacant to Tyriano, or dull at best. But the old Watcher knew that such a thing as unhappiness was impossible for the beast. "He does not know loneliness. It is something that slips pass him as easily as a breeze would. He is oblivious to emotion."

"How can that be?" Dezriak questioned, as all young beings would.

"Because that is how he was built. He was made to be numb, to be naïve to the time that moves over him ... He has the memory of a goldfish." Tyriano's voice echoed between the stars and the apprentice stood in awe of his teacher's knowledge.

"Fascinating," said Dezriak, though Tyriano knew this response didn't mean the youngster understood.

Indeed, none of what Tyriano had said was true. Temelephas was more knowing of this than Tyriano or any of the Watchers that came before him could ever fathom. It was his memories that haunted him and the pain of those memories that drove needles into his heart. He remembered his very first memory, his favorite by far ... simply because it *was* his first. Tyriano should remember it as well, since he was there. It was the first time the two had met ...

Life before that time had been a blur for the elephant. Every few minutes or so his mind would be wiped clean of all memories, and his realization of being would appear anew once more. It was a miserable existence, living that way; trapped in an endless string of singular moments. Whatever engulfed his mind in those minutes would be a lifetime to him.

If he happened to be hungry in that moment, it was an empty, painful life of starvation. If he happened to stub his big toe, it was simply agonizing, the pain so new and fresh to him each time. And the moments he was completely alone were the saddest of all—filled with terror ... alone in the dark.

In such a life as Temelephas', there were more sad and painful moments than there were happy ones. He existed in abusive, small glimpses of an actual life. But on the day of his first clear memory, it was the booming voice of another teacher that somehow flipped a switch in his mind, compelling him to remember.

"He feels nothing," Tyriano's teacher had told him then. "That was how the Maker designed him ... to feel nothing, to know nothing, to remember nothing ... he isn't really alive at all."

"So, he has no memories, Uncle?" Tyriano had asked.

"None-what-so-ever."

"Fascinating," Tyriano had said, just as his own student would over a millennia later. Temelephas had heard it all and his small, goldfish-sized mind spun crazily with thought. No memories, *he thought to himself,* no memories? How can that be? I am alive; I know that because I breathe. I can feel; I know that because my feet are sore. I *am* real. How can I not remember?

That was when everything changed for the giant elephant, his mind determined to remember everything possible. He forced his little brain to store every little memory, painting the inside of his skull with all he heard and saw. It caused him great pain to accomplish this, but he found that it slowly began to work and the pain subsided. He remembered everything from that day forward.

As he walked in his circle—which he quickly decided was monotonous, Temelephas worked his mind to store more new knowledge. That was when he first noticed those that fed and washed him. They were so peculiar to him, so different from the larger ones that merely stood guard over him. He began to study them, anxious to learn all he could about these new creatures.

They were very short—those that took care of him—far shorter than Tyriano's kind. Their faces were tiny and held clear blue eyes that reflected the fires that glowed around them. Shaggy hair of crimson fell around their faces in wavy curls. They referred to themselves as Minikins, and they dwelled in the caverns of the earth's core, much as Temelephas had.

Minikins would enter Temelephas' hollow at random times, wheeling a large cauldron before them. They would stir the smelly gruel it held continually, trying to thin it out a bit, before ladling it up and extending it to the elephant's eager mouth. It tasted awful, but what choice did Temelephas really have but to swallow the swill. At the very least, it would fill his empty stomach.

The Minikins would speak openly to him as they spoon fed the monstrous beast—not knowing that he was slowly understanding and remembering their words. That was how he learned all he knew about the center of the earth, from one sided conversations with Minikins.

One time, upon hearing a Minikin talking to Temelephas, Tyriano chuckled lightly. "He cannot understand a single word you say," he chanted gently.

"Why is that?" the Minikin asked in a squeaky voice.

"Because he was not made to. He was made only to slowly walk, nothing more. To turn and turn his heavy wheel, to spin the earth like a top till the end of days. Never to stop."

"What would happen if he did stop?"

"Oh, we will never know, because he never will. Nothing

can stop him, since he is so very big," Tyriano proffered in his eloquent voice as he bent to meet the Minikin's eye. "And nothing can make him want to stop, because he can never want."

Temelephas cried softly then, silently, as little tears ran the labyrinth of his cracked, gray face. It had been his first experience with sorrow, and it had hit him hard. His heart sank and his head wallowed about clumsily. He had no idea what the little drops were that fled from his eyes, but he knew he did not like them.

It began that day, a defiant desire to stop the walk. He so desperately wanted to stop, if just to see if he could … to see if he had the strength to break the chains that bound him to his wheel. He tried to build himself up to it, but found himself falling away from such a rebellious act. It was not the consequences that kept him from trying. The truth … he decided, would kill him.

Truth has a way of interfering, a way of making those that long for it fear it, as well. It's strange just how threatening truth can actually be. In Temelephas' instance, the truth could mean a sheer absence of will, on his part, if he were unable to stop. It would mean that the poor elephant was nothing more than a machine, an automaton meant to do the will of others. It was a truth Temelephas could not bear to meet.

He would rather live a horrible life, forever shrouded in mystery and doubt, rather than bask in the light of the truth that damned him to it.

The truth has a way of interfering,

a way of making those

that long for it fear it,

as well.

2

It's an ancient truth, one proven time and time again, that babies are gifted with the ability to fit through oddly small openings. From the more comical instances involving staircase railings to the more macabre dark well or sewer drain—daring babies fear none. If it's true that curiosity killed the cat, then it was surely the adventurous wanderings of toddlers that caused the demise of parents around the globe.

Franklin, as it turned out, was no different. He—chubby arms and all—was able to crawl clear across the parking lot before his mother had even noticed he'd gone missing. His face glowed with excitement; his chin glistened in the sunlight, covered in his own spittle.

He had been safely hidden away—with the aid of a bush—when his mother started to scream, calling out his name. Babies don't understand these things though. Franklin just continued ahead with his ambling crawl, his little diaper drooping behind him.

He came across a small hole in the ground that shared his hiding spot behind the bush. It was surrounded by tall grass and would have been nearly invisible to most, but not to a crawling babies, their faces so close to the ground. The hole was the perfect size for small animals or inquisitive babies to fit through. And as sure as Franklin was a small baby, down it he went.

Babies—while not altogether dumb—know little to nothing about the intricate workings of the humungous universe in which they live. They know nothing, for instance, about wormholes or tears in the fabric of time and space, and time has yet to find any meaning at all for them. So how was Franklin to know that he had slipped through a crack that no one even knew was there?

Franklin showed no sign of worrying over the unfathomable workings of the physical universe, or anything at all for that matter. He merely giggled as he fell into the darkness and out of earshot.

Watchers live astoundingly long lives. As stated before, they are human like, but subtle differences in their appearance give their anomaly away, especially their bright, fiery eyes. By some previous inhabitants of Earth they have been called angels or aliens, and those from the distant past may have even called them gods.

But in all actuality they weren't as wondrous as gods or angels, although they are powerful creatures. They serve more in a middle management capacity, overseeing the day to day machinations of ordinary life across the cosmos. Some supervise dead star systems, yawning widely as they watch the lights of their galaxy blink out. Others merely manage street corners on earth and the children that hopscotch down their sidewalks.

Then there was Tyriano, taxed with overseeing the center of the earth itself and the origin of its spinning, the great ancient elephant called Temelephas. It was an honor to be selected for such a position, especially since it meant falling under the tutelage of his uncle, Tyrimus. It was during that training that Tyriano learned much about the humans that walk the earth.

It fell to Tyriano to monitor the great elephant and the Minikins that fed and bathed him. The Minikins were good workers—never causing any real trouble—so he treated them more than fair, often doting over them. In response, they loved and respected him.

After his many centuries of dutiful service, it finally came time for him to train his *own* replacement. Dezriak was young, only a century old or so, but no different than Tyriano himself—when he began his own training. Tyriano was one of the last of the Great Ones, who'd been born into desolation and hardships. This younger generation came into being during the burst of technology, the excitement of it running through them all, much like the electricity that ran through the gadgets they coveted.

It didn't matter to Tyriano much; he couldn't keep his station forever, though many before him had tried. He could only hope his training would mold this young Watcher into the tenacious shepherd that the post demanded. Looking at the shorter creature beside him made him both happy and sad. To think he had ever been so young.

The student stood by Tyriano in the brilliant light that hovered in the midst of the cosmos, listening intently, all the while taking mental notes. His teacher was staring off into the distant nothingness of space as he narrated a brief history of man. That day's lessons were on war, which seized Dezriak's interest.

"Once there was a man from Troy, named Paris," Tyriano told him. "He was enamored by Helen, the beautiful Queen of Sparta. It is said that Helen returned his love, though being married to King Menelaus. Others claimed it was the Goddess Aphrodite that made her love him back. Either way, it led to war.

"So it went, as things do between humans. The Greeks united against Troy and sailed across the sea, led by Agamemnon—brother of the King—and fueled by the fearlessness of their greatest hero, Achilles. They took the city of Troy, burned it to ruins and enslaved its people; stamping its name into history and myth. Many died and all for the love of a king."

"Amazing," Dezriak chimed. "So humans are led mostly by emotion and not by logic?"

"Of course ... fear, love, greed, faith in a god ... they all can lead to war. You see, humankind has done some amazing things through their short time on earth because they are a very clever, but sly race ... so it only makes *sense* for them to have done some crafty and terrible things, as well. Many times, they do these things with the best of intentions, no matter how wrong they may be."

They stood there in the shimmering light, enjoying the silence of vacuous space around them and the time for reflection it allowed. Tyriano knew that war was an inevitable necessity of mankind. There couldn't be *that* many people on earth without the occasional war.

"Of Course, the victors write the history," Tyriano explained, "wiping their foes off the face of the earth and out of the memories of its people." He pondered all the lives lost to war and cultures destroyed. The books and music and poems never written, laughter never heard, loves never consummated, all the terrible and good gods created and forgotten, perhaps demonized, perhaps lost forever. So much loss.

Tyriano saw that look in Dezriak's eyes, the unmistakable gaze of one dreaming of the glories of war. It was only natural for the young ones to dream of glory. War is a young man's game, so the saying goes. There was a pop in the air behind them, drawing the attention of both from their individual thoughts.

They turned around in time to see a Minikin fall into the light, his little bottom bouncing as he landed. "My, oh my," Tyriano called out as he went over to help the little one up. The old Watcher held him steady as the Minikin rubbed at his backside, whimpering from the slight pain.

"Something has gone wrong, Tyriano," he shrieked, his crimson hair bouncing with terror.

"What happened?"

"An outsider has entered the center of the earth!" The Minikin trembled as he let the last words slip from his lips, falling to his knees.

"Well, that's impossible," Tyriano chuckled. "There's no way for an outsider to pass into your world, with all the protections in place and secrets needed to traverse the doorways." Tyriano bent over and helped the little fellow up to his feet once more, holding a confident smile on his face.

"It's not a man," the Minikin began again, "It's a baby! I saw it with my own two eyes!" Tyriano stood in silence for a moment, his old eyes peering off as if they would find the answer in the ether. He brushed back his gray feathers and turned back to his apprentice and the small creature.

"Oh, my," Tyriano muttered as the answer came to him. His mind went back to the old days, before man became so curious, before magic and protections were even necessary. There were passageways. There had been doors. He remembered them well, openings that had burrowed down into the core.

No man could squeeze through them, not those holes. They were far too small. But a baby—with no doubt, no fear in his mind—could have easily made its way through. "The child must not reach Temelephas."

Edward left his office early that afternoon, abandoning work to be resumed the following Monday, anxious for the weekend. He snuck from his office floor in a way he imagined a deft ninja would, slinking pass open doorways, sneaking down the halls. He sighed with relief upon making it to the bank of elevators.

One more day—he had survived. He had escaped the inevitable requests for assistance and the trapping demands from higher-ups to stay late into the night. Down the elevator took him, till he could dash off to the parking garage. No one tried to stop him. Safely in his car, he pulled out of the shadowy tomb of the garage and headed towards the suburbs.

He hoped to get some final Christmas shopping done before going home; after all, the holiday was fast approaching and he had yet to find Lily the *perfect* present. Internet shopping became little more than a quagmire of fruitless, hellish searching, and endless scrolling lists. With modern technology failing him, he was left with one option—something he equated to an iron maiden—the mall.

He should have known that the mall would be chaotic, that it would have been filled with people selling and buying their wares in the midst of packed halls. He was looking for, only that it would hit him like a thunderbolt when he spotted it. All of the gadgets and gizmos they offered were thrust upon him, but none seemed to carry that special quality a gift for her had to have. He wasn't even sure what

The mall—he quickly decided—was a war zone, strewn with the slack bodies of teenage lollygaggers and overbearing mothers waving credit cards as if they were little, white flags of surrender. He had a difficult time moving through the mob, which could have been mistaken for an evacuation center. People screamed and shoved one another; Christmas packages slid across the foot trodden floor in their oversized bags. Edward gave off a cry as he felt an elbow jab into his ribs.

Commercialism did this, he thought, destroying his favorite holiday. Edward had never been a religious man by any definition. He neither relied upon it nor turned his back on it, always swaying somewhere in the middle. He attended church as frequently as the holidays came around, always guiltily dropping money into the donation basket.

To him, Christmas was a time to spend with loved ones, giving gifts and sharing a lavish meal and a handful of well-known carols—all the while sipping rum infused eggnog. And yes, at some point on Christmas morning, his mind would be overtaken by images of Christ lying in a stable. It was always simple for him.

Today people speak of presents they bought for family and friends as if they were trophies, birthing a sentiment of competition. Big flashy cars, surprisingly bigger TVs, and near microscopic phones. Whatever happened to the idea of a nice sweater or—to be extravagant—jewelry? Jesus' name fell away long ago to make room for Apple, Xbox, Abercrombie, and his dastardly clever comrade Fitch, the new deities of America.

It were these thoughts that rattled about in Edward's head as he slipped out of the tumultuous river of humans, seeking refuge in a small jewelry boutique. Soft music bounded through the little shop, but softer yet were the pink lined display cases. The light was dim, allowing the precious metals and gems displayed there to shimmer and sparkle—like thousands of tiny, watchful eyes.

The shop was eerily empty, and a little woman sat behind one of the glass cases, too busy reading her romance novel to notice the arrival of a likely customer. All that could be seen of her was a tightly bound silver bun, knotted upon her head. The rest of her face was hid in the pages of her book; the sultry kind of novel with the standard shirtless man with flowing locks emblazoned on the cover, grappling an ample, blonde vixen.

She just sat there reading away as Edward walked around gazing into the backlit displays. Every once in a while Edward would hear her mutter something under her breath causing him to smile. Not wanting to scare the oblivious woman with his sudden appearance, he gave off a subtle cough.

She jumped a bit in her stool, giving a little hoot as she slapped the paperback down to the counter. "Hello," she said, her face red, though still beaming with a wide smile. She wore glasses low on her long, wrinkled nose, below eyes that appeared younger than the rest of her. She was indeed tiny—especially after she'd hopped down from her stool—but her ears were bigger as if they never heard they needed to stop growing.

"Looking for a *special* present for a *special* lady ... hmm?" she asked, walking around the counter spryly.

"Yes, ma'am," Edward answered, smiling down at her as she sidled up to him; bravely grabbing his hand, leading him towards the cases.

"An engagement ring, perhaps?"

"No, she has one of those already," he said. She "awed" smarmily, nearly giving off a guttural applause. She then pulled him off to another counter on the other side of the sales floor. She stood him before the case, making sure he wouldn't move, before darting behind the velvet covered counter.

She disappeared under the counter top, "And now, what to get the girl who has it all ... hmmm?" her muffled voice called out. Edward quietly waited, examining earrings that hung atop the counter. "But, do you *REALLY* love this girl?"

"Excuse me?" Edward asked, obviously caught off guard. The little woman popped up from under the counter with a tiny black box in her small hands.

"It's a simple question, answerable with a mere yes or no. But it is a very important one to answer ... do you *truly* love this girl?" She held him in a steady gaze with a thin mouth and questioning brow. She was more than a saleswoman, Edward could see then.

She was a romantic, aside from her novel—that most likely belonged in a set that lived on her bookcase back home. No, he saw the sentiment of love was far greater to her than the gems and metal bands that men pawn off to women on a daily basis. To her, selling jewelry to an untruthful lover was equivalent to a pharmacist filling a prescription for a junky.

"Yes," he said in earnest softness, "with all my heart." The woman cocked her head slightly, relaxing her face into an easy smile with twinkling eyes. She then slowly raised her hand and pressed a wrinkled finger to the tip of her nose.

"Perfect answer," she exclaimed suddenly with a wink. "I can tell by your eyes that you aren't lying ... all women can." She beckoned him closer to her, even closer still, till he was hovering low over the countertop with her as she held up the little, black box.

"I wanted to make sure that *you* were the right man for this certain present," she said quietly as if sharing a secret, all the while eyeing the little, black box.

"And what's so special about this gift?" he asked as he absentmindedly pushed his glasses back up the length of his nose, he himself now fixating on the box.

"It's only the sweetest gesture a man can make towards the woman he loves," she said matter-of-factly as she slowly opened the box. "Imagine giving her the peace of mind ... *never* doubting, *always* knowing exactly how you feel ... forever."

She pulled a locket from the box; an ornately trimmed silver heart. It was stunningly crafted; detailed finely, giving it the look of a museum piece. It could have easily been the spoils of a crown jewel heist. 'I am loved' was etched into its satiny finish.

"Beautiful," Edward said, mesmerized. He looked over the locket with wide eyes and ran his index finger over its smooth surface.

"I thought you might like it," she said confidently as she began to coil the locket and chain back into its little, black safe haven.

"How much is it?" he asked. She snapped the lid shut and gave him a stern look, chiding him with clicking, pursed lips.

"You can't think of it like *that*," she said as she slid the box away from him. "No, no … *never* like *that*."

"Well, how should I think of it?"

"Anyone can just *buy* a waffle iron … or, *buy* a DVD player. But, *you* … *you* know better," she lectured, giving him a wink. "You know that this locket is a symbol of your love … and like this locket … your love is priceless."

Edward fixed his eyes once more on the little black box. He imagined the look on Lily's face when she'd first hold it up before her, imagined the little pictures it would hold. It was a done deal. All this lady had said, it was exactly what he wanted to give to Lily; it's what she deserved.

The caverns of the underworld were built like a labyrinth, its many turns and dead ends made harder to traverse by its perpetually dim light. It was always winding and spiraling downward in confusing ways, slender passages that held an eerie glow within molten rock walls. Echoes bounced about, bringing the high pitched voices of the Minikins and the sound of the eternal grinding, creaking wood to any who walked its paths.

Franklin had been crawling through those caverns for hours, his chubby baby legs tiring with each knee shuffle. His body was more worn down than it had ever been in his short life. To put it simply, he was pooped.

His little body gathered dust, just as much as a box of old photos would that had been retired to a spot beneath the sofa. His face was coated with the gray film, driving him to sneeze as he moved forward, collecting pebbles in his chubby legs and hands. The passage he followed began to descend, so he slowly began to slide forward. The slope grew deeper and he giggled louder and louder as he slid faster and faster.

"What was that?" one Minikin asked another as they pushed a wheelbarrow full of rocks along a ledge below.

"I don't know," the other answered as the loud 'weeeeeeeee' of an infant shot off like a bugle. A little, chubby, dusty thing spiraled out of the passage above them and slid off into another cavern, descending further into the depths of the earth.

"You think that was the *baby* we were to keep an eye out for?" the first asked of the second. The other Minikin merely gave a shrug of his tiny shoulders as an answer.

Franklin fell with great speed and showed no fear as he plummeted. The wind swept through his wispy hair and whistled in his baby ears. He could see nothing, especially the Minikin he was about to land upon. When he did land on the one known as Tibil, it was with a great thud and the impact splayed the Minikin out beneath him.

Tibil gasped for the dark air and rolled the unscathed baby to his side. He sat up—himself unhurt due to years of hard labor—and glanced at the baby that sat before him. "You," Tibil yelped in his high voice, causing Franklin to chortle hardily.

"We've been searching all over for you," Tibil said as he slowly stood. He brushed off his green trousers and looked down at the baby with curious, clear-blue eyes. "What ... can't you speak?" Franklin could only shoot off a long raspberry in response and spittle down his chin. "Oh, that's right, you're only an *infant* human. Well humans must be *big* for you to be considered small."

Franklin peered off into the darkness with large vacant eyes, sighing with the boredom that began to settle in him. Infants can be so fidgety, after all. "Well, Tyriano will be happy to see you," Tibil said as he wrapped his short arms around the baby, trying to lift him. It proved to be an impossible task, the little baby being more combative than a large rock.

"My, you're heavier than you seem." Tibil tried then to pull him to his feet in hopes of simply walking along with him. This method was nearly as difficult as the first due to Franklin's lack of balance and leg strength.

Tibil struggled repeatedly until his own strength fell away. He stepped back and breathed a heavy sigh as his tiny brain moved in thought. The brain of a Minikin *does* in fact move in thought. It remains still when simply following orders, but upon creating their own ideas their little brains wobble like wind-up toys.

"Wait here," Tibil commanded, "I need to get a wheelbarrow and then we'll go to see Tyriano, alright?"

"Gooba-da-swwwwwwweeerrp?!"   Franklin answered. Tibil felt sure that the little baby understood, especially after motioning firmly with an open palm. Then the small, red-headed creature ran off to find a wheelbarrow so that he could be the lucky one to present this intruder to Tyriano.

Franklin was on the move again just as the little man was out of sight, bored with the surrounding darkness. He crawled off to a small opening in which he disappeared, only to resurface later.

Unknown to Tibil, this oversight would cost him his job and lead to his banishment to the surface world.

Poor Tibil.

Temelephas had heard the ruckus and gossip that was constantly swirling around him. The Minikins spoke excitedly of an invader. Temelephas' large, old heart beat harder at the news, so loudly did it sound that it drew the attention of his Watchers, shining a light on his sudden joy.

He stepped with more resolve as he waited for the moment when he could finally see this invader, the one that could bring so much woe to the underworld. *What is this that I'm experiencing? Why does my heart beat faster ... why do I feel—if that's even the right word—different?*

There were many questions in Temelephas' mind and even more wondrous things happening in his chest. He had nothing to compare this sudden existence of joy to. Before then he had only the dreary lull of sadness and stinging pain of monotony. The thing that captured his attention most, though, were ideas of what it might be that drew nearer to him?

They must be fierce, Temelephas thought, *why else would the little ones be so frightened?* Temelephas continued to speculate as he walked, his large feet keeping the rhythm of the earth.

Edward drove home as quickly as possible; his hand lightly tapping Lily's present as it sat in the passenger seat. He had had it gift wrapped with beautiful paper, tied tightly with ribbon and topped with a delicate bow. He couldn't wait for her to rip it all to shreds. Christmas seemed even further off than he remembered—too far. His heart beat quickly as he pulled up in front of their house.

The house they shared was in an area of Columbus called Clintonville, a warm and welcoming neighborhood filled with growing families and promise. They lived in a house that was both thin and tall, with brown paneling; a cookie-cutter home for the middle class. The only thing that set it apart from the rest of the houses that lined their street was the lonely pink flamingo that lived in their front yard all year long.

He hopped from his car with haste, nearly slipping

on black ice before steadying himself against the car. He marched through his yard, passing the frozen flamingo as he pushed up his glasses, bounding up the steps. The heat of his home slapped him in the face as he opened the door.

He glanced about, searching the living room for Lily, but catching no sight of her. All he spotted were boxes marked 'Christmas Decorations', some empty; others overflowing with holiday cheer. Lily *loved* Christmas. Edward was never the type to go all out for the holidays, but he wouldn't deprive her of her traditions.

"Lily," he called out.

"I'm in the kitchen," she called back. He followed her voice with determination as a predator would its prey. He found her eating an orange over the sink. She had fruit juice dripping down her chin and a look resembling a dog that had been caught with its nose in the trash.

"I'm sorry," she said with a mouthful as she set the orange aside. "I know how much it annoys you ... me eating over the sink. But I *really* hate doing dishes for silly things."

Edward grabbed her sticky hands and pulled her to him so they could share a citrusy kiss. "Do what you like," Edward softly told her, his glasses slipping down his nose. She pulled her lips from him and eyed him confusedly with a wrinkly face, still in his grasp.

"You aren't going to ride me about this *ever* again?" she asked as she gently pushed his glasses back up the length of his nose. She waited for his response with a doubting smile.

"Life's too short to worry about the little things," he said before kissing her cheek.

"Aww ... thanks," Lily said, eyeing the remainder of the orange as it sat less enthrallingly on the countertop. "But *now* it's not as fun," she pouted.

"Then wash your hands and follow me," Edward said excitedly as he abandoned the kitchen.

"Why?" she asked as she dropped the sad orange into the waste basket.

"I have a gift for you," he shouted over his shoulder. Lily quickly ran her hands under hot water and doused them with soap. After scrubbing her palms with the care and vigor of a child, she rinsed and dried them furiously and left to follow him into the living room.

"A gift?" she asked as she fell upon the sofa beside him.

"Open it," he said, laying the little package in her lap. She looked at it with tempted eyes, her fingers playing with the ribbon and bow.

"Eddie," she began slowly, "as much as I would *love* to, I think I should wait until Christmas. At least I should wait till Christmas Eve."

"Open it for me then … because, I can't wait." Lily let the idea stew in her mind for a quick moment before ripping the shiny paper from the small box. She opened the black, velvet lid and out twinkled the silver reflection that spoke those three sweet words. *I am loved.*

"Oh, Eddie," she said with a hushed breath. She looked it over with teary eyes. "It's gorgeous."

"I thought you should always know," he said, kissing her forehead. He slipped his arm around her and she nestled into his chest. Her eyes swelled, she sniffled and then whispered a 'thank you' to him.

Later she thanked him once more for the gift. It was done so in private, in the darkness of their bedroom. Edward imagined that the second 'thank you' could have rivaled anything found in a novel emblazoned with a shirtless man and a buxom blonde.

Tyriano saw that look
in Dezriak's eyes, the
unmistakable gaze of one
dreaming of the glories of war.
It was only natural for
the young ones to
dream of glory.

3

It was the middle of the night when Tibil was forced from his underground home and into the strange place known as the surface world. Not many Minikins have gone to surface before and any who had have long since died. Rumors were all he had to rely on and stories remembered from his time as a young child, stories only meant to scare him.

He remembered those tales, told to him and his eleven brothers as they lay safely tucked in their bed back in the burrow where they grew up. They would cower beneath their quilt, listening to stories about the burning star that would broil their flesh, and of wild dogs and cats that would hunt them. There were stories of the waters that would sweep them away to be swallowed by giant monsters that lived in desolate places called oceans.

But of all those stories—all the ones that made him quiver in his bed—they all paled in comparison to the Kyroclypto. He was an evil creature that hunted down Minikins once they came to the surface. He was said to have skin the color of ash and a sense of smell that could stalk anything to the ends of the earth. To go to the surface was a fool's search for certain death, a gruesome end for any bedtime story.

Those stories stayed with him. All those horrible images were frozen in his mind. He had never dreamt of coming up here, but there he was.

At first he was frightened, worried of the star that would cook him alive and of the wild animals that would search him out as a quick meal. But even if he were to survive those immediate threats, there was always the ferocious, tenacious hunter—Kyroclypto—to contend with.

He cried softly, icicle tears that fell slowly from his clear, blue eyes and fell to the dirt. He thought back to those warm nights in the burrow and longed for the company of his brothers. Even faced with the horrors of the stories he was told at bedtime, those tales were far better than knowing the truth.

It was dark on the surface when he was shoved out. But a soft glow captured everything around him. There were noises, hoots and cackles and a crunching sound that he assumed were foot trodden bones. He shook with fear, his little arms wrapped about him, trying to keep warm.

He felt eyes on him, as if the Kyroclypto had already spotted him, laying an invisible target upon him. He wished he could have returned home ... back to the Underworld and the days of hard labor that he had abandoned. But now he was sure he would die in this strange place. He waited for something to happen, his little body filled with terror.

Then—much to his surprise—nothing happened. He still stood on his own two feet; afraid and cold, but nothing came for him from out of the darkness. There were no nets or spears or rushing waters to sweep him away. It was only quiet.

And as that moment grew longer, the realization that no harm would befall him crept in. He was able to relax a bit and even breathe his first surface breath. He still missed home and was still afraid of this new world, including the unknown things that moved around him in the dark. It slowly dawned on him that maybe the stories he was told were just that … stories.

He walked between the trees, the frozen leaves crumbling beneath his small feet. The air was so cold that it burst from his lips in thick clouds. Every now and then a bush would shake from somewhere in the dark, but it would quickly cease as a small animal would shoot out from its roots, darting away from this type of strange creature, new to them. *Maybe there was nothing to be afraid of all along*, he thought as he came to a clearing that seemed to glow in the dark night.

There was a field before him of crystalized grass that glistened in the faint moonlight. Tibil felt tears welling up beneath his eyes. There was never such beauty in the underworld, nothing so clean and shiny. He knelt down and ran his hand across the blades, feeling the coolness of them. The light seemed to dance across them all.

He looked up for the first time and was silenced by the overwhelming night sky. He'd never before bothered looking up in his own world. Up was much like forward, behind, and below … nothing but rock.

But here on the surface, up and down and left and right and all of the other directions were so different. But nothing was quite like the sky. The moon was near full overhead and swallowed the darkness with its light which fell upon him. His eyes went wide to take it in, along with the stars and midnight clouds that crept by it all.

"Beautiful," he whispered to himself, falling back as he tried to see it all at once. The frozen grass was so cool against his hot flesh. *Why hasn't anyone spoken of this*, he wondered. The sky was a massive blanket of lights and possibilities and where it fell to meet the earth. The horizon was even more explosive with lights that twinkled and danced.

He would go there he decided. It was his best chance to find humans and maybe even some food. Maybe the stories were true and he would be heading to his own end. Or, perhaps it was a path that would lead to a new beginning.

In the Underworld, Tibil had always been a cog in the machine, a part of the secret that made this rotating world possible. Tossed from the only home he knew, he was now left to find his own way. The journey would be frightening, he knew, surely it would be tough. But that is how life is, he figured.

Tibil, now a broken cog that had slipped away from that machine, would need to adjust. No more would he have to worry about feeding schedules or breaking and clearing away rock. For once, instead of being a spur to life … he could simply be a part of it.

Edward woke the next morning with Lily lying across him. Her arms were tucked snuggly around him—like a comfortable quilt. He stretched as much as he dared, not wanting to disturb her slumber … wanting her dreams to carry on. It was a Saturday, anyhow, giving him no need to rush. There was no workday beckoning to him; the inbox could wait.

He actually had no plans at all for the day, a rare but welcome void in his week. The day would be as lazy as he would allow it to be. And at that moment, all he wanted to do was lay in bed while Lily slept, smelling her penny-colored hair.

It was a treat no other man would ever experience. He inhaled deeply, breathing in the scent of her conditioner. It was like breathing in a strawberry patch, bathed in the light of a spring morning. She rolled over suddenly and gazed at him with sleepy, green eyes between strands of chestnut hair.

"Are you smelling my hair?" she asked with a throaty voice and coquettish smile. He could only shrug and smile at her, letting out a heavy sigh. She just rolled back onto him and slipped her mouth over his, laying her nose against his. For Edward, there was no better way to begin his mornings.

Lily pulled away from Edward and his eager lips, looking at him. She just gazed upon his face in the way women do, as if studying each little mark and pore. She ran the tip of her finger along his nose and then brushed the unruly hair from his forehead. With a smile and a sigh she was off, rolling out of bed and skipping away.

Edward only laughed, knowing he had been distracted and therefore beaten to the bathroom. That meant waiting while Lily showered and groomed, all while singing along to the radio with her delicate, pitchy voice. Edward could only lay back and listen as he waited his turn.

When he finally made his way downstairs—freshly showered and shaved—Edward found his sweet fiancée sipping coffee and flipping through the paper. Her hair was fresh and clean, still wet from the shower, and most likely had met a brush. It would be hard to prove then, though, as she busied herself with the task of re-tangling it with her nimble fingers. Edward smiled at her as he sat and kissed her soap-scented cheek.

"What should we do today?" Lily asked as she poured him a mug of steaming coffee.

"Whatever you want," he said. Lily let out a pouty lipped sigh and slid into his welcoming lap. She nestled against him, kissing his neck carefully as she spoke between her smooches.

"Well," a kiss on his neck. "We could …" a kiss on his cheek, "stay in," another on his neck. "I'm sure," kiss, "we could," kiss, "find … *something*," kiss, "to do." Ed smiled as her lips worked effortlessly over him, repeatedly finding a new bit of him to adorn with her lips.

"Sounds good to me," he said goofily, never having

been able to rid his voice of the awkward, eagerness of a teenage boy.

"I thought it might," she said with a devious grin. "Too bad, because we're off to the zoo."

"The zoo?"

"Yes," she said, dancing away from him and out of the room.

"But, it's freezing out there," Edward called out to her as he rose from his seat.

Lily's head popped out from around the corner, wearing a knitted cap and a colorful scarf. "All the better to wear a coat, my dearie," she said with a theatric voice and a prodding smile, her fingers masquerading as wolf ears atop her head. Edward couldn't resist Lily or her many smiles.

On the other side of town lived a man named Nicholas Forrest. He was middle aged and so was his mind, which is normal and would be perfectly adequate if it weren't for its lack of stability. Not that *his* mind shuddered and spun in his skull, but that its perception of things around him did.

Case in point: He told all who would listen to him that he was homeless—which was an utter lie. He wore clothes that would be more at home scrubbing the sides of dump trucks than hanging from a body in public. If he were to put out a personal ad, his hobbies would include watching clouds pass overhead and rummaging through other people's trash cans.

He actually lived with his older and somewhat saner sister, Camilla. She thought herself to be of the psychic nature, mostly believing she was some sort of medium, and would pass on the deceased's howdy-ya-dos on a regular basis to those many strangers she met. She was otherwise harmless, with hair the color of a bird's nest that was always done up in a likewise fashion.

They lived in a tall, skinny home that was squeezed between other tall and skinny homes. Their yard was overpopulated by garden gnomes and spotted with a handful of birdfeeders. A plastic reindeer had lived in their yard at one point, but some rowdy neighborhood kids found it a more proper home—smashed and scattered in the street. A teary eyed Camilla buried its remains in the narrow back yard while Nicholas leaned against a nearby tree, playing his sad harmonica.

Camilla made her money in a grocery store where she committed acts of ringing up foods and household goods and the bagging of said foods and household goods. While she slaved away in her 'mercantile prison' with walls made of ground beef and whole wheat bread, Nicholas wandered the streets with an empty coffee cup, rattling it in hopes of getting loose change. He was always wearing those raggedy clothes that smelled of last year and a matching jean jacket. He normally did pretty well for himself.

His way of making money had always made Camilla sad, thinking she was unable to provide a life for Nicholas that made him truly happy. But it wasn't the *money* that provided the life for Nicholas; it was the *life* itself that made him smile. He always hated living indoors, those dark corners and confining walls, all that unnatural light. So he chose the lifestyle of a vagabond. Somehow, even with her psychic eye, Camilla was never able to see well enough to understand this side of Nicholas' life.

But at that moment—as Edward and Lily readied themselves for a cold afternoon at the Zoo and Camilla stuffed paper sacks with heavily preserved foods—Nicholas sat upon the roof of his narrow home. In reality it was not a tremendously marvelous place to be, with the chilly wind and uncomfortable tiles pressed against his bottom. In his mind, however, it was a rumbling locomotive, like one from a Tom Waits song or a song Tom Waits should have sung.

Slow and steady, his train moved forward, its tall and lingering smoke stack flowing thickly behind him like black cotton balls strung up to the heavens. Beneath him, the train's cars shifted and rocked as they noisily crept down an unseen track. Chugga-chugga-chugga-chugga, the engine pumped hard beneath him.

"Wooo-wooooooooo!" he screamed over the cold neighborhood, mimicking the gentle cry of his imaginary train. His steamy breath flew from his mouth as he made each of his long, wailing calls. Neighbors watched safely from within their warm and stable homes, watching the mad conductor of the neighborhood. They always wanted to call the police, but their sympathy for Camilla kept the phones at bay.

Nicholas watched the make-believe landscape as it rolled by, driving his stationary train onward. He never knew what *truly* lay before him, though. He could imagine what lay over his phony horizon, but never would he surely know the future, or what would come from a chance encounter.

Tibil walked freely amongst the humans as if he had done so his whole life. The people he walked by couldn't help but notice his small stature or strange appearance. He looked more like a child's doll than a person—with his small stature, big head with red locks, and impossibly clear blue eyes.

Tibil was increasingly shocked with every passing second he spent amongst them. *The clothing they wear,* he thought as he brushed pass the gloriously soft and brightly colored fabric. *Look at how tall these buildings are, much bigger than the deepest ravines back home.*

Everything was so new to the little Minikin the

he believed even then that he was dreaming. Maybe he had died and never felt the teeth of whatever wild beast had devoured him. Death was irrelevant to him then—everything was so beautiful. Bright lights that didn't bounce from wall to wall and noises that didn't echo down caverns and in his head.

And the smells ... he loved the smells most of all. The flowers and the grass from the field where he appeared—even the people somehow smelled like flowers. Smells that were so sweet and so new that they coated his tongue. Much better, he decided, than the gruel that he ate and Temelephas' waste.

"Hot dogs!" he heard a gruff voice call overzealously, like a town crier. Tibil ducked quickly and his eyes darted about searching for the large monsters, but he found none. The cry came again, loud and booming, and he saw a man standing behind a large, wheeled cart made of battered yet shiny metal.

He waddled up to the chubby, tall human in a very cautious way. The man was messy looking and had more than stubble, a shadow of a beard—a nine o'clock shadow. He wore stone washed jeans and a blue t-shirt beneath an apron that at one time had been white. Now it was a kaleidoscope of condiments, reds, yellows, and greens swirled about. There were other stains there too, but it would be best not to venture a guess as to their origins.

The man continued to call out, peddling those blistering hounds, his eyes scanning the crowd beyond our little friend. Tibil stood patiently, waiting to be acknowledged. After a total of ten minutes—having not been noticed at all—Tibil gave off a soft, high pitched cough, then tugged on the man's trouser leg.

The man looked down at Tibil for the first time and a slight, controlled smile peeked at the corners of his mouth. It was the sort of smile you might experience upon seeing something new and peculiar, the kind of smile that sneaks up on you. Of course, the vendor had no way of knowing how rare and peculiar that little man that stood beside him truly was. "What can I do for you, my friend?" he asked Tibil as he bent down to his eye level.

Tibil took his eyes off the chubby, mustard stained man and lifted his nose to the hot dog cart, taking in deep sniffs of the aromatic meat. "You like the smell, my friend?" the vendor asked with a puzzled smile. "You want a hot dog?"

Tibil glanced back to the man and tilted his head, his crystal blue eyes fluttering like little blue butterflies. "Hot dog?" he asked in his high pitched voice. The vendor couldn't place the slight dialect in the small fellow's speech, but America was a melting pot.

"Yes, it's a type of American food."

"Food? American's eat dogs?"

"No," the man laughed out. "It's fast food."

"I know dogs are fast, but why would you eat them?"

"Look," the vendor started, some of the whimsy gone from his voice, replaced with frustration. "There's no dog here ... it's food ... you eat it." He held out the cylindrical meat substance, held firmly by a fibrous wheat fold. Across the top of it was an aromatic, yellow sauce that squiggled its way from one end of the "dog" to the other.

Tibil inhaled deeply, the mixture of tang and salty goodness filled his head. "I ... eat it?" he asked, looking pleadingly at the hot dog salesman.

"Yes," the vendor laughed again, his fast cheeks forcing his eyes to squint; and in that moment Tibil's tiny hand swiped the fare from the hand vendor. "Hey," he called out, no longer amused. The slim sandwich was already shoved into Tibil's little mouth. His jaw worked quickly, making a paste of it before swallowing it down in a selfish act of nourishment.

Those crystal blue eyes beamed up at the vendor in pure joy as he hummed jubilantly, trying to swallow it down. "Tasty!" the little man said cheerfully, wiping his arm across the yellow smear on his chin. "Thank you!" With that, the weird little man turned on his heels and ran off.

"Hey," the vendor called after him, "you owe me for that dog!" But it was already too late, the little tourist from beneath the crust had vanished into the crowd. *What a strange little guy*, the vendor thought as he started on with the rest of his day.

🐘

Deep in the core of our revolving rock, Temelephas continued his walk. His large feet stomped as his mind swelled with the joy of knowing that he may soon see a new face in his home. The feeling came tinged with the anxiety of not knowing what to expect, but he couldn't identify that emotion. It was all so new to the monstrous elephant.

He wondered about where this thing came from and if it had to travel far to be in his home. *How many different places could there possibly be?* He didn't know of many places to begin with, only his cavern and the caves that fell off into the dark around it. He knew the Minikins dwelt somewhere there.

As to where the Watchers came from, he had no idea where to even begin in wondering that. He knew they didn't live in the caves, seeing how they always wore such clean clothes and their hands were always that nice and clean purplish color. Hands like those weren't meant for hard labor.

The Minikins, however, had deceptively small hands. One wouldn't guess by looking at them that such tiny hands could do all the strenuous work that came with the life they led. Yet, their palms were rough and cracked from their lives in the center of the earth, their reward for crawling through the dark.

Temelephas had seen those hands up close many times before, felt them upon him as they fed and cleaned him. They were such small creatures, yet so sturdy. The Watchers and the Minikins couldn't have been more different from one another. One was like an eye, hovering ... always watching. The other was more the gentle hand that caressed and doted over him.

I wonder which one this intruder will be like more. There was no way of truly knowing and Temelephas wasn't very good at wondering, anyhow. Temelephas had only been exposed to those two types of creatures, the Watchers and the Minikins, making them the only things for comparison. Temelephas imagined a balanced mix of the two and smiled.

"He smiled," Tyriano said from above Temelephas' stomping circle. "But that cannot be," he raised a lone finger to his gray beard and swirled it through its fine feathers. He thought feverishly for a moment, trying to pinpoint a cause for the sudden happiness. When that moment was done he was left with no answers.

It was simply impossible.

"What could cause that old beast to smile?" he asked aloud to no one but himself. His mind wrapped around that one, solitary question and spun a thick web of thought around it. Soon, his mind was lost to that question, like a spider trapped in its own, sinewy web.

He thought and thought and thought, forever pulling at his feathery beard. Tyriano's mind stretched back to his first meeting with the elephant, but it was no good ... nothing came to him. Further and further back he thought, as far back as he could ever even know about, all the way to the beginning ...

Long ago, before the surface had yet to sprout a single seedling—before fish swam the waters that flooded it—Temelephas had always been at the center of the earth. The giant elephant had been created by the Maker to spin this rock as it glided through space, to allow its weather to change and aid in the turning of time.

The Maker—knowing that for a creature to do this for all eternity, it would have to be dim—created his pet to be naïve to all things that he held dear. Love, pain, fear, happiness ... all these things were denied Temelephas. He would be as numb to emotion as the stars would be to the existence of one another.

Could the Maker have underestimated his own creation, Tyriano pondered. *Could it be that Temelephas has learned to feel? Could it be, simply—that over time—this great elephant has taught himself to break his own nature?* Tyriano's face brightened as he continued to explore all the possibilities.

"What could this lead to?" he asked aloud again. Whatever it would lead to would not be good for the High Council—those who oversaw all in the Maker's absence. Tyriano, so lost in his own thoughts, failed to see the Minikin as it sidled up to him.

"Excuse me, Tyriano," the Minikin called, dragging the Watcher back to the here and now.

"Yes ... did you locate the intruder?" he quickly inquired.

"No, sir," the Minikin said, looking up at his boss with his head craned, his red hair fell back, away from his face. "We still search for the baby. I was sent to retrieve you."

"Retrieve me?" he asked; a befuddled look upon his face. "For what purpose?"

"It's the High Council; they wish to speak with you." With that the Minikin turned away from Tyriano and bounded off into the dark of an adjoining cave.

Good, the Watcher thought, it was the perfect time

to meet with them, to inform them of his discoveries. He allowed a brief smile for himself before bringing his arms down to his sides and holding himself straight and tall. He cleared his mind of all other things in that moment, something that takes great discipline.

He thought only about the High Council and the place in which they meet. He took a deep breath as he solidified that thought in his ample mind, holding it firmly there. "Yes, High Council?" he called out at last.

As the last syllable rang out from his lips his body pulled directly from the spot he stood. He shot straight up and out of the core, paying no heed to the laws bound to physical mass. He flew up, through the crust and passed between the stars.

He was moving so fast that his surroundings became nothing more than a bright, sliding blur of light to him. He felt nothing more than a wind passing his face, no pain or discomfort came to him. It was as if he were only standing in one place. Just as it had begun suddenly, so it had ended; abruptly, with his feet planted on a fluffy floor that resembled a cloud.

At first, all he could see was a brilliant, celestial light—blends of red and gold with a splash of cerulean. His eyesight returned and before him he could see the ancient table of the Council. It stood there as menacing as it was beautiful—as tall as it was long—carved from white stone. The whole front of it a sort of chiseled diorama that showed the conception of the Universe.

Given the time, one could trace it from its first, beautiful and fiery birth all the way to its close, which will most likely be as equally violent and poetic. In between is the molding of stars and their planets, the breath of life that surrounds it all. A sort of Universal history of us all.

High above it sat five figures behind the table, their forms and faces hidden by their robes that glowed white hot. It was important that they be able to preserve anonymity since they themselves were nothing more than Watchers that had achieved a higher office. Power can pervert even the strongest minds—the only way to protect such power is to hide it.

"Greetings, Tyriano," they said collectively, in a harmonious tone.

"Greetings, High Council," Tyriano returned as he bowed as low as his old back would allow.

"For many long years," the first of them began, "you have served us ... and for that we are grateful."

"The honor is mine, Councilman," He said as he lifted his head. "I was pleased to hear your call, for I have just discovered something that may very well deserve your attention."

"In due time," a second Councilman said. "But first, we have some information that was brought to us from a third party." Tyriano didn't like the sound of that at all, the tone of Councilman's voice being that of a reproving mother. It was hard to tell which way this conversation would go, especially without being able to read their faces.

"We have been told," a third started, "that an outsider has intruded upon the underworld ... Is this true?" Tryiano felt his mouth go dry and his tongue shrivel up like a burning leaf. It was a surprise to him that his mouth didn't cease up completely.

"It is your Excellency, but I have sent out all available Minikins in search of this intruder. The fact is that this outsider has proven to be furtive and rather intelligent."

"Is it also true, Tyriano, that this intruder that has proven to be *so* furtive and intelligent is nothing more than an infant human?" asked the same Councilman in a haughty tone. The rest of the table bubbled with a gentle sniggering, though one of the Council remained silent and stoic, as if quietly studying them all.

Tyriano also didn't laugh, in fact his face turned into a tragic mask. He felt his heart deflate and slowly sink into his gut as they laughed at him. Words, his only true companion through life, had left him there alone, undoubtedly hiding away in shame. Tyriano only nodded in answer to their humbling question.

"Should we be led to believe that you are not smart enough to deal with a baby?" a fourth Councilman asked. The sniggering continued, but this Councilman's words held venom and its bite did its harm upon Tyriano.

"It is the system," Tyriano mumbled, head lowered in shame.

"What was that? The last, stoic Councilman asked with apparent interest. Tyriano did not repeat himself, feeling his words may draw more negative fire; he just stared ahead into the brightness of the oblivion beyond them. "Speak up, Tyriano."

Somewhere inside Tyriano, a little ember spat and fought against the dark. It clawed at the walls inside him, growing stronger with every breath he took. The spark ignited him and Tyriano burned with its strength.

"There is a flaw in our system," Tyriano said finally, his head lifted once more, his words as strong as he was then. The High Council grew quiet, shocked perhaps by the great calmness that seemed to possess the being before them. "Not me."

"That is impossible," the first Councilman said, breaking the silence.

"And why is that?" Tyriano demanded loudly.

"Because the Maker is infallible," the second one shouted, slamming his fist into the stone table. "Saying *otherwise* is blasphemous! Besides, the Maker is not on trial today."

"Is that what this is?" Tyriano asked coolly, his arms crossing before him. "Am *I* on trial? If so, I demand to know who is accusing me of being insufficient," Tyriano added as he approached the stone table with his head high, hands bent at his waist. Tyriano was shaking he was so full of rage.

The High Council said nothing, merely sat there, frozen. "Who was it that gave you this information?" Tyriano tried once more.

"If the accuser wishes to be known, he may show himself now," the first Councilman said. Tyriano looked about, waiting for the vile being to appear. Just as he had appeared moments before, another popped up through the floor and landed sturdily before them all. His face carried a wicked smirk and he had scowling eyes that burned, fueled by arrogance.

Tyriano looked upon his accuser and sighed with regret in his heart. "I should have known," Tyriano whispered, shaky once more; his eyes glazed over with sadness. He had to look away, hiding the tears that slowly came. "How *could* you, Dezriak?"

Deep in the core

of our revolving rock,

Temelephas

continued his walk.

4

"It had to be done, Tyriano," Dezriak said through clenched teeth. It was as if Tyriano wasn't looking at his student any longer. He knew it was Dezriak, but he seemed older now, rougher around the edges. It was as if this act of betrayal had aged him; perhaps it was the pure hunger for power that had done it to him. Power has that effect on people. "Your ways of doing things leave much to be desired. We need a change."

"Change?" Tyriano shouted, throwing his arms up in despair. "The system needs to be changed, not I." Dezriak simply laughed at his former teacher, a slow, thundering grumble of a laugh. The laughter flooded over Tyriano and he stared towards his unwitting student; his eyes became thinner and burned with rage. "You hope to take over my position?"

Dezriak smiled, a pretentious smirk was his answer, but it was Tyriano's turn to laugh. Dezriak's leer slowly slipped into a scowl and his eyes burned like hot coals.

"Do you honestly believe this *child* will be able to take the helm?" He asked, turning his attention to the High Council. "This ... sniveling ... ignorant thing?"

"I have plans," Dezriak snapped, stepping forward.

"Oh, *do* you?" Tyriano asked with a chuckle. This

time his laughter didn't have the effect on Dezriak he had wanted. Instead, he gave his former teacher a kind of hungry grin, the sort reserved for predators.

"Yes ... I do," he said, circling Tyriano in the way a vulture would a slowly dying tortoise. "You see ... while you complain about the system, I plan to change it. As the times change ... so shall the system." Dezriak stepped to Tyriano, his horrid breath beating against the older one's face. He seemed to have grown a number of inches as he stood before him, but Tyriano also knew that it could have easily been himself shrinking away.

"What are you saying?" Tyriano asked in a near whimper, for lack of anything better to say.

"Well, Tyriano, as they say on the surface ... you dropped the ball." Dezriak loomed over Tyriano with his long, beak like nose. "Maybe you should just fade away." He grimaced at Tyriano, nearly salivating as he gave a low growl.

Even the most civilized of creatures has an underlining that is primal. Just as hungry dogs that have been cornered may bite, the same could be said of any man, even Watchers. Dezriak had Tyriano cornered with a look on his face that demanded a fight and the teacher wasn't so old that he wouldn't deliver it.

Tyriano lunged at the laughing creature with his claw-like hands extended, glowing with an eerie blue light that cracked like breaking twigs. He felt two shadowy arms grab him, pulling him back before he could lay his lethal hands upon the traitor. Tyriano saw the silhouetted hands that restrained him and looked over his shoulder to see the listless, dark face of the Gloom, the bloodcurdling henchmen of the High Council.

He had never had much interaction with the Gloom before, which suited Tyriano fine. They are a vile, malicious thing that live wherever darkness can be found, a dangerous snake waiting to spring forth. Where ever light is not, obviously the darkness reigns, but where there *is* a light ... a shadow dwells nearby. And from out of the tiniest bit of dark can stretch the sinister, skeletal arm of the Gloom.

They feed on fear and sadness and—like all other sentient beings—have learned to cultivate it. They call to it, pulling it from the miserable souls they embrace. They go as far as to lurk about the surface at night, descending on sleeping children and creating nightmares. That was why Tyriano dreaded the cold touch of their wraithlike hands.

"What is the meaning of this," he cried out, already hearing the dreadful whispers of his ghostly assailants.

"Calm yourself, Tyriano ... they will not hurt you if you don't fight them," the stoic Councilman said. "They are only here to restrain you." Yet, Tyriano spied more of the Gloom slinking out from hidden dark spots. They fell upon him, practically drooling over his growing misery.

"Then ... why do they ... whisper to me?" he wept. The fifth Councilman stood from his spot and lifted a white hand that then showered the Gloom with an invasive, white light. It pulsed over them in three, short bursts and the Gloom loosened their grasp on Tyriano, their grave voices fell from his mind.

Dezriak continued to smile from ear to ear. He bent over to peer into his former teacher's eyes as he was now on his knees from the pain. "First order of business is to get rid of you," Dezriak nearly sang. Tyriano trembled and his eyes glazed over in defeat and sadness and the Gloom savored it. "Then get rid of your stupid pet."

"My pet?" Tyriano asked with a quaky voice.

"Temelephas, of course," he said with a sickly grin. "You know ... the big, smelly elephant?"

"But, what about his duty? He's essential to all life on earth."

"Dezriak has suggested we replace him with a machine," the Second Councilman said, which started

Tyriano's blood to boil. "It will be a more efficient way to turn the earth."

"And what of Temelephas?" Tyriano asked, his voice cracking in weakness as the Gloom hovered ever closer to him. "What will be done with him?"

"He will be disposed of," the Councilman said.

The air was still and only the gentle sobs of a tired man could be heard as Tyriano wept. The fragile tears rolled away from his dulling red eyes and fled into his beard. The Gloom cackled about him, smoke spurting from their terrible mouths as they drank in his sorrow.

"But you can't just *kill him*," Tyriano said in a meek, miserable voice.

"Of course we can," Dezriak began, enjoying it all far too much. "*We* created him and anything we create … we can destroy."

"That is a lie!" Tyriano barked.

"SILENCE!" The first Councilman bellowed, slamming his hand upon the white, stone table.

"Tread softly," the fifth Councilman urged of Tyriano.

"It was the Maker who created him!"

"That may be so," the second Councilman began, "but you know as well as we that the Maker has abandoned us. All that he has created has been left in our knowledgeable hands." The Councilman couldn't hide the mirth in his voice, it was the one thing the white veil could not disguise.

What he said was true though, Tyriano knew as much. When the Maker left all those centuries ago it was to be only a short while, but he never returned. That was when the High Council inherited their god-like power and began to wield it as arbitrarily as they pleased.

Yet Tyriano wondered if the Maker would have done things differently. Maybe he might have handled everything just as callously as they, but he had never met the Maker. Not many alive had met him; he had been gone so long. But he refused to believe he would be so dismissive of life. But none of them could possibly know that Temelephas was truly alive.

And it came to him; like a gentle breeze blown over the sea, it came. It was an idea that may very well save the old elephant from an unnecessary end. "But, he's alive," the old watcher called gently. "You keep speaking of him as if he were a book to be shelved, or a trunk to be stowed away ... but he lives!" Tyriano called out as he struggled against the Gloom.

"Enough," the third Councilman screamed back. "He may be alive, but not in the same sense as you and I."

"But he is! He feels!"

"Impossible," muttered the fourth.

"BLASPHEMY!" sounded off the first.

"TAKE HIM AWAY FROM OUR SIGHT!" shouted the third.

The Gloom surrounded the frail Watcher, falling upon him like a thunderhead. Tyriano writhed from the pain, crying out, but for the sake of Temelephas not his own. The ravenous darkness would have torn Tyriano apart to get at his fear and sadness, if it weren't for a pulsing, white light.

It came flooded from the open palm of the fifth Councilman, scattering the black smoke of the Gloom away from its would be victim. "Take him to the center of the earth and lock him in his office until we decide how he should be punished," the fifth Councilman demanded.

The Gloom seemed to cower before the Councilman and the white light he commanded; they obeyed, dragging Tyriano's unconscious body away. Dezriak had to restrain a laugh that edged its way up his throat.

The only thing gloomy about the zoo was Edward's mood as he and Lily walked through the frozen menagerie. The afternoon sun was quick to leave—as it normally is that time of year—and night was creeping in. Clouds overhead shut out what little of the day remained, threatening to unleash white death on the ground below.

Most of the animals were tucked safely away, not accustomed to these frigid temperatures. Those that made the decision to appear before the masses looked as if they regretted it. They seemed frozen in time, like animal popsicles ... animopsicles.

The young couple walked about, their arms intertwined, hoods pulled snug against their icy faces. Edward was miserable for it, but Lily helped ease the cold by pressing her body against his, keeping a patch of warmth between them. They strolled slowly even though the winter air badgered them to abandon the outdoors for a cozy fire. *'Isn't it cold out?'* the wind seemed to ask with its harsh, push of a voice.

Yet the two carried on, their hearts further distancing them from the savage weather. Edward would be the first to crack under the pressure of winter's ugly attack. He wobbled with each gust and shuddered; it felt as if icy needles touched his face. "It's bad enough when the animals are always sleeping," he complained to his beautiful companion. "Now we have to deal with them *literally* hibernating?"

Lily just rubbed his back gently and pressed her face closer to his. She whispered a slow and steady 'shhhhhhhhh' into his red ear—her warm breath defrosting his cheek. It was enough to momentarily silence his criticisms, though Edward continued to pray for the end to come.

As the final light of day slipped over the horizon, little statues of light hemmed and hawed their way to life. It wasn't long before the area around them was filled with brightly lit animal replicas. "Wow," Edward chimed as little, hidden speakers began to pipe soft Christmas music out into the chilly night air.

"See," Lily said with a soft voice, "Isn't this worth it?" Her bright eyes watched as Edward glared about his cold surroundings at the glowing figurines. Children gasped and laughed nearby, pointing mitten cloaked hands to the trees and statues, all aglow like Christmas morning. Edward—remembering Lily beside him—nodded with a steamy sigh.

As if spurred on by the joy of the children—anxious to be a part of the merriment—snow began to fall. White, fluffy bits fell from the darkened sky, pirouetting against the blue-black of night like tiny ballerinas. Being the first snow of the season, it was met with jovial cheers and smiles.

Edward and Lily headed towards a growing crowd, joining them around a barrel that belched flames. They stood, slowly getting warmer as the snow thickened in to wet, sticky flakes that clung to people's coats and hair. The little ones sang and danced through the snow as it brought to mind a forecast of snowballs and days off from school. They all sang, singing along to the carols that swam in the air overhead.

It was beautiful, the scenery, the night—even the crowds that came together; they were nothing more than strangers to one another, but they would always share this one, beautiful memory. Edward chuckled and squeezed Lily tight against him, whispering, "I'm glad I didn't listen to the wind."

Nicholas was sitting outside the United Dairy Farmer's—his favorite panhandling spot—as the delicate snow fell around him. Night had come for good that day and cars drove by slowly, their headlights burning bright. Nicholas liked to squint at them as they went past, making them appear like a parade of shooting stars.

The employees at the UDF never gave him a hard time, mostly because he never bothered their customers. Other panhandlers generally assaulted them as they left the store with oddly vivid stories as to why they needed their change. Running out of gas was a popular one.

"Hey, man ... help me out," they chanted one after the other, a barbershop quartet of the needy—a chorus line of down-and-outers. Nicholas just sat quietly by a trashcan, demanding nothing, yet it seemed to rain change over his empty cup.

"Thank you," Nicholas would say warmly to all who gave as they continued on their way with serendipitous smiles on their faces. Nicholas would go back to humming Christmas carols for no other purpose than to hum them. Sooner or later he would always feel the looks of disdain emanating from those holding empty cups.

He could tell that they didn't want him around; it was easy to see on their faces, but he also just knew it inside himself. It wasn't any special powers like his sister claimed to have, just a sense of not being wanted. He glanced down at his foam cup and saw that he had amassed a small fortune and knew he could afford to leave.

So, Nicholas slowly stood and looked both ways before heading off. It was time to get moving anyhow, his back had gotten tight from sitting still for so long. He began to whistle 'Jingle Bells' as he stepped between the snowflakes. It wasn't long before he found a new place to sit and wait.

It was a little market that smelled musky, dimly lit by slowly dying neon tubes. They had lunch meat and milk and other cool treats packed away in old coolers with rusty racks. The counter was small and surrounded by cigarettes and cigars. It was definitely a neighborhood store, small but busy—owned by a Korean couple.

Nicholas sat outside by a Coke machine for an hour

before the husband had seen him sitting there and came out to investigate. Nicholas thought for sure that he was going to be shooed away like a wayward dog. He just smiled at the shop owner and asked how his night was going. The owner looked him over for a quick moment before answering with a stern face and returning to his counter inside.

The store would be safe for Nicholas—for the time being—and he was able to collect an extra dollar and seventy-three cents. He began to think that maybe this new store would be better than UDF—a Mecca safe from ferocious beggars.

The streets had emptied, the wind and trains were the only sounds to ring out in the night. He stood up from his little nook and ventured in to the small store, his pockets a-jingling with change. He slid his hand in to his pocket and stirred the nickels and quarters with his fingers.

The Korean couple eyed him suspiciously for a moment and then diverted their eyes back to their paperwork as he flashed them a smile. Nicholas made his way through the store, swiping up a package of bologna, a box a crackers, and a small bottle of apple juice. He carried them towards the counter and set them down gently, amongst an assortment of smoking apparatuses that lived there.

The woman rang him up and bagged his goods. He counted out the change on the countertop and handed it over to her with a quiet, "thanks." The couple watched him as he headed out the door, letting the December wind in as the little bell rang overhead.

He stepped out into the blustery, snowy night on Summit Street and the husband called to him, "Have a good night." Nicholas nodded to him with a grateful smile and left.

"What a nice man," the wife said to her husband once the stranger had gone.

Things seemed to be ending pretty well that night on earth, but below its crust things were only starting— slowly edging onward, coming to a boil. Tyriano was locked away in his office, which was nothing more than a small burrow that housed an old, wooden desk surrounded by stacks of books. None of the Minikins had noticed his disappearance; he would often hide away in his office.

Temelephas continued in his eternal circle as Dezriak moved silently through the caverns, quickly seizing reign of power. "I'm in charge now," he issued to every Minikin he came across. All of the Minikins seemed confused by this but quickly accepted the new change and proceeded with their work.

Dezriak found himself standing on the shelf that overlooked the tired, old elephant in the midst of his arduous task. He imagined what it would be like when Temelephas was gone, replaced by his dream machine; cold and metallic, a construct of gears and cogs, turning in small circles, ruled by bright and blipping lights. He imagined it wobbling and clanging loudly, turning the earth and progressing time.

A Minikin stepped up to him and stood by, awaiting orders. "Have you found the baby?" was all Dezriak said.

"No, sir," he answered obediently.

"You better," Dezriak continued, "And when you do, dispose of it … or, I will dispose of you." Even as he threatened the life of that inferior creature, he never took his eyes off of the elephant and what he envisioned in its stead. After all, Minikins are lesser than Watchers, and making eye contact with one would be beneath him. The Minikin trembled with fear while he scampered away, off to preserve his life by ending that of another.

Temelephas could feel Dezriak's cold stare and was not very fond of it. *Something has changed,* he thought to himself, *I don't know what for sure, but I know the change is there.* He wondered where his Watcher had disappeared to; he missed his soft voice resonating off the cavern walls.

Temelephas had just gotten into a great train of thought—which was always a heavy task for him to take on—when it was suddenly derailed by a new noise. It was light and bubbly and trailed off at the end. It came from close to the ground, so he half expected to see a Minikin there when he looked.

He looked and there was no Minikin. Instead, there sat a very happy and dirty baby human. The elephant couldn't help but smile and give off a bellow from his long, gray trunk. Franklin giggled at the great beast and clapped his chubby ... little ... baby, human hands.

The little ones sang and danced

through the snow

as it brought to mind a forecast of

snowballs and days off from school.

They all sang, singing along to the carols

that swam in the air overhead.

5

Edward and Lily were sprawled out in their bed, listening to the enduring hum of the blustery, winter night. His arm was tightly wrapped around her as if he felt a sudden, dreadful fear of losing her. She purred with content against him; her hair splashed across his shoulder. "Nice night," she cooed as she watched his closed eyes.

"Mm-hmm," he responded mindlessly, then went back to deep breathing and balancing on the edge of sleep. As his chest heaved and sank with his sleepy breathes he could feel her attentive eyes upon him.

"What do you want for breakfast?" she pried, denying him sleep, but he remained defiantly silent. She repeated her question, but only after a short, quick elbow to his ribcage.

"Anything you want," he answered obediently. He had been so close to sleep when she had called him back. Sweet dreams laid just before him; lush, green trees amongst flower sprouting bushes, fairies quietly beckoning him with come hither fingers. Then she yanked him back with a violent elbow.

"Well, I want some of that melon we have and some toast … maybe some orange juice," she half whispered to him, her eyes glued to his face. "Sound good to you?"

"Mm-hmm," he murmured, mouth half open.

"But, we're out of orange juice ... so, I'm going to need you to grab some from the store in the morning, ok?" she asked.

"Mm-hmm," he murmured again. Her questioning ceased then and she slouched against him, but not before giving him a quick peck on the cheek. Their conversation left Edward with nothing except the sweet, deep seeded desire for sleep. He soon obtained it and raced off towards a dreamland where nothing ever went wrong and you never ran out of orange juice.

Nicholas—at that very moment—was perched atop his trusty roof once more; the snow from that day soaking into the butt of his jeans. This time, though, he knew his rooftop was not a train. There was no scenery racing past him, no smoke stack billowing skyward. It was just a roof.

He stretched back and looked up to the foggy stars, hidden away by straying clouds and the biggest nuisance of city life—light pollution. It left him at a disadvantage for stargazing and somehow left him feeling homesick. He sighed from time to time, releasing his slight frustrations with each steamy breath.

His sister was inside, dozing in her favorite armchair as the television gently hummed before her; its abnormal light dancing upon her. In her lap lay a medium's manual, face down and half read. It was entitled *I Can Reach Beyond the Veil* and was written by a leader in the field, Marcel Delacroix. On its cover was a bearded man—presumably the writer—gazing out mysteriously with a lone, arched brow. His hands were held out in a manner that would lead you to believe he was about to do something remarkable.

Nicholas steered clear of Camilla's books and the same went for the television. Nothing good ever came from it, he realized at an early age. He just didn't trust the thing, it was too unnatural. It only served to distract him from the more interesting things around him, such as a sky full of stars.

Even as a child, all he wanted to do after the sun went down was to take in the night sky. All the children at school ever talked about were *the Twilight Zone, Batman,* and *My Favorite Martian.* None of it held any interest for Nicholas. *His* fall line-up consisted of Pegasus, Andromeda, and her mother Cassiopeia. And when he grew tiresome of those same, old constellations, he would just create his own—naming them for his family members.

The more he gazed upon the sprawled out stars, the more he wished he could walk amongst them—like a gardener through his lilies. He would step across the intergalactic dust clouds, leaning over to smell those burning buds of gas. And when they were in full blossom, he would pick them from the sky and rest them in a giant vase.

How laughable, he thought, thinking back to those days. It's funny … the flexibility of a child's mind and the things they dream; all their thoughts so open and fragile. He clung to that philosophy of dreaming, and strove to continue through life embracing it—to be a scraggily, grey haired child.

If only he could pluck the stars tonight.

Tibil was lying out on a park bench, admiring the same night sky. His belly was full with the dog he ate earlier and a mystical thing he found in a "bar" called "peanuts". His stomach was settling as he took in the blanket of stars overhead, the magic of their brilliance; radiating through the darkness. They winked at him as if welcoming him back.

He felt strangely at home beneath the open, night sky, but this nagging loneliness swept through. He had never felt so free in his whole life than he had that day, but something tugged at him … making him wish to be home once more. He tried to shake the feeling, but even the night around him couldn't drown it out.

The wintry wind blew over Tibil and he felt the chill he thought he'd forgotten come racing back to him. He shivered once and then wadded his little body up as he slowly began to doze. He thought again about what it was he could possibly be missing. He smiled, knowing "missing" was not the right word.

Sure, he missed his family, but they rarely saw one another anymore. He didn't miss the work, the heat, or the gruel he ate. He simply refused to believe he could ever miss the Underworld.

Then his mind found Temelephas; that giant, slow, lumbering beast … turning his wheel in the back of his mind. He was the only one he truly missed—felt bad for. He was the innocent one in this wicked game they were all forced to play—a mindless slave to creation.

If only Temelephas was with him, that behemoth that spun the world. He could nearly imagine him, lying beside his bench in a snowy patch in the park. *What would he think of this wondrous night sky*, Tibil wondered. *Would his eyes be as big as mine? Would they twinkle in wonderment of the stars as well?*

It was thoughts of Temelephas that gestated in his mind as he fell asleep, keeping a smile on his face through the night.

The baby just sat there … his sleepy eyes struggling to a hold its gaze upon the huge creature that Temelephas truly was. The elephant—on the other hand—was busy trying to figure out whether or not the little thing feared him; or more importantly, if *he* feared *it*. Their eyes met with every turn Temelephas took, and the baby neither moved nor whimpered. *He must not be afraid,* Temelephas reasoned, doing a bang-up job at his first pass at reasoning anything at all.

Temelephas came to an agreement in his mind that he liked the little thing, even though he couldn't pin down a reason why he would. He wanted to touch it, to feel another living thing, but it remained too far away. It stayed hidden between two boulders, sitting there for a long while now. He wished he could talk to it, ask it questions and have a *real* conversation. The only noises he was able to muster were grunts and bellowing blasts from his trunk.

So he kept on walking his circle, wondering about this new visitor and how he got to be here. *Has he always been here? Why have I never seen anything like it? How long will it be staying?* Temelephas thought on all these things, his mind busier than it had ever been. Then he noticed that the baby began to slowly close its eyes.

The little lashes would bob up and down, staying down longer than they did up. When the baby realized that they were down, his head would rock back and up the eyelashes would come. Drool began to spill out of his mouth, forming a pool on its chin before beginning a slow trek downwards.

Up and down his head bobbed; each time it remained down for longer and longer. His head finally slumped onto his chubby, little shoulder and his eyes remained closed. His tiny chest heaved greatly for such little breathes.

It was asleep. Temelephas found himself feeling something he had never felt before. It was an urge that suddenly came into being within him as he thought what only women are compelled to think in such situations. *I just want to hold it!*

It's funny ...

the flexibility of a child's

mind and the things

they dream; all their thoughts

so open and fragile. He clung

to that philosophy of dreaming,

and strove to continue

through life embracing it—to

be a scraggily, grey haired

child. If only he could pluck

the stars tonight.

6

When he woke the next morning, with Lily's hair on his face and her hand in his shirt, Edward had completely forgotten his nocturnal promise. He got up—as was routine—showered briskly in scalding water and brushed his teeth till they could be brushed no more. All the while his mind struggled to remember something, plagued by the vow he made, chiding him from the other side of consciousness for forgetting something so simple and silly.

He dressed quickly with no thought on fashion and made his way down to the living room. He settled onto the couch as he turned on the television with a push of a button. He flipped and skipped his ways through the channels with the ease of an expert channel surfer. He watched a bit of news, a bit of a cartoon, and even suffered through a small, but intolerable bit of a shopping channel.

There was nothing on, he decided, which was somewhat odd considering the number of channels he subscribed to and the amount of money he paid for the luxury of exercising his right thumb. But he felt assured that it would be wise money that was placed on him in a thumb wrestling contest ... him and the Mighty Thumbo.

Thumbo's workout came to an end, though, as he ceased the channel flipping and stopped on the weather channel—with the idea that he might as well learn something new. Settled on his channel, he stretched out across the couch, searching for the hidden impression he had perfected over the years. It was around this time that Lily plodded her way downstairs with heavy, morning feet.

Her hair was a tousled mess of red, flying about, giving off the impression of an ancient Celtic warrior woman. She stumbled through the room with her eyes squinted—having not found their place in this new day. She glanced at the TV in a way that made it seem as if it was painful to her and then looked accusingly at her fiancé.

"It's very important," he said defensively. She just shook her head cynically and stretched out on top of him. "No ... seriously, it is!"

"Sure," she said dryly. She rubbed her face into his chest in an effort to rid her eyes of that stubborn sleep.

"Look," he said, guiding her eyes with a finger to the screen. "There's a storm system over Indiana and it's coming right for us."

"Well, that's there," she said, "this is here." She then yawned her tired breath into his neck and continued to watch nothing at all. She laid atop him in a way that always reminded Edward of a cat; nestling into him until she found a nice, soft spot that made for easy napping.

"You're reminding me of my dad ... he watches this junk," she said with the least amount of enthusiasm any human has ever used while saying anything at all. *"All ... the ... time."*

"Good, then we'll have something in common," he said as he watched a Meteorologist talk about how storm systems move. "Then we can discuss matters involving cold fronts and warm fronts. We can bond over quiet chats about hot flashes."

"I hope not," she said with short laugh, "neither of you are menopausal ... at least I hope."

"The point being that ... maybe he won't hate me so much."

"He doesn't hate you," Lily said, glancing at him with the defiance of a cat that had just been startled awake. He just looked up at her with an all knowing eye and she looked away from it. "But I guess it can't hurt. This *will* make the holidays ... much, much more boring ... just so you know."

He clicked the remote again, sending a signal to the boob tube that shot it over to a children's show, no longer being able to sit idly by as weather was discussed ad nauseam. Lily just continued her luxurious breathing, taking in the scent of his neck. Edward would always remind her it was only soap, to which she would always reply that 'it smelled best on him'. This time, though, he merely smiled.

"Did you remember my orange juice?" she asked finally, breaking the still air and sentencing Edward's smile to a quick, painless death. He refused to answer, just breathing air sharply in through gritted teeth. "You didn't ... *did* you?"

"No," he answered.

"How am I supposed to have breakfast?"

"I'll go right now," he said as he slowly wiggled his way out from under her.

"No ... don't go," she said coyly, "this couch isn't as comfy as you."

"No," he said with bravado. "I promised to get you juice ... I'll get you juice." He found his shoes beside the arm chair and quickly went about tying them up. "If I can't remember the little things, then how can I ever remember the important ones?"

"What about the Indiana storm?"

"I won't be gone that long," he said with a mild smile. "Besides, I'm sure it can get along without me."

"Fine, but no dallying, young man ... you get

the juice, come straight home … and squeeze right back between me and this couch." Lily gave him a look that made him wish he had remembered to run to the store earlier. In the back of his mind his subconscious self was screaming, *I told you so!*

🐘

The baby woke with a yawn—his face forming a toothless abyss—and stretched his little arms. Temelephas, who didn't know how to sleep—let alone what it entailed— was completely confused by this foreign ritual. The baby's eyes grew big as he examined his whereabouts for what might as well have been the first time. Everything seemed brand new to him till he spied that great elephant, which he regarded with a smile.

He started to move as babies do, in a crawling fashion out from his hiding spot between the boulders. He came to the front of the large rocks and sat back on his haunches. He smiled again, showing off his budding, baby teeth and gave a fat fingered wave, Temelephas returned the wave awkwardly with his trunk and smiled back the best he could, which wasn't very well.

The baby giggled at him and began to move closer and closer to Temelephas, which worried the great giant. He discovered that he was definitely more afraid of this little one than it was of him. He still had no idea who or what it was. As the baby came closer, the idea of it shot both glee and terror through his thick hide.

Was this what the Minikins were so afraid of, he asked himself. *Why?* He didn't see such a small thing being such a big threat, but maybe it was. Temelephas would know soon enough as the baby continued to slowly move closer.

He could hear the shrill cry of a Minikin from the other side of the cavern and looked over in time to see him hopping away quickly, calling out anxiously. The great elephant didn't know much—that much he was sure of—but he got the *feeling* that this was not a good situation. He could only hope that his new, little guest of his would remain safe.

Temelephas continued in his circle as well; his eyes shooting about, on the lookout for any sign of trouble. None had come yet, but he was sure that it would sooner or later. Whatever came for the little one, he was sure he would be ready for it, and still the baby came closer.

The baby began to move quicker then, as if he were heading towards a giant teddy bear rather than a living, breathing mammal. His dirty knees were scuffing and scratching along the rock floor, yet still he came.

Temelephas saw the baby right beside him, mere feet away, but he continued on his predestined path. When he turned his head away, he saw him there, a strange man with blue feathers that Temelephas couldn't place. The man stood there with a red-faced scowl and his voice was booming.

"There you are!" he cried. The baby jumped and saw the man with strange hair and his smile immediately turned upside down. "You have caused me many headaches, little one." Dezriak took long strides to reach the baby quickly, which only upset Franklin more and brought wailing tears to his eyes.

Temelephas swung his head around and saw the small, horribly contorted mouth, hearing the yowls of sadness flowing from its little spout. The baby cried wholeheartedly, either because he knew his fun was over or because the feathery hair scared the bejesus out of him. "Stop your crying at once," Dezriak demanded as he stood over the baby.

"What should we do with it?" a Minikin asked as he came to his new master's side.

"I don't know," Dezriak said honestly. "Find a deep, craggy hole and throw him down it, I suppose."

The Minikin didn't seem too happy to hear this order. Temelephas wasn't happy with it either.

The elephant looked at the child, whose face was red, tears running away from tiny, clamped eyes. Then he looked at the vicious creature that stood over him—and vicious he was. Temelephas' eyes squinted in anger and a loud bellow erupted from inside his chest. Dezriak swung his attention to the elephant in time to see its large trunk come swinging at him.

Dezriak gave a short, high pitched scream as he was punted clear across the cavern. He flew as gracefully as his feathery hair would allow before slamming into the hard, cavern wall. The whole Underworld shook mightily from the crash and Dezriak slumped to the ground.

The baby's crying stopped as suddenly as it had begun. He gazed up at his rescuer with glassy eyes and an unsure mouth, not quite ready to smile. Temelephas gave him a gentle wave with the same trunk that had just flung the scary man across the room.

Franklin giggled and waved back.

Edward scurried down the street through the cold air. The wind had picked up and began to blow his overcoat to and fro. He was on a mission, a small one, *but nonetheless a mission*, he thought. He had to prove himself to be a good provider, even if it *was* only orange juice.

He came to the door of his neighborhood shop and pushed it in, setting off the tinny ring of its overhead bell. He nodded to the quiet woman that was perched behind the counter then shouted a hello to the man in back.

It was a little market that smelled musky, dimly lit by slowly dying neon tubes. They had lunch meat and milk and other cool treats packed away in old coolers with rusty racks. The counter was small and surrounded by cigarettes and cigars. It was definitely a neighborhood store, small but busy—owned by a Korean couple.

He was met by a slap on the back from Mr. Lee as he headed for the coolers. Edward had always like the couple that owned the market. He couldn't get *all* of his groceries there, but did as much business with the Lees as he could.

After exchanging their normal niceties and inquiring about one another's families, Edward headed to the cooler to get his trophy—the bottle of orange juice. With it tucked safely beneath his arm, he headed to the register. He was rung up with efficient speed, Mrs. Lee's nimble fingers tapping at the keys, and Edward asked for five, one dollar scratch off tickets. With his bag of goodies in hand, he headed back out to the cold and blustery morning of Summit Street.

He was about to begin his walk home when he came across an older man sitting in a warm, little nook between the Coke machine and the wall, hiding from the cold with a foam cup in hand. He didn't know why he felt so compelled to do so, but he walked over to the strange man and stared down at him. "Hi," Edward said warmly.

"Hey," the man said back. He was thin and rough around the edges, with hair that had once been dark but was now graying; losing its battle against time. It seemed to Edward as if the man had met more bad days than good.

"Pretty cold out, isn't it?" Edward asked as he looked the stranger over. "At least for a jacket and a Zeppelin shirt."

"Sure is," the man answered with a shivering smile.

"I would give you some change, but I haven't any, but a few pennies, and that would be more of an insult than anything else," Edward clumsily said, feeling foolish even as the words fell from his lips.

"No worries," the man said with a bristly grin.

"Well, I do feel bad," he said nervously, "especially since I just brought it up." Edward gave a quick laugh and then remembered something suddenly. "But, I can give you a bit of hope." He reached into his bag and withdrew one of his lottery tickets, a green and red one with Christmas stockings, and passed it to him.

"We can all use a little hope," the man said with a smile as he looked the ticket over.

"Merry Christmas," Edward said with a nod.

"Merry Christmas," the man said back, his dirty hand sliding the ticket into his worn jacket pocket.

"I'm Ed," he said, extending his hand to the man crouched before him.

"Pleased to meet you," the other said, shaking Edward's hand. "My name is Nicholas."

The Minikins tried repeatedly to get the baby away from the elephant's track, but they always had Temelephas to contend with. No matter from which direction they came, trying to pierce his protective circle, Temelephas could always swing his trunk or kick out with a heavy foot. Dezriak remained sitting against the wall, rubbing his bruised head. He continued to scream—spitting out orders, curses, and threats—but no one heard him over the terrible racket of Temelephas defending the baby.

The little, red headed Minikins caused Franklin to laugh uncontrollably as they flew off and rolled away—little clowns for his amusement. He leaned back and began to clap erratically and fell further back, sliding into Temelephas' well-trodden trench. The old elephant hadn't noticed—being busy with the Minikins.

Temelephas smacked the Minikins around with such ease and talent that he was almost proud of himself. He looked for the baby as he made another pass, but was shocked to see it had disappeared. It was not where he remembered seeing it last, but he was forced to continue his walk, step by step.

Lifting his foot again, he went to place it before him … a simple task he had done mindlessly for forever. Then, he heard it … the slight coo of the young one, calling out from beneath his raised foot. Every bit of Temelephas wanted to put his foot down … squashing the baby under his weight as he continued his walk.

It wasn't a desire to kill the baby, that wasn't what drove Temelephas … he would rather kill himself than harm the little, defenseless thing. But nothing could stop him … he had heard it time and time again. His foot was held frozen in air for a moment, but that was all it took.

He had stopped.

Order fell away as chaos stepped in. The wheel had halted and the only sounds were the rumbling of the earth around them and the solitary scream of Dezriak, screaming because he had witnessed the one thing that should never have come to pass.

He had his purpose. He had a reason to exist that was so imperative that none had questioned whether he would continue in his walk. But Temelephas had stopped, and so had the world around him.

They had been shaking hands at that moment, a rumble came crawling up from the earth beneath their feet. "What was that?" Edward asked; Nicholas shrugged. The earth shook and gave off a long, slow grumble, like an upset tummy.

And in an instant, the sky tore open. The wind became violent, throwing Edward to the ground where he flopped around like a tattered ragdoll. Nicholas kept hold of his hand and braced himself in his little nook.

The wind pulled on Edward, wrenching him upwards, tearing the clothes from his body and his bag from his other hand. His eyes followed them and he shuddered with fear as he saw them being sucked right into the sky. The wind pulled him with more vigor and all Edward could do was scream as the sky tried to swallow him.

What did I do to deserve this? All I wanted was some juice!

"Hold on!" Nicholas screamed over the disgruntled wind, both hands now fixed around Edward's wrist. Glass was shattering all around them; shop windows, house windows, and street lamps ... all shattered, all pulled towards the sky.

"He couldn't have stopped!" Dezriak screamed over the din of the world coming apart. "It's impossible!" Temelephas, ignoring the quaking earth beneath his feet, bent over and grasped the baby with his trunk. He pulled him up in front of his face and looked at him, his chubby legs dangling effortless beneath him. Franklin smiled at him as the walls of the cavern cracked about them, showering the floor with pebbles.

Lily was rocked off of her couch and scrambled along the floor as it, too, shook. Picture frames and little knick-knacks shot out from their usual spots, exploding in glass. She screamed loudly as she crawled quickly towards the nearest threshold, the only thing she remembered about surviving earthquakes.

She huffed and puffed, tears streaming down her face as she clamped her hands over her ears; trying to lock out the noise. *Dear God,* she prayed; probably for the first time since Sunday school, *please ... watch over Edward.*

Little couch cushions and other unidentifiable

objects flew out the pane-less windows, pulled by unseen hands; the wind tossing things about like a child in the midst of a tantrum. Lily just huddled there, fending off the racket as she sobbed and prayed; if it were to ever work … then, was the time.

Camilla woke in her favorite chair to the sound of exploding glass. She was jump started like a car and shot straight up. The wind was whipping pass her, tearing at the corners of her clothes. "Nicky!" she screamed. "Nicky … please God, where are you Nicky?!?!"

The lamp on the table beside her was sucked through the window, which was now nothing more than a gapping mouth. She screamed as she dropped to the floor, ripped pages from paperbacks streaking through the room.

"Oh, God!" Edward screamed, his eyes busy watching trash cans and mailboxes as they rolled down the street before being engulfed by the gray and ominous sky. "What's happening?"

"Hold on!" Nicholas screamed for what could have been the hundredth time, but he knew his fingers were slipping from Edward's wrist. He readjusted his grip with his second hand and prayed it would work. But by then he could feel the pull, too. He felt the hungry sky trying to devour them, pulling them into the murkiness above. He looked beyond Edward's legs and saw clouds racing past so fast that they appeared as one—a great, black, rippling sheet.

Nicholas's legs began to weaken; he steadied them again and felt his old knees cry out for relief. He wondered when his knees would give or when the pain would get to be so great that he would cave to it. He prayed it would never come to that. *Hold on*, he screamed to himself, *please, God … hold on.*

🐘

Temelephas swung Franklin up on to his back, unaware of the turmoil that unfurled about him. The baby grabbed a baby-sized fistful of long, gray hair and giggled, his legs sliding into it. The big elephant could feel the small creature nestling its face against the crown of his head.

He could feel its little giggles radiating through his skin. Temelephas smiled.

🐘

Edward was dangling by one arm then; his other arm was sucked backwards, his clothing no more than tattered fabric, rippling like a war-worn flag. The air was filled with the rumbling anger of the sky above and the cries of countless other people, all facing the same havoc. The cries continued on in a morbid chorus, but some faded off into the vacuum of space.

Edward cried, all he could think about was that he would never see Lily again. That they would never be married; never be together through sickness and health. That he would be sucked up into the stratosphere and be tossed about until he be dead.

Nicholas' legs started to give out and he was suddenly pressed with that horrible choice. Should he let go … save himself? Or hold on to this virtual stranger and accept *his* fate as his own. He continued to hold on, his sweaty hands clasping tightly on to Edward's. His legs buckled and they were dragged out into the street.

Edward cried out to him, but Nicholas held fast. They were pulled upward; their bodies together then in a tearful embrace. They began their ascension to the heavens.

🐘

Temelephas, with the baby on his back, resumed his walk once more. Dezriak watched with furious eyes. The Minikins stood idly by, afraid to step any closer to Temelephas and his wheel. Franklin rode on the back of his neck, his fingers intertwined in his mane.

🐘

The wind began to fade away as the two strangers were being rushed towards their inevitable deaths. When it did, they fell back to earth just as fast as they left it. Nicholas' body fell into the windshield of a car that had been sliding down the street. Edward's fell into the hood of the same car, their hands still joined.

The young girl that had been driving the car freaked out—for good reason—and screamed as she leapt out from behind the wheel. She had just gotten her driver's license and knew that her mother would find *some* way to blame this all on her. She prayed to God that her parents wouldn't murder her.

And everything else that had found its way climbing through the sky fell to earth as well. Trash cans, bikes, plants … think of anything, no matter how trivial, and it probably fell as well, somewhere. Many died during that eerie storm that swept across the globe, but many more were thankful for simply surviving.

There were also many half-miracles to be thankful for. Little things that people took as signs of a benevolent spirit that watched over them. It was something people clung to in order to feel more comfort with the unknown universe around them.

For example: a small dog fell back to earth, landing somewhat safely in a tree near its home. It was a cute dog, able to capture and hold the attention of the media. Misty—the little morkie—was found sitting in the tree as she barked at the sky.

7

"This morning, the world was struck by a ghastly storm," the woman said from the studio of a news station. She was in her late twenties, but could have been deceptively older; with honey hair, perfectly molded ... smiling with blood red lips.

"The freak storm—that we once thought was only focused over Franklin County—appears to have occurred across the globe. We now go to our correspondent in Washington D.C., David Mathis, who is now waiting for a statement from the President. David?"

The screen split down the middle, allowing room for a clean cut man in a gray blazer and yellow tie. He was standing in the crowded press room of the White House, surrounded by his peers—all of whom seemed anxious for answers. His face was bright and cheerful, even though the news he would speak of would be horrifying. To be a journalist takes a lot of courage ... or at least a little obliviousness.

"Thank you, Denise," he said, pausing to take a quick breath. "What happened this morning is in fact a mystery, scientists and meteorologists around the world continue to debate as to whether or not it can even be classified as a storm. Reports continue to roll in concerning the so-called storm and the damage it has left behind.

"Earlier this morning, we received word from China that bricks from its Great Wall were pulled into the sky by the high winds. Once the incident had ended, the bricks—along with everything else from the area—fell into the China Sea."

"Oh, that is a shame," Denise chimed in, her slight smile purposely turned down, her head shaking. There was a short pause from David's end, just a toothy smile and a quick shudder. Then the correspondent took a deep breath.

"Yes ... Denise," he said quietly, "Yes it is. We can expect the President to appear shortly to give an official report to the people and answer a few, brief questions ... In fact, here he comes now."

The camera swung around to a podium that carried the seal of the President, a modest flag stood in the corner behind it. A stout man with receding hair and pockmarks as a reminder of his childhood stepped up to it and announced the President. Flashes went off and immediately the members of the press began to speak, shouting questions and pushing one another about.

The President stepped up to the podium with the utmost air of confidence. His face was strong, but only in the way that would calm the people that followed him. He stood there for a moment, waiting for the crowd to quiet. When it did not, he held up one hand to call the room to order. *Showtime*, he thought to himself as he opened his mouth.

"Good afternoon America ... and I extend a warm welcome to our brothers and sisters around the world ... I say that ... because we all now know ... that America was not a lone victim to this morning's storm." He allowed his words to sink in and flashes to crack off. If anything could be said about the President, it was that he had quite a stage presence.

"Some crazy stuff happened," he continued. The press was in hushed bewilderment and the President wished he had taken more time to prepare. "We don't want it to happen again ... So, I've put together a committee of Congressmen ... at this very moment, their busy brainstorming ... getting to the bottom of this. I have been assured ... that they all received high science grades back in college."

"Mr. President," a squirrelly man in a brown coat said from the front, "Wouldn't it be wiser to bring somebody from an official scientific field in as an advisor to the government, rather than exhausting their limited knowledge?"

The President licked his dry lips and looked at the reporter briefly as his mind worked towards an answer. There were always roadblocks ... no one got to the highest office of the nation without steering around them. "That's a good question, Stanley ... I appreciate that ...See, we as a people ... we as a country, matter of fact; we need to stand on our own two feet ... We don't *need* the UN ... we can handle our own problems. That's why I have ..."

"I meant, shouldn't we use *real* scientists to find the source of this morning's catastrophe instead of Junior Congressman?" The galley was filled with murmuring and the sound of flash bulbs popping off. The President's eyes shifted back and forth as sweat gathered on his tanned brow. *You got yourself in a* real *pickle*, he told himself.

"Stanley ... do you know how to make a tornado out of a couple of empty pop bottles?" The President snapped back; hands together, fingers laced with his head bobbing up and down.

"No, Mr. President ... no I don't" Stanley answered with a wry smile.

"Well, I've been assured that Congressman Joe Sanders from the great state of Nebraska *does*."

🐘

Orange juice ... I have to get orange juice, Edward thought. He was unconscious—but had no idea that he was. His body was bruised and battered, but he didn't know that either as he slipped through his dream.

In his dream he was lying on a couch—much like the one from his living room—floating through the clouds. He looked over the side, through the wispy, cirrus strands and saw fields of yellow and brown. He needed to get down there—he had the *urge* to get down—but knew he couldn't fly. So ... he lay back down and watched as the sky crept by overhead.

After a bit of a rest, he looked over the couch's edge again, but this time—to his surprise—he spotted a giant, orange juice factory. It was a shiny, metal dome, with a giant orange atop it, surrounded by orange groves. Obviously, an orange juice factory is all it could have been. *Orange juice*, he thought again, *I need orange juice.*

Just as in childhood, in dreams we come up with astoundingly ridiculous ideas ... plots to skirt around obstacles that are otherwise impossible except for our dreamy way of thinking. In Edward's case ... the puzzle was how to get from a couch floating thousands of feet in the air to the ground below. The astoundingly ridiculous answer to that, of course, was a makeshift parachute, MacGyver'd out of a throw blanket that was miraculously draped over the back of said couch.

With each of the blanket's four corners clasped in his hands, two a piece, he slid off the edge of the couch and fell. The fall was short, a quick blast of air shooting pass him; it filled the blanket—pluming it open. The blanket-chute caught hold of the air and held him up, his feet dangled beneath him as he began his descent to earth.

The air was cool against his face and Edward was shocked to find he was not afraid. He looked around himself and saw the thin clouds moving through him, tickling his nose. *It's nice up here*, he thought. The further down he went the more he saw, the giant orange factory growing beneath him.

A gaggle of geese flew slowly by, their long wings flapping lazily as if they swam though gelatin. They looked so peculiar to him, much funnier looking than any geese he had seen before. They flew by him and continued on to whatever destination they had. Edward wished he could follow them.

But, Edward had other plans to see through, so he just continued his gentle fall. In Edward's mind, this falling to earth thing was taking a rather long time. He had never done it before, but he had always imagined it would be a much quicker chore, something that could easily be fit in between two other errands. A last minute add on.

A white swan flew pass him and Edward gazed at it and its beautiful, shiny, white wings. Edward had never seen anything as beautiful and elegant as that swan. He was genuinely sad to see it go. As if hearing his thoughts, the sleek bird turned about and flew back to him and began to circle him slowly.

"Never mind the juice, Edward," the swan said with its orange beak.

"I can't ... it's for Lily," he calmly replied—as if this wasn't his first exchange with a bird. The swan turned in a graceful circle worthy of a Tchaikovsky symphony and began to shed her glossy white feathers. There was a cloud of feathers then ... a sea of them in midair and they fell slowly away. When they did it revealed Lily ... floating in a golden, unworldly light, her body enshrined by clouds.

"Never mind the juice, Edward," the vision repeated, floating closer to him. *"Just come home to me ... please?"*

"But, I promised you orange juice," Edward said proudly, beaming with the bravado that has adorned mankind since its inception. The vision of Lily floated closer still and

gazed into his eyes, her face glowing warmly as a candle only could. She brushed her hands across his face and laid her lips gently upon his cheek.

"*Just come home to me,*" she whispered in his ear. Her slight voice rippled through Edward's subconscious and he swooned at the mere timbre of her voice. He smiled like an idiot, entranced by her.

"*Ok,*" he said with glossy eyes and a wide smile. "*I'll come home.*" She held her arms open, welcoming him to her. He released the corners of the blanket and threw his arms out for her.

If she had been real, he would have felt her in his arms. He would have held her in a beautiful, levitating embrace. But she wasn't real ... so he couldn't.

What had been the vision of Lily burst in a cloudy explosion—little bits of her floating off towards the heavens. Edward was left grasping nothing but thin air, immediately hit with an 'uh-oh' moment. And so he fell to earth.

"Can you hear me?" a distant voice called out, echoing as if being tossed down a long hallway. His eyes were blinded by a brilliant light. He couldn't get away from the light—it was so bright and intrusive. All he could think about was closing his eyes, getting away from the light—but he couldn't.

He murmured, trying to beg the light to leave him be, but his words were jumbled like a freshly opened jigsaw puzzle. As if controlled merely by his will the light went away, leaving him in a dark confusion. All that surrounded him then was the murky fog and the loud, steady thumping of his heart.

He laid there, his mind swimming. Did he fall? He seemed to remember a fall, the air sweeping pass him. There was a fall, he was sure of it, but he wondered how far he fell … even why? Everything else was lost to him.

"What's your name?" the voice asked from the other side of the black haze. *What a silly thing to ask*, he thought. Such an easy question … who wouldn't know the answer to that? He opened his mouth to answer, but nothing came.

What's my name, he wondered. He had to have a name … even the lowest, most hideous *thing* on earth has a name. What was his? He was too afraid to ask.

His vision started to come back to him like brilliant pieces of colored glass falling into place in a stained-glass window. Then the details as the glare faded from behind the colorful pane. Then it was all normal again.

There was a man hanging over him. He seemed to be looking closely at his face with a mild look of concern. "What's your name?" he asked, his voice ringing.

"I don't know my name," he answered, his voice dry and harsh, "I don't think I have one."

"It's more likely you are suffering a bit of amnesia."

"Is that normal?" he asked.

"It is after a fall … and you had a bad one. You were found on top of a car."

"Am I at the hospital?" he asked, rapidly blinking his eyes.

"No, I'm afraid the hospital was full, there were a lot of accidents today during that storm. We had to set up an emergency site here at Medary Elementary School. I'm Dr. Bomser."

"What storm?"

"Man, your brain must be like Swiss cheese," Bomser said.

"Well, do you know who I am?"

"Yeah … your name is Nicholas Forrest."

"I don't feel like a Nicholas," he said as his head swam.

"Don't worry about it … I never felt like a Michael, myself," the doctor said. "We've contacted your sister, she should be here soon."

"I don't remember having a sister," he said.

"You won't remember a lot of things, but with rest and help from your sister ... I don't see why you can't fully recover it." The doctor stepped away from the cot that Nicholas occupied and began to scratch little chicken scratches on a clipboard, leaving Nicholas alone.

The idea of being trapped inside your own mind would terrify anyone, the walls to your own memories too high to scale. Nicholas was oddly at ease with the notion and simply just went about the errand of trying to remember any and all things. He tried to push against the metaphorical walls in his mind, but they stood firm, tall, and unmoved.

All he could really remember were the things the doctor just told him and he really didn't think that counted much. But inside him lay a sleeping desire. It was a need that was knock, knock, knocking at the inside of his skull like a woodpecker.

The object of his desire wasn't for him, though, it was for a beautiful woman. He remembered a dream, vaguely, and in it there was a woman calling to him. Everything was so blurry, though. In his dream, he knew her ... knew her name. But now he had diddlysquat.

What was it that he wanted for her so badly, he couldn't remember. He kept pushing on that wall in his mind. He could feel it reaching out to him, the memory, from the other side of the wall ... wanting to be found. He touched upon it, like a weed pushing through rocky soil, begging for the sun. And it came to him.

"Orange juice?" Nicholas said aloud. Dr. Bomser looked over at him inquisitively, setting the clipboard aside.

"Sorry, Nick ... we don't have any orange juice here."

🐘

On the other side of the school gymnasium lay the body of Edward Crosby. It had no broken bones but was scratched and bruised, beaten by the hood of a car. The only thing that was wrong with the body was that Edward Crosby wasn't in it. It was currently being occupied by the mind and soul of Nicholas Forrest. His—or rather Edward's—body ached.

A nurse had been in earlier to check on him, but she had been called away by a strange, woeful wail from another cot that sounded strangely like an injured cat. The young nurse gave a heavy sigh, closing her eyes and rubbing her forehead. She promised to return later as she dashed off, calling him Mr. Crosby as she hurried toward the crying cat.

Nicholas didn't feel the need to correct her; the place was loaded with the broken bodies of hundreds of injured people. It was pretty safe to assume that they all had their own names. She was bound to confuse them once in a while.

He couldn't see much from the cot he laid upon. His back ached thoroughly and they had no strong drugs on hand to alleviate it. So he kept his eyes closed and soaked in the noises around him; the crying, the beeping of machinery, the idle chatter of people who could only wait.

It was all so sad, the turmoil and disorder that filled this room as easily as the air they all breathed. He wished he could be of some help, but his own body remained riddled with pain and stiffness. All he could do was lay there, one arm tucked behind his head, reliving the events that led him there.

What a hell of a freak storm, he thought. *Pulled me and that other guy clean off the ground. Must have let up after a bit, 'cause I wouldn't be here otherwise.* The nurse came back minutes later, as flustered as ever, carrying a clipboard. She smiled broadly to hide the chaos that lurked behind her tired eyes.

"Well, I'm happy to say that you are free to go," she said as she watched him sit up slowly. Nicholas despised even the slightest movement of it for the pain it shot down his spine. He rubbed at his back, wincing softy as his palm tried to drive the soreness away.

"A woman's here to take you home ... I'm sorry, I forgot her name," she said with a poor attempt at a frown. Nicholas had always been pretty good at reading people. Her face was saying, *I'm glad you're okay, but I'm happier to see you leave.* Of course it was reasonable for her to feel that way. No doubt she had no desire to spend the whole day tending to injured people in an elementary school.

She went away again, leaving him alone—sitting on the edge of his cot. He pulled at the flimsy cloth that covered him, the drab blue found in any hospital. He waited patiently for his sister to appear at, screaming and crying all at once. Instead, a small face poked in, freckled and sad, with auburn hair tumbling down around her ears.

She was very frightened, but Nicholas couldn't help but notice her unsettling beauty. Her eyes were glossy; tears had run down her face recently, their dried up trails the only evidence of their passage. She ran to him in a burst and flung her arms around him.

"Thank God you're alright," she whimpered in his ear, tears springing up again and running freely. Nicholas felt awkward in her embrace but gave her a gentle squeeze in return. It was only the polite thing to do.

"Who are you?" he asked after she had finally released him.

"What?" she asked with a bit of a nervous laugh. Her mouth twitched, unsure whether it should smile or pout. "Are you serious?" Nicholas looked at her blankly. "I'm Lily ... your fiancée ..."

Nicholas looked hard at her, trying to catch any tell that she was playing some sort of sick joke on him. Her eyes were glassy and in the iris of them he could see himself as he stood before her. It wasn't the same, old, raggedy face he was accustomed to. It was younger, bruised, but younger ... his hair was windswept but dark and his face had grown glasses.

It wasn't him at all, Nicholas realized. The face he saw in her sweet, caring eyes ... was that of the man he tried to save. His head spun at the sight of himself.

He stumbled back a half step at the shock of it. His stomach churned and tumbled as he looked once more into her eyes at the vaguely familiar face that glared back. He felt as if he would pass out.

He remembered the feel of himself before and only then realized how it differed from how he felt now. The youth of this body—the newness of it—was masked by the pain from the fall it took. He looked at his hands and saw how smooth they were, how soft.

What happened to the other guy, he wondered. *Where did he go to?* He asked the questions in his head, releasing them to the universe in hopes that answers would come. They didn't though.

He was gone and somehow Nicholas had taken his place. One major thought seeped into his brain. It was a morbid thought and Nicholas was happy not to know from where it came. That thought was this: could he really take another man's life?

In an instant he knew that he could. It had been forced on him anyhow, this new body he inhabited ... the life it came with. *A new beginning for an old soul,* he reckoned. Would he miss his own life at all? Or could this new life— with a beautiful woman that loved him—be enough to make him forget it?

He looked back over at her and her shock stained eyes, her mouth hanging open. He felt her look—fragile and caring—and it pulled at him. It was a look that was hard to evade. Even as afraid as she was, she was still a beauty.

"I'm just kidding, babe," he finally said with a smile. Lily exhaled heavily, as if she had held her breath the entire time. Then she hit Edward in the arm with a meaningless fist.

"Dickhead," she cried, laughing nervously. She smiled at him, allowing herself to accept the horrible joke he had played on her. It would be hard not to, the way her heart reached out for him. She pulled him to her, planting her mouth on his.

8

Dezriak stood smoldering on the dark edge of the Great Cavern. His eyes, once like smoldering coals, now burned like a raging inferno; his face quivered, his brow furrowed, and his teeth were grinding away in his mouth. He stood, hushed in the shadows, his fists balled up at his sides. He bore the grimace of sheer animosity.

It steamed from within him—this hatred—and it was reserved for only one living thing in existence. That living thing was Temelephas. The old elephant had no idea how hate worked or even how something like it could drive people to do terrible things. He had no idea that he should be afraid.

Dezriak turned his back on the abhorred beast and its wheel and stormed off, seeking Tyriano in the one place he could be found. Two agents of the Gloom peeled away from the shadows as he walked and fell obediently in line behind him. Any Minikins they came across fell quickly against the walls, afraid of the dark guards that now always followed Dezriak like wisps of smoke.

His mind seethed with anger as he marched down the dimly lit corridors, teetering over the edge of madness. All his plotting and hard work ... gone in a flash. *All because a dumb elephant somehow refused to squash a baby. Who was he to stop his walk?* The only thing that kept him from shrieking aloud was the soothing knowledge that he *would* get his revenge.

He came to a halt outside a round, wooden door with an ornate, matching set of knob and hinges—made from brass. He brushed his hands through his feathery, blue hair as he tried to regain some of the composure he lost in the cavern. He couldn't let Tyriano see him flustered—he knew that much. He was glad to find the door locked, just as he had left it.

The Gloom fell flush against the shadowy walls behind him with a hiss and begun to wait in silence as they always had; in hiding. Waiting and watching. Dezriak pulled a key from his pocket. The door groaned as he pushed it inward.

There, in the middle of the room sat Tyriano, hunched over his desk. He held his head in the palms of his hand, his eyes peering down upon an open book on the history of colds and viruses. He looked up at the groaning sound of the door, his face remained apathetic as he saw Dezriak. "Good to see you again," he said calmly.

Dezriak knew that his old teacher must have learned of the events of that day. In his mind, he wondered if one of the Minikins had betrayed him, ran off at the first sign of trouble to whisper to their beloved friend through the oak door. Then the question became not if ... but how many. They never liked Dezriak.

"You too," he said back, his eyes hollow and weak, closing the door behind him.

"As you have most likely surmised, I already know about the current conundrum concerning Temelephas," Tyriano said, lifting his head heavily from his hands.

"It's hardly a conundrum," Dezriak said, doing his best to act calm and sure; picking up an ancient text and ruffling through its yellowed pages.

"The world stopped spinning ... Dezriak," Tyriano

said with a huff of laughter. "What *would* you have me call it?"

"It is nothing more than a mere setback."

"And does the High Council know of this *mere* setback?" he asked as he gazed at the back of his student's neck. There was silence. Dezriak brooded over the question, despising the older one's savvy.

"I'm sure they do," Dezriak said as he turned again to peer at him. "And I'm also sure they know that it was *your* pet, not mine, that stopped the turning." Dezriak tried his best to smile confidently, but it failed upon his lips.

"It happened on *your* watch," Tyriano said calmly, nearly in a whisper. "Do *not* think they will overlook that tidbit." Dezriak knew he was right. His blood boiled at the thought of being dismissed, demoted, or even banished. He couldn't face it … he would rather tear it all down around him then to be sent away.

He looked again at his former teacher, looking for something … some sign of wisdom hidden away. All he saw was the cynical smile of an old fool that had lost everything. Tyriano had once been such a strong and admirable Watcher … now he seemed broken. Dezriak would not be pulled in by him … he would not share in his fate.

"I think you had something to with this," Dezriak said with a sudden inferno of hate in his eyes. No calmness remained in his tone. His voice took on the chaotic tendency of a caged ape. It would have been fitting if he were to start beating on his chest.

"*Me?*" Tyriano asked sharply as he stood. "What could I have possibly done? How could I have had anything to do with this, locked in here like some rabid dog?" He would have moved towards Dezriak, he wanted to … but, he knew the Gloom lay in wait, just beyond the door—and no door can keep out the Gloom. "Why would I do *anything* to jeopardize this world?"

"I don't know," he said slowly, cautiously choosing each word. "Perhaps you're distraught, being fired can do that to people, right?"

"That's ridiculous," Tyriano said with a worried smile. "Who could ever be so mad as to stop the Turning ... destroying the world itself." Tyriano was eyeing the younger being then, watching his eyes flicker and the way his mouth contorted in miniature spasms. "Who in their right mind would do that?"

Dezriak smiled, but it was an empty sort ... a sad smile, meant to hide nefarious thoughts more than in joy. "People can do anything ... you've said so yourself."

"But, those are people ... human beings. We are the Watchers! We are meant to know better ... we *live* by higher standards!"

"We are closer to humans than we admit."

"Even humans wouldn't destroy their own world."

"You would like to think so," Dezriak said with a wry smile. "What about Vlad the Impaler? Killing tens of thousands of people ... leaving their bodies on pikes, like grotesque trophies... burning villages, people and all, to the ground.

"And what about Genghis Khan? It is said he is responsible for the deaths of millions of people—innocent people—as he murdered his way across Eurasia. He, too, burnt villages as he went along ... humans sure do love their fire, it surely is ... effective."

"Look at yourself," Tyriano said in an unforgiving growl. "You can't help but smile ... you say these things with an envy stricken tongue." Tyriano stood with clenched fists, rage seeping from every pore. "Has it dawned on you that those things happened centuries ago ... that maybe people have changed?"

"People haven't changed; they've only perfected the horrible things they do. I learned that from you. Nuclear weapons, biological warfare, pollution ... it's all evidence of the insolence of man. The world is filled with people, all of them clamoring for power and resenting those who have it.

"The poor hate the rich for the gluttony they represent, and the rich hate the poor for being just that ... poor. Religion keeps the people as separated as oceans once did, and race isn't too far behind. All of those people, created by the same Maker, and they are at odds with each other over the most frivolous of things. It's like watching children fight over candy.

"The world is already broken, Tyriano. It spins like a glass globe in space, cracked ... waiting for that final hammer to come down upon it." Tyriano glared at him, unable to believe the appalling things he said. Dezriak all but offered himself up as that hammer.

It wasn't unheard of for Watchers to become dissident; it wasn't even a rarity since the Maker left. Power has always drawn attention, like bees to sugar canes. But, Dezriak wasn't just being rebellious ... he was the incarnation of insanity and destruction.

"You've gone mad," Tyriano said. Dezriak laughed loudly, but never took his eyes off the old Watcher.

"Maybe ... but, I have the power now," Dezriak said coolly. "I think you've gotten too comfortable here, locked away in your den. I think you should be locked in a cage, like a bothersome bird."

The Gloom had been listening from the other side of the door ... the Gloom was always listening. They flooded around the door; even seeped through its boards like black bile. The Gloom came at Tyriano with hungry mouths, dripping black saliva as they swam through the air around him.

Tyriano was overtaken by the black tornado, nipping at his ears and whispering their terrible words. He buckled and fell to his knees, gasping and clutching at his throat as he felt the air being pulled from his lungs. Then consciousness escaped him and he fell over in a silent lump.

"Lock him away," he said to the darkness. Dezriak turned on his heel and marched out, leaving the echoes of Tyriano's bitter cries in his wake. He was smiling as he went.

Edward—having being told he was a man called Nicholas—sat in the passenger seat of Camilla's 1984 Dodge Aries; it was cluttered with books and the discarded wrappers of fast food chains, french fries sought refuge in the seats hidden creases. The car smelled, but he couldn't guess if it was oil or gas. He looked at the person he was told was his sister and studied her.

She had tangled, graying hair that whipped out in curls. It so resembled a nest that Edward thought squirrels might jump out and scamper down her. Her face was soft with chubby cheeks and only the beginnings of wrinkles growing about her eyes. The eyes themselves were more youthful and a dark brown.

She didn't spark anything in Edward's mind. He didn't remember having a sister, but that was normal, or so he was told. He then looked at his own face in the vanity mirror. It was old; wrinkled and rough, and his hair was wild in dark tangles with gray streaks.

He felt younger than he looked. Edward ran his fingers over his face, crossing the wrinkles around his wide mouth. The stubble on his cheeks looked like it hadn't been managed in days. He imagined there were monkeys that were better groomed than this.

"Do you know how worried I was over you?" she finally asked, breaking the silence. The question froze in the air, hanging like a pail of water—waiting to dump over some poor person's head.

"I don't really know anything right now," he said

gruffly with a clumsy, confused smile. "I don't even remember you." She looked over at him then, her eyes glazed over. He wished he could take it back, but it was already out there—running free.

"At all?" she asked.

"Sorry," he said, looking at her sheepishly. Edward wished he could remember. He would give anything to remember her … himself … or anything. He would pay a king's ransom for a memory of a distant birthday party where as a young boy he ate too much cake and threw up in a potted plant.

But nothing came to him. He sat silently in the little, sputtering car as the sun began to run from their section of the world—leaving for another day. There were no more words to be spoken. They were all already said or too far gone to be found in such dim light.

Camilla sniffled in her seat behind the wheel and Edward tried hard not to notice. He knew why she cried and felt horrible for being the reason. But after all, what could be done about it? It would take time and rest.

"I need a drink," Camilla said.

"Me too." The car made a sudden turn down Bethel road, heading off towards neon lights, cold beer, and good people.

While Edward was trying hard to remember how to be somebody he wasn't, Nicholas was getting pretty cozy being Edward. It was really easy for him to do so—he found. The clothes he wore were cozy … the house was cozy; even the couch he sat on was cozy.

He had just gotten done marching through the house, staple gun and plastic wrap in hand, searching for broken windows. He was quick to cover them with plastic when he found them—two layers to be sure—and stapling it down. Lily followed him, sweeping up the glass and marveling at the masculinity he exhumed while doing the chore. Edward must not have been too handy, Nicholas guessed, but jobs like this weren't foreign to *him*.

The couch he sat on was plush, not the kind Nicholas was accustomed to—found mostly in second hand stores. His body sank right into it and the soft flesh of it cradled him like a baby. Surrounding his little cocoon were mementoes of Edward's life, knick-knacks and photos that each offered a little insight into the mind and heart of the man he was now to be.

He stood and went to investigate the photos, peering at each one carefully, absorbing the images and the clues they offered. They were stacked carelessly, in disfigured frames and broken glass—courtesy of the storm. He picked them up, one by one, glancing at them.

Most of them were pictures of Edward and Lily, smiling—as young couples usually do. The poses were generally the same, with different backdrops. One on a beach, their skin burnt lobster red … another on a snowy slope, the two of them burdened with ski gear … and so on.

Outside the shrine they built to themselves were scattered snapshots from their lives apart. The pre-Lily/Edward era, before the two had met—the dark days. But those days didn't seem that dark as Nicholas looked over the photos.

Pictures of Lily's enormous family were present, countless brothers and sisters, all smiling out from pictures as they enjoyed family vacations. Edward peered out from another, small and fragile as a cub scout, smiling broadly as he hoisted a Pinewood Derby trophy. Lily laughed in another, sandwiched on prom night by her best friend and her date, whose smile spoke his unsavory hopes aloud.

Life seemed to be fairly good for the two of them. It's unreasonable, Nicholas knew, to assume that their lives were completely carefree; no one ever took photos of children as they cried, there were never good photo ops at funerals. But overall, the two seemed happy.

Above the array of photographs hung book-lined shelves. There was a lot of fiction, some heavy reading that Nicholas guessed was there for show. Hidden amongst the Tolstoy, Hemmingway, and the like, were small sci-fi paperbacks, squeezed in.

On the end of the bottom shelf lived old law books. Their corners were worn and torn from years of flipping through them—yellow sticky notes sticking out the ends. Nicholas would never have guessed that Edward was a lawyer, but here the proof lay.

Lily walked in from the kitchen, two plastic trays still steaming from the microwave in her hands. "Reminiscing?" she asked, seeing him hovering around the photos. He smiled back at her and picked up a photo of the two of them at a Halloween party with friends.

"Yeah," he said slowly. "Just realized how close I came to losing all of this today."

"Hey, we're lucky only the frames were broken," she said, sitting on the couch. "They could've been sucked out the windows, I heard on the radio that that's happened."

Nicholas smiled easily, looking over at Lily as she sat, blowing on the hot food in her lap. "I meant *this*," he reiterated, "My life … I could be dead, instead of standing here."

"I knew what you meant … I just didn't want to think about it." Lily smiled weakly and patted the soft cushion beside her, beckoning him. Nicholas moved around the couch and fell into the seat and she moved closer to him, kissing his cheek. The warmth of her lips ran through his body, forcing him to wonder when the last time was that a woman had kissed him.

"Well, I'm glad you're still around," she whispered, her warm breath sending a tingling sensation down his back. She kissed him again, her lips on his, her breath flooding his mouth. Nicholas wrapped an arm around her and pulled her to him, the other hand holding her cheek.

She giggled in his mouth and pulled back, looking at him with accusing eyes. "Well, haven't *you* gotten aggressive." She smiled and Nicholas blushed, upset at his own eagerness.

"It's been a long day," he said meekly, "There was a chance I was never going to see you again."

Nicholas had always had a way with people, knowing just what to say or do to get what he wanted. It was a gift he had always had, ever since childhood. His mother had figured it out—his *talent* for reading people— and warned against using it to manipulate others.

He went to kiss her again, but she stopped him with her small palm against his mouth. "We better eat our dinners before they refreeze," she said earnestly, "don't you think?"

And with a sad nod, Nicholas set aside his lustful desires and went about eating the frozen dinner. Salisbury steak with mashed potatoes, Edward's favorite—according to Lily. It was, Nicholas had to agree, a pretty good meal.

Tibil was frightened. What occurred that morning is what nightmares are made of and his people have long feared it. He never thought it would come about, just as all the stories he heard about the surface turned out to be no more than fables. Yet, there he was on the surface; a witness to the chaos.

He was in a bar in the midst of the city, surrounded by sad and angry people that shouted their best guesses as to what happened. Some were marred with injuries— bandaged and rubbing bruises. Others simply hovered over empty glasses, crying softly.

He went unnoticed in the busy room, no one saw

him sipping colorful liquids from tiny glasses that had been abandoned on tables. They were all too absorbed in their own fear and sorrow to notice anything as small as him. It suited Tibil just fine; he liked the taste of the drinks and they made his head feel funny.

He saw a box hanging high in one of the corners of the bar with a tiny man inside, talking about what happened earlier in the day. He made guesses and promised to learn more later, but Tibil knew he would never have the truth. Tibil was perhaps the only creature on the surface that knew the true reason for the chaotic storm that morning. It was caused by the sudden, yet short halt in the earth's turning. Something had happened to Temelephas.

It became a pain in his stomach, thinking about Temelephas; wondering about what could have become of him. He thought back on his day, all the wondrous things he saw and experienced. He was happy on the surface. He loved all it offered … the moon, the stars, and the breeze that rippled over him.

Everything he saw held a bit of his heart. Thinking about abandoning it all never crossed his mind, he was so happy. But the more he thought of that sleepless giant, the more he longed to return to him.

The Gloom had

been listening from the

other side of the door

... the Gloom was

always listening.

9

Franklin laid still in the nook of Temelephas' neck, his head placed upon his own chubby arms—his eyes lulling toward sleep. The heaving of the great elephant's rib cage slowly rocked the baby, its heartbeat playing a lullaby. Temelephas himself could feel the baby tangled in his mane and enjoyed it immensely.

No one ever touched him. Not in that way, at least ... not gently.

He walked at his normal pace again and had no idea what commotion he had created when he had stopped. He was calmer then, with the little baby on his neck, his little palms stroking his scalp. He barely noticed the Minikins around him as they plotted and worked to get the small child down.

"Simply extraordinary," Tyriano said, peering out from the cramped cage in which he sat. It was similar to a bird's cage and hung high above the cavern in which Temelephas stomped. A loyal Minikin stood on a nearby ledge and nodded his agreement. "You say he picked the child up?"

"Yes," the Minikin chirped in excitement, "Just after he stopped his walk."

"He would rather stop ... than harm the child."

The Minikin didn't know what to say in response to that—didn't understand the significance of it—and only stared at his former master. It was a sad sight to behold, Tyriano in the hanging cage, his old body folded within its brass bars.

"Don't give up hope," Tyriano said upon seeing the shift in the little one's mood. "These things always have a way of working themselves out ... I can't be contained here for long."

The Minikin let his eyes meet those of Tyriano and he forced a rough smile to his lips. Tyriano gave him as warm a smile as he could, sighing deeply as he settled back in his cage. The Minikin stayed for a bit longer, long enough to see the old Watcher fall into a slumber. He thanked the Maker for giving Tyriano some peace and then headed off to spread the optimism of his captive friend.

Life is a very complex and beautiful thing. It's made of many wonderfully odd events, most of which are the byproduct of chaos and spontaneity. They can be happy events—worthy of celebration—or they can be tragedies that bring people together in mourning. It was the latter that Edward found upon stepping into the darkness of Dimarco's.

The bar was filled, spilling over with the regulars that normally haunted the dwelling on afternoons and weekend nights. The jukebox was blank, made powerless by the storm. It fit the eerily dim room perfectly, lit only by warm, shifting candlelight that burned softly from the tabletops. The air was filled with the somber chatter of ne'er-do-wells and the smell of stale beer.

All the electrically defunct business had to offer its weary patrons were bottles of slowly warming beer that ate away what little ice remained and straight shots of liquor. They drank it all the same ... never ones to turn away from a good time—no matter how bad it all seemed.

Many faces turned to Camilla and Edward, nodding and calling out various greetings, not happily, but anxious to see more people upright and well. It wasn't Edward's name that they called, however, but he had no way of knowing that. He simply nodded back to them and moved to claim a spot beside Camilla at the crowded bar.

Many bodies cluttered around the bar and flooded over onto the tables and into the stretch of carpet that lay before the dartboards. The mob pushed clear back to the door and onto the patio, where smokers sat, huddled around picnic tables as if in communion. It would have been an epic night, one to remember, if it weren't for the bitter taste of the memory it would carry.

The man behind the bar had seen them walk in through the crowd of sad drinkers and approached their end carrying two bottles of beer. "Hey, Nick," he called over the heads of those between them. "That storm ... or whatever ... knocked out the power, so the beers a bit warmer than normal."

He was shorter than most and a bit scrawny, with hunched shoulders and a block "O" cap pulled down low, covering his eyes. He set the beers down with care and quickly wiped his damp hands across his shirt which coined a simple request across its front, 'tell your breasts to quit staring at my eyes'.

"Do you remember Doug?" Camilla asked him. The man named Doug glanced at him then shot Camilla a confused look.

"What happened?" he asked.

"Nicholas bumped his head during the storm," she explained, matter-of-factly, "he's suffering from a bit of amnesia."

Doug looked shocked at first, perhaps a bit worried for his friend. But years of bartending had left him with some skills, one of which was putting troubled minds at ease. "Sometimes it's good to forget," he said with a chuckle. Edward felt a smile peeking out from the corners of his mouth. "I hope your brain gets better."

Doug scampered off then, down to the far end of the bar to tend to other people and their drinks. Edward sipped his warm beer, slowly gazing around. Everyone seemed a bit beaten and weary, like socks that had been mangled by a shoddy washing machine.

Some wept while others consoled them. Still, others laughed, finding some shred of hope in the dim light of this place. It warmed Edward, knowing that this place must truly be a second home for those around him. Maybe for some, the people here were the only family they had.

With the thought of family on his mind, he turned his eyes to Camilla and saw the worry on her face. "Anything coming back, yet?" she asked, her voice dripping with hope. He wished he could say yes, but the fear of never remembering sat in his chest, clinging to his heart.

He shook his head slowly and looked down at his beer. Tears gathered in his eyes and swung low beneath them like dew drops on a leaf. He tried to hold them back, but one slipped out and raced down his cheek. He was quick to wipe it away, feeling a sudden stab of loneliness.

He felt Camilla's hand on his back, rubbing softly as if to drive away his fear and sorrow. "It'll be okay," she said in a tone that only an older sister can muster. And he believed her.

Through the fogginess of his own mind, he truly believed it would be okay ... that things would be just fine. As if by magic from an unseen hand, the lights came on and the jukebox came to life, pumping out Lynard Skynard. The crowd cheered and Edward laughed aloud, choking back the unneeded tears.

He watched as most sang along and some of the braver ones danced. The room became livelier then, as if the collected sadness of all those present just slipped away.

Things will be okay, he reminded himself as he watched those around him, celebrating the simple fact that they were *still* there, and more importantly … together.

🐘

Nicholas was getting entirely too comfortable in his stolen body, lying in a stolen bed, lights out with a beautiful woman lying beside him. He watched as she slept with her back to him, her curves covered—a picturesque bottom pointing at him through the dark. He leaned towards her and brushed away her short hair to plant a kiss on the back of her neck.

Lily moaned delicately as his hand rubbed her hip. She pushed back against him and turned her face to kiss his mouth, his hand now wrapping around her—his fingers on her belly. She pulled away and sighed heavily.

"Sorry," she whispered through the darkness, a hand caressing his bruised cheek.

"For what?" he asked, equally hushed—so close to her face that he could count her freckles.

"We can't tonight," she said rolling over to face him. "I've got a busy morning … and we both had a pretty rough day."

Nicholas sighed. She smiled at him with pursed, pink lips, a bit of white teeth shining through. She brushed her fingers across his chest, dragging them down and across the tender, deep purple bruises around his ribs. Nicholas winced slightly at the gentle touch.

"Besides," she whispered. "I don't think you're physically up for me." She purred into his ear, rubbing her face against his. Her mouth found his once more, but for only a second, before she rolled over to find dreamland once more. Nicholas lied there … wide awake and frustrated.

Sleep was the furthest thing from Nicholas' mind. He thought about trying to rouse her again, but knew it would only end in the same manner. He got out of bed slowly and slipped on a robe. He looked back, making sure he hadn't disturbed her, before heading for the window.

He slowly pushed it open and felt the cold air beat against him. Nicholas shivered as he caught his breath and then climbed out onto the roof. The wind was wild and smelled of snow. He sucked it in deeply, his mouth puffing out steamy air, he thought of trains.

He climbed to the house's peak and straddled the roof. He surveyed the area and found that the streets were quiet and abandoned. He filled his lungs again with the freezing air, till he felt they might burst from the load. Then he let out a long wail, mimicking the cry of the great iron monsters he loved so much.

He chugga-chugga-chugga-ed away, the landscape around him transforming in his mind, rolling pass him like a country side. He cried out again and paid no attention as the neighborhood came alive with the sound of barking dogs, little lights erupting from once dark houses. He was oblivious to them ... even to the light that turned on, casting a silhouette in the window below him.

10

Being small—as his kind tends to be—Tibil was able to take a path similar to that of Franklin's. It was a bit scary at first, with all the slopes and sudden drops, but it offered a secret backdoor into the underworld. He had to remind himself that he was still banished to the surface and the last thing he could expect was a happy reception. He certainly didn't want to bump into the Fir Bolg.

They are the ever grumpy goliaths that hold up the tectonic plates, responsible for every little movement of the crust. They have dark, grimy skin, dark hair, and smell horrible all the time. The Fir Bolg stand for long, laborious shifts; their backs, shoulders, and hands holding up the world.

They are humungous and indefinably strong and frightening to creatures as small and delicate as Minikins. Any of his kind that had had the misfortune of finding themselves in the company of the Fir Bolg returned with stories of their drooling stupidity. They possess stomachs twenty times larger than their brains and an indiscriminate attitude towards what they eat.

He had never heard of any Minikins being devoured by the giant men, but Tibil did not long for the honor of being the first. So he stuck to the whipping and twirling slides, a straight shot to the center. It was nauseating, but Tibil made it through with little vomiting. He was happy to find that the rest of the trip would have to be made on foot.

The caverns were hot and muggy, as they always were, much like a baker's oven as it preheated. The darkness was nearly thorough, save for the rippling glow of far off flames that bounced off the bowing cavern walls. He had only spent a short period on the surface, but Tibil felt the sadness of being back soaking into his bones. He would always remember the moon and the stars and the other great amenities the surface offered.

He worked his way around the sleek corners and down the spiraling passage ways, his eyes slowly growing accustom to the eternal night of his home. It wasn't too long before he came close enough to the core to hear the sound of Temelephas' heavy steps, a sound that surprisingly comforted him.

Soon, he saw other Minikins—some that he knew—and he greeted them and their surprised reaction to see him again. They seemed more somber than usual. Some were so overly stressed that the weight of their sorrows showed on their sunken faces. He asked one in particular what all the sadness was about.

"Tyriano has been replaced," the Minikin answered. "And Dezriak is a cruel and unforgiving slave-driver." Tibil was unsettled by this ... the Minikins knew no one would be as kind to them as Tyriano always had. But it was not their place to decide who would be their boss.

"What happened to Tyriano?"

The others told him the story from the beginning, of the baby's contact with Temelephas, of Dezriak's betrayal of Tyriano. They even told him of the bad conditions they now lived in. They worked longer, harder shifts; forced to carry heavier loads. Their food supply had been cut back, leaving their tiny bellies nearly empty.

Any who defied Dezriak or his orders were snatched

up by the Gloom, his shadowy assailants, hiding in the walls. They were then dragged off, deep into the darker caverns. The only evidence of their existence being the screams that fled out into the faint light. Tyriano's loyalists were the first to be dragged off.

Tibil slumped back against the damp, rock wall and thought of the life he hated and how it would now be worse. He worried for his family, especially his mother, who was nearing the end of her life cycle. This was no life for her, this was no life for anyone. His eyes had gathered cool pools of sparkling tears that he was unaware of.

The sadness was overwhelming and made his legs seem heavier, as if he were already in the Gloom's dreadful embrace. It would have suited him to just continue sitting there in the dark, let the world go on without him until he took his last breath. But painful memories of all he saw and all he had been through pounded in his mind.

Even before his banishment, life had been barely tolerable. Now it only promised to be worse. He couldn't stand to see his people tortured and ran into the ground from exhaustion. Couldn't bear to see the young ones crying, alone in the dark—their bellies empty.

Stand up, he commanded himself, *there's no room in this world for quitters … not even in its depths.* He slowly stood; his eyes squinted with anger. "Where is Tyriano?" he said with unfettered determination.

Edward stood in front of a mirror, illuminated by the dull morning light of winter that trespassed through a tiny bathroom window. He studied the face he was told was his own, tracing the wrinkles that spread out from his eye lids with a fingertip. His chin—which was really that of Nicholas—was covered with thick, graying stubble that flirted with the identity of a beard.

His eyes were sunken and swung dark bags beneath them like worn pillows. He looked older than he guessed for himself, not a bit of his face triggered any recognition. He leaned closer to the glass and stared deep into his own eyes, hoping to jar some lost part of his mind loose. He gazed, long and hard; losing focus. In the end they still remained the eyes of a stranger.

He gave up in frustration and turned on the cold tap, gathering a pool in his cupped hands before splashing it over his face. He rubbed the sleep away and a small part of him hoped to rub the old facade from his face. But—with his chin dripping—he was saddened to see that old mug still staring back at him.

His face was bruised and seemingly caked with dirt. He thought maybe cleaning up a bit would uncover a more memorable face. With that hope in mind, he searched for a razor, but found none around the cluttered sink. He looked in the cabinet below and found a dull one, hiding in a dark corner.

He found it pointless to search for shaving cream and just went about the painful task of scraping the hairs from his face. With that done he showered, washing away countless days of grime and most likely a layer or two of skin. He slicked back his gray hair and admired the dapper, old man in the mirror and felt more comfortable in this strange skin.

He put on some clothes, a pair of slacks that still bore a crease and an untouched dress shirt he found buried in the back of a dresser drawer. Feeling there was nothing left to do; he headed down stairs to greet the day and anything it had to offer. He strolled around the ground floor until he found the kitchen and his sister sitting at the small round table.

Her eyes went wide at the sight of him. She had to set her heavy coffee mug down so as not to drop it. Edward didn't notice her look of shock at first; his attention went straight to the hot, pot of coffee and the empty mug, begging to be filled.

"Oh my stars," Camilla called out with a laugh. Edward turned to see her and smiled.

"What?"

"I haven't seen you clean shaven in ... I don't know how long," she said. Her face contorted as she tried to do the math. It looked as if someone had just asked her a difficult riddle.

"You have to be kidding me," Edward said in his gruff voice.

"No, in fact ... come to think of it," she began, shaking her finger at him. "I gave you those clothes two Christmases ago ... and never once have you worn them. But you refused to wear anything except for those grubby clothes of yours."

Edward stood there silent, looking more and more like a constipated porcupine, trying to remember anything. The doctor told him his memories would come back slowly. He didn't expect a miracle, but hoped things would be clearer in the morning light.

"So, what can you tell me?" he asked. She sat there for a moment, staring into the steamy abyss of her coffee. She thought on it for that moment, trying to piece together the delicate words she needed to use. The truth can hurt— Camilla was aware of that—the last thing she wanted to do was hurt him. But anything less than the truth can be harmful as well.

"What can I tell you?" she said, looking at him with soft eyes. "You are my brother ... and I love you with every bit of myself." She smiled at him, tears building about her crow's feet. "But ... you have *always* ... been a burden to me."

Edward felt a stab of discomfort. He tried to muster the courage to hear her words, but he felt it slowly slipping away. He looked down at his rough hands as he twiddled his thumbs in a feeble attempt to distract himself.

"You have always been … *different*. You were a below average student … someone that *never* followed what they call the *normal* path. Not that it's such a bad thing … Lord knows it's not a horrible thing," Camilla said with a chuckle. Edward tried to share in her jovial moment, but the pain of what she said bit too deep. All he could manage was a gurgled chuckle.

"When you were a child, running around in the woods and climbing trees was acceptable … it was expected. But as you got older, you stuck to your solitary lifestyle … remaining alone … watching the world spin out of control around you." She reached her hands across the table, seizing his fumbling hands.

"In fact, this is the longest we have *talked* … in a long time." She beamed at him, tears flowing down her cheeks, framing her face. Edward placed a hand over hers and patted it softly, his own tears now tumbling down his freshly shaven face.

"I appreciate your honesty," he said with a jerky voice. "But … I was actually only hoping to find out the little things … like, where do I work?"

Camilla burst out in riotous laughter. She pulled her hands from his and clamped them to her cheeks. "Oh …" she sighed faintly as she settled, smiling at him. "Honey … you haven't worked a day in your life."

Lily sat on the floor, surrounded by broken glass and scattered keepsakes. She busied herself, sorting pictures and mementoes from the rubble left from the storm. She carefully picked each photo up and blew the debris off them before setting them in a pile on a nearby table.

She wasn't in any of the pictures … this wasn't her house. She took her time in doing so, glancing over them, trying to find a way inside the captured moments. Steal herself away for a moment, hide out in their little stories. And when the story became bland, she would set it aside once more and move on to the next.

"Katie?" she called into the kitchen, where her friend was busy cleaning what little dishes remained from the freak event. "Who's this guy dressed as a clown ... giving the camera the finger?"

"That's my brother," she said with a huff of breath. "It was at some Halloween party he went to in August."

"August?"

"Yeah," Katie said, coming into the room, looking at the photo as she dried her hands on her pant legs. "Don't ask ... he has some *weird* friends."

Lily shrugged, placing the photo with the rest of the disheveled memories. She stood up then, stretching her back as a cat would in the afternoon sunlight. "I need a break," she yawned, wiping bits of glass and dirt off hands.

"Good idea," Katie said as she gazed out into the backyard. "I need to keep an eye on my little demon, anyway." They shared a laugh as they walked out to the back patio. There was a large table with ornate chairs, which reminded Lily of *Lord of the Rings*. After the storm they had been scattered about the yard and had to be retrieved. One of them ended up on the roof; unbroken, but terribly lonely.

They sat down in front of mugs of coffee they had abandoned earlier. The afternoon sun had melted away the frost that had taken over the table overnight. Lily had hoped it would also keep their coffees warm, but was sad to discover hers cool to the touch.

They sat there, drinking their lukewarm coffee, watching as the little, yellow haired girl that lived there ran around wildly, giggling with abandon. She darted around the snowy yard, chasing a large black dog that was fair enough to slow its running anytime the little girl fell too far behind.

"Addison!" Katie called across the frosty yard. The little girl stopped suddenly, snapping her head in her mommy's direction, bearing a look of guilt that rivaled that of criminals. She huffed and puffed, her little shoulders rising and falling with each gasp.

"Yeah, Mommy?" she hollered.

"You need to put your hat on, it's cold out here," she called across the distance to her daughter, easily twenty yards off.

"'kay, Mommy," she said in her cheerful soprano, "I will ... inna minute, 'kay?" With that, her chase began again much to the dog's chagrin, who had already found a warm patch of sun to lie in. Addison's golden hair bounced in the sunlight and her laughter began again as if she had never been interrupted.

"She never gives you a break, does she?" Lily asked with a slight laugh.

Katie shook her head and rolled her eyes as she sipped her coffee. "She'll be the death of me," she said, pulling the mug from her lips. "But, it's a death I'll welcome. So ... how soon after you tie the knot will you two start trying for a baby?"

"I don't know," Lily said solemnly. She had been thinking about Edward all morning and his weird behavior, the open window and the screaming from the roof. He seemed different to her, his aggressiveness and awkwardness around the house. She tried to convince herself it was nothing.

"You know I was kidding, *right*?" Katie said quickly, seeing the change in Lily's demeanor, a deep, somber look on her face. "Kids weigh heavier on the pro side than the con."

"No, I know," Lily said, trying to smile. "I just don't *know* anymore."

"What does that mean?"

"Eddie's been different," Lily said slowly before

sipping her coffee, "ever since the storm ... and the accident."

"How so?"

"It's like ... he's a stranger; he doesn't know where anything goes or even how we do anything ..."

"Well, it was traumatic for him ... it was for a lot of people."

"He kissed me last night, and ... it was like making out on prom night; his hands were all over me. He was just different ... aggressive, even."

"Sounds good to me," Katie said with a sly smile. "What passes for foreplay around here is a belch and a firm slap on the ass." Katie laughed then, trying to ease her friend's mind. "It sounds like you're getting cold feet to me ... just relax. You guys will be married forever, trust me."

"Yeah," Lily murmured, her eyes following Addison as she fought with the dog over a knotted rope. The little girl eventually won when the dog let go, sending Addison falling—bottom first, into a muddy, snowy mound. Addison simply chortled and righted herself to run some more.

They sat in silence for a while, Lily deciding not to go further into detail about her worries; she didn't need anyone knowing about the rooftop incident. They simply sat there, enjoying their coffee, the sunlight, and the chilly air. It was a stale sort of quiet, with both participants struggling to find a topic for conversation.

Addison continued to run, always at full speed; her heavy boots more of a hindrance than a help. She continued to fall—as clumsily as all children do—each one quickly followed by an *'I'm okay"*. Then off she ran again. Lily only wished she were that young and carefree again.

Tyriano was curled up in his bird cage, dozing with his hands together, squeezed between his feathery face and the cool bars. The cage slowly swayed, rocking him in his slumber. The only sounds he heard in dreaming were the steady thumps of Temelephas' steps and the gentle creaking of his cage.

He was only roused from his sleep by the gentle calls of Tibil, hooting to him from his hiding spot in the dark. Tyriano shook his head, glancing about foggily until the call came again. "Who goes there?" he weakly called in a hushed voice.

The small creature crept out from the shadows, looking around cautiously as he waved. "It's me," he whispered over the gap, "Tibil."

"Tibil?" Tyriano gasped. The Minikin shushed him quickly and waited for the echoes to cease their bouncing through the dark tunnels around them. "What are you doing back?" Tyriano continued in a whisper.

"I just had to return after what happened," he explained.

"Yes, tell me," he began again as he shifted in his cage, angling himself into a squatting position. "How was the surface effected?"

"The sky began to devour everything," Tibil began, waving his arms around as a storyteller might. "Everything was sucked into the sky." His face dropped, thinking back on it. "I was lucky … I was in a grocery store at the time, sampling little things called cheeses. The building shook and rumbled with the anger of the Maker.

"When it stopped, we went out in a group, looking to the sky and all around. There was so much destruction … so many deaths." Tibil's face was a mangled and morose sight.

Tyriano looked down, his eyes glossing over with sadness and regret. "I didn't even think of those on the surface," he muttered, to himself more than anyone else, "… not of them." He dropped his feathery chin; a single tear slipped from the corner of his eye and fled, quickly down his burning cheek.

"I was too busy, too concerned with what was going on down here," he explained. "I never stopped, not once … to even *guess* as to what chaos we might have unleashed up there. All those lives … lost."

He had studied humans all his long life, more than was required; learning of their complex emotions and desires. He knew, for instance, that the average human heart beats seventy-two times a minute, pumping a little over five liters of blood in that time. He knew that a human will take 151,200 breaths in a week.

Fifty percent of humans have their first kiss before they turn fourteen years old. The average human experiences twenty-eight first kisses in their lifetimes and will spend 20,160 minutes of their lives perfecting the art. Tyriano even knew that in the average lifespan, a human will cry enough tears to fill one hundred and twenty liters.

All of those numbers swam through his head and he realized for the first time what they truly were … only numbers. They were little facts he had acquired over his life, memorized to help him do his job better. They were numbers … and nothing more.

He had never met a human, never shook one's hand, nor received one of the thousands upon thousands of hugs they may give away in a lifetime. He'd never heard them laugh or watched them dance, both things he learned they love to do. He'd never seen them smile or frown … never seen them coyly flirt back and forth.

So, he wept freely in his dangling cage. He cried shamelessly, tears cascading down his face as he thought of the countless, faceless humans that perished in that quick moment. Tibil looked away; allowing his friend privacy to shed his pain.

It was then that the thought came to Tyriano, in those calming moments when his tears had begun to slow. He was crying for humanity … a people he was meant to protect, but never knew. He spent his time in these dark caverns, never even setting foot on the surface. He snuffled and ran a robed arm across his face.

"But, why return to this place?" he asked Tibil in a sluggish voice, not even looking at him.

"I knew you would need me," he said softly. "I wanted to be here to help."

Tyriano smiled, thinking perhaps that humanity was infectious, spreading like a germ. Its incessant need to intervene manifested in the little creature before him. He was so small … so fragile. But even with his faults he was fundamentally willing to do what was right, no matter the cost.

He glanced down at the ancient elephant as he walked, watched as he ran his trunk over the tiny baby that nestled atop him. Humanity was there, too—he knew. As much humanity as there was in any man or woman.

Perhaps humanity filled Tyriano as well. *Like a flickering candle, perhaps it burns softly within us all. It isn't the factoids or numbers that dictates humanity; it's the choices we make… it's how we live our lives that defines humanity.*

All will be fine, he silently vowed, *all will work out*. Then, Tyriano was filled with hope … it pumped through him as it always had through the history of humanity. All he had to do was use that hope, harness it … bend it with his will.

He wondered how much the High Council actually knew, and was a bit worried about how little they might care. He imagined in his mind, trying to find a path through the situation, a way to right the wrongs. And, as if struck by lightning, he had a plan … a loose, but promising one. "Tibil?" he asked through the silent darkness. The Minikin's face lifted meekly. "You couldn't possibly pick this lock … could you?"

11

Edward flipped hastily through that day's classified section with the aid of Nicholas' old, wrinkled hands. The idea of not working bothered him. It seemed odd to not have felt the drive to be productive before, to *want* to contribute to the great effort of the working class. He skimmed through the paper, passing the ads for used cars, escorts, and those depressing parts about homeless cat.

Camilla stood shocked in the corner, her coffee cold, mug clasped in her white-knuckled hands—like a hawk's talons around a field mouse. It was a new thing for her to behold. Part of her was simply thrilled at the new determination Nicholas now exhibited; yet there was a darker, doubtful side of her, screaming in her mind that her brother would never do such a thing. She had trouble deciding which thought deserved to float at the front of her addled mind.

"Legal Assistant!" Nicholas screamed out, his face beaming at her.

"You need a degree for that job, sweetie," she reminded him, smiling as she sipped her coffee. College, the end all and be all for tomorrow's youth. It was, honestly, the most plausible gateway to a successful future.

His borrowed face crinkled in thought. He dug

down deep, with his mental fingers, into his cloudy cerebrum. It was nothing more than a giant, black wall, evasive of all memories. But, then there came a flash … foggy recollections, bleeding through the dark bricks.

His eyes went blank as he flashed back to law school. He remembered the classes he took, even the smell of the second hand books he nearly broke his back carrying down the halls. The stuffy professors that ran him ragged, the long hours at the library on Friday nights as parties burned like bonfires through the night, and the cute coeds that the cozied up to him in a ploy for his study notes.

"But I did go to college … I remember it," he said, instantly ignoring the laughter from his sister. "Why didn't I do anything with my law degree?" he asked aloud, as easily as if asking someone to pass the creamer.

Camilla's face went white; her hands went numb and the coffee mug she had been holding went falling to the enamel floor, shattering, spilling its Colombian goodness. Words couldn't find their way to her mouth. It was as if her mind had been locked down, quarantined from the rest of her faculties.

The only place words lived were trapped in her mind's creases and wrinkles. They begged to be released … spoken into the silence that engulfed the room since the mug blew apart against the floor. But, all they could do was exist in her mind as a pure thought. *This is not my brother.*

Deep in her mind, a part of her lived—dormant most of the time. It was ignored and overlooked all other times. It laughed now, *I told you so.*

Tyriano crept through the caverns, his footsteps echoing down the dark tunnels; Tibil was nothing more than his little shadow, close in tow. They moved slowly as if studying each step before taking it. Tyriano wondered what he would say when he found Dezriak, undoubtedly sitting behind *his* desk.

Would he yell, chastising him as a bitter grandparent would, shaking his boney finger towards him? Probably not. That would only attract the unwanted attention of the Gloom, their grim figures surely lurking about in the shadows.

That was certainly not something he wanted to relive ... the invasive touch of the Gloom. He shuddered upon remembering it, that glassy, cold touch of theirs; their claws ripping at him, drawing out his fears and sadness. He knew he would not survive another encounter with them.

How could he keep Dezriak from calling for them? That would prove harder than he previously thought and the time for planning was quickly fading away. *Time* ... he thought, if only he had more of it.

It had to be quick, it was decided, quick and simple. If he ran off, hid away in the expansive tunnel system of the underworld, Dezriak would surely discover his disappearance and the element of surprise would be lost. It had to be quick and simple, he reiterated. *Like ripping a bandage off,* he imagined.

They turned a corner and found themselves before that familiar, circular, oaken door. Tyriano glanced around, holding Tibil still behind him as his eyes searched the darkness. As he had surmised, he spotted a cluster of the Gloom lying in wait within the shadowy walls. Their eyes were sunken and shut as they slumbered. He wondered what cruel, depraved things such a creature would dream.

Tyriano crouched, pulling the tiny Minikin close to him. He placed a long, bony finger to his lips, begging for silence. He then pointed to the sleeping shadows, their ominous forms just barely hidden. They watched them feverously, but they never stirred, not even to draw a breath.

"Stay low, my friend," Tyriano whispered, again

pointing to the Gloom. Tibil trembled involuntarily, and his eyes went wide in sudden fright. No Minikin had ever survived a scuffle with the Gloom.

"They sleep now," the old Watcher whispered on, calling the Minikin's attention back to him. "There's no telling how long they will remain in that docile state. We must be quiet ... we must sneak in, take Dezriak by surprise."

"How will we do that?" Tibil asked, his whisper like a squeaking chain.

"I will bind his hands with my belt, and you move to cover his mouth with your scarf. But be quick about it, we cannot chance him calling out for his stealthy assassins." Tibil heard him, but his eyes fixated at the dirt beneath his feet as he tried to muster up any courage that lay dormant inside him.

Tibil wished he wasn't there at that moment, so much lying on his puny shoulders. He would give anything to be anywhere else for a time. He wished there was a way he could be there in the physical sense alone, his mind off somewhere more peaceful. He was afraid.

He remembered then, the dark sky of night; swirling black and blue with a splattering of far off stars. It was a frightening time for him then, but the stark beauty of the vast ceiling of twinkling lights was enough to ignite a slender flame within him. He had faced his fears then, survived the surface to return once more to the bowels of the earth.

He knew it was in him, the courage he needed. That flame, while small, still flickered inside him; it burned like a candle, spilling over with the wax of trepidation. Tibil just needed to focus on the candle and its dim light, feed it until it grew to a blazing pyre.

Sure, his hands shook and his knees quaked—all the tell-tale signs of fear. But he would do what needed to be done. *Stop your shaking*, he commanded of his hands; *quit*

your quaking, he ordered his knees. He stood with sweaty
fists, clenched at his sides; his jaw was set with a grimace.
He looked to Tyriano with steady, fierce eyes and nodded.

Tyriano smiled at the strength he saw before him.
He marveled at the Minikin's courage, how it overflowed
from him, spilling out onto the ground. To think, a creature
constantly stepped on and overlooked was capable of such
courage.

"We only have one chance, let's make the best of it,"
Tyriano said, patting his friend on the shoulder. Tibil only
nodded, no sign of fear on his small, round face. He only
hoped some of the Minikin's courage would pass on to him
with that slight contact.

Temelephas stomped about with his heavy feet,
small clouds of dust puffing up in his wake. The sound
of his fallen steps filled the cavern, its thunderous cadence
spilling down the dark, twisting burrows. It shook the
walls themselves; yet it did not even jostle the sleeping
child, nestled in the elephant's tangled mane. He was a
warm spot at the nape of Temelephas' neck ... slow, steady
breaths from his heaving chest.

Though he felt as if it were just he and his young
rider, Temelephas never forgot the little Minikins that
circled him. He heard them talking, always chattering
away, talking about the baby. They said the child was
asleep, some said it lay dreaming. Temelephas had never
slept before, so he didn't understand the concept.

All Temelephas knew was that the baby seemed at
peace, not whether it slept or dreamed. *What is dreaming,*
he wondered. Just the word, rolling through his mind,
sounded pleasant. Temelephas wanted to dream ... wanted
to lay still and just breathe.

Sadly, dream, he could not. The only relief from the

constant dread of his own endless errand was the ongoing soliloquy in his own mind and the gentle caress of his only friend. He could feel his chubby, little fingers brushing his hair, scratching his rough scalp.

Maybe this is a dream, he believed. His eyes smiled as he continued to walk his tireless circle, a friend and keepsake at the nape of his neck.

Lily returned home and found the house quiet and dark. The door was unlocked, an odd thing for Edward to forget, and his car keys still sat on the small table by the door. She called out for Edward, but no answer came. She felt the ache of that morning's labor burning in her shoulders and back and a sense of loneliness in her chest.

She stepped through the house and found that the mess she left behind that morning was still there, the only thing waiting for her. Edward had said he would tidy up, but apparently that promise had been forgotten, just as the door lock had been. Edward never used to be so careless. He never used to be so blasé when it came to the promises he made.

She tried not to let these thoughts, these mild accusations seep into her mind, but found it hard to close them out as she walked into the kitchen. There on the counter lay the dishes of his lunch, scattered like cleaned, sun bleached bones at an archeology dig. She felt as if the mess and clutter was overwhelming her, drowning her in her own home.

This was the last thing she needed, something else to worry about, another thing on her epic list of things to do. The wedding was fast approaching and the stress of planning alone made her second guess getting married at all. Then the storm came, dark and loud and tenacious, seemingly ripping her life apart and leaving a shell of a man behind.

He was fine, she knew ... bruised and scratched, but at the physical peak of his life. But something nagged her at the back of her mind, pointing an accusatory finger at her soon to be husband. There was just something off about him.

They were all little things—really. The new, bizarre sense of humor and lingo he picked up from somewhere. The laziness he exuded and a passive attitude towards life, the unlocked door, the forgotten keys, the messy kitchen, and the broken promises. Even the way he touched her was different ... almost invasive. It was like she was sleeping beside a stranger.

She briskly cleared away the mess of Edward's lunch—unwilling to leave such a welcome mat out for bugs—then retreated to the dim light of the living room. She sat back in the recliner and let the warm air wash over her, calming her mind. She pulled her phone from her pocket and dialed Edward's number, waiting patiently as the phone dialed out.

It rang twice before she heard his phone chirping in the background. She pulled the phone from her ear as she stood, following the intermittent waves of sound like a game of Marco Polo. She traipsed through the dark of her house—her ears ready to steer her—into the foyer. She discovered the phone there, laying on the floor under the table by the door.

She knelt down and ran her fingers across its worn, gun metal finish as it gave off its final ring. It lay silent then, and Lily couldn't help but feel as lifeless as the small, inanimate phone that sat beside her. She fell against the wall and held the phone in her lap, sleepily gazing at it. Edward never left his phone behind. Her mind was racing, worried.

Life shouldn't be like this, she imagined. She never thought things could go bad between the two of them; her life was fine just days ago, but now it seemed something had gotten away from her. *Ever since that damned storm.* She'd never hated the weather, so much as now.

Life was now much like the shattered glass she spent a good part of her day sweeping up. It had become messy and nothing more than a chore. She couldn't live a life like that. That wasn't in her future, not in the plans she had made. She wondered if Edward would ever *truly* come home to her. More importantly, would she even be there waiting for him?

She didn't even notice that she had been crying; tears snuck slowly down her cheeks without a sob falling from her lips. She didn't bother wiping them away, choosing to leave them there to fester. They would dry, leaving their little slick, little paths as a memento of this sad day gone by.

Not far from where Lily sat in misery, Edward's body sat high up in a tree, full of Nicholas. He stared down at the children as they meandered about with sleds and random toys, trying to make the most of the fading light. They seemed happy, but Nicholas knew they longed for more snow and dreamed of schooldays being canceled due to the white death.

He liked looking down on them, their feeble minds unaware of his viewing. He felt at home in that tree, a man sitting outside the realm of his own belonging. Disconnected … that was how he felt.

He hadn't shaved that morning, as was his normal routine—or lack thereof. Nicholas was sure Eddie shaved every day, perhaps even going as far as stashing an electric razor at the back of his desk drawer at work. That wasn't the sort of thing Nicholas did; he wasn't Edward.

A little boy found a spot to sit against the roots of the tree in which Nicholas hid, leaning back with a videogame in his hands. Nicholas watched the child carefully as he alone with his head cocked, staring down at his ever-changing console screen. Occasionally, other children would wander past him, stopping to ask him to join in their fun. The boy would only brush them off and shift his attention back to his game.

Nicholas frowned, watching the boy and his solitary game. He thought about his own upbringing and how it seemed to parallel that of this young boy. He called down to him but the boy didn't hear. He called again, louder, causing the boy to look around quickly before shifting back to his game.

Frustrated, Nicholas grabbed at a lost acorn that had somehow remained untouched by squirrels and dropped it, bouncing it off the boy's head. The boy gave a quick shout and rubbed the crown of his head as he glanced upward. There wasn't much shock in his face at seeing a grown man in a tree. You would think it was an everyday thing for the young boy.

"What was that for?" the boy called up, a miffed look on his scruffy face.

"Sorry," Nicholas called from on high, "I only meant to get your attention."

"Well, you have it now ... what do you want?"

"I was just wondering why you weren't playing with the other children?"

"I don't want to," the boy said callously.

"Why?"

"I just wanted to play my game," the boy explained with an agitated tone in his throat, angry at being bothered at all. Time can be so fleeting to the young; a week goes by in a blink if an eye. When they get older they will hypothesis that the days are *actually* getting shorter.

"That's not normal," Nicholas passed down from his limb.

"Neither is grown man in a tree ... watching

children play," the boy said loudly; the agitation set free from his throat.

"Sorry," Nicholas said with a humble voice, "I was only concerned."

The boy huffed and stood up, sticking his game in his coat pocket. He then glared up the tree, through the branches to Edward's soft face. "Well, you can take your concerns and shove them up your ass, Fuck-head!" he screamed as he stuck up his gloved, middle finger, displaying it solely for Nicholas' displeasure.

With that, Nicholas was quieted and he watched as the boy ran off. *My, how children have changed*, he sadly thought as he lay out across his branch. He never remembered having the balls to tell *any* adults off, let alone complete strangers. He figured the world had changed, and not for the better. It wasn't the children's fault, they were victims of it too.

Where did the world go wrong? When did it begin to spiral out of control? He couldn't help but wonder why God had stopped caring. His mind sat on that thought; it sank deep into his mind. Like Jonah in the belly of his whale … his mind sat, thinking.

Dezriak awoke suddenly as the door to his office burst inward, his eyes blurrily gazing about. He saw a tall man come at him quickly, barely recognizing Tyriano before he slammed into him. He fell from his chair and unto his back, absorbing both the fall and the weight of his attacker—knocking the air from his lungs.

He gasped for air—trying to summon the necessary breath to call for help—but it never came. Tyriano's hands quickly moved around his wrists, binding them with a strap of leather. The skin burned beneath it and he jerked his head back and forth, trying to throw off the older man.

"Tibil," he heard him call, "the time is now!"

It was then that he saw the Minikin move in from the side, his scarf stretched out between his tiny fists. He moved to his mouth and Dezriak gasped hard, all of his will trying to gather if even a small breath, but again ... none came.

The scarf was in his mouth, the taste of sweat on his tongue. He could feel the hot breath of his smaller captor on his face as the Minikin finished tying the gag. And as quickly as it began, it was over and Tyriano was the victor ... standing tall over Dezriak's sore, bound body.

"Good to see you again, Dezriak," Tyriano whispered as Tibil made quick work of binding the fallen man's ankles. "You are looking well ... power suits you."

Dezriak was beaten and he knew it. All he could do was lay there, let Tyriano stand over him with a smug look of satisfaction splayed across his aged face. Dezriak may have given off the appearance of a caged rabbit, jittery and frightened, but inside he burned with the rage of a tiger.

He liked looking down on them, their feeble minds unaware of his viewing. He felt at home in that tree, a man sitting outside the realm of his own belonging.

Disconnected ... that was how he felt.

12

"I knew there was something off about you," Camilla said as she paced back and forth in her kitchen, the old floorboards crying out beneath her with every step. Edward sat at the table, his head pressed between his hands like a vise. "I could sense it with my third eye ... your aura is completely different from before." He gave a quick, sharp laugh like a hiccup exploding from his mouth.

"*Don't* you mock me," she demanded, shaking a finger at him. "I *knew* deep down inside ... you dress differently, speak differently ... Christ, you even showered without me having to fight you about it! You shaved!"

"Thanks, been doing it a while," he said quietly, rubbing his forehead. So many thoughts were barreling through his mind. The prevalent one being: is what she claims to have happened even possible?

Camilla sat heavily in the chair across from her brother's body, her elbows planted firmly on the newspaper that was spread out atop the Formica table. Her face became quizzical and her stare burrowed into the man she once thought was Nicholas. "So ... if you aren't my brother ... who are you?"

"Maybe my brain is just rattled ... because what you're saying is impossible," he said.

"Anything is possible," Camilla spat, "even the impossible."

"That just doesn't make sense."

"Just think," she ordered, reaching across the table to grab his hands. "Close your eyes and think ... we'll figure it out together." He drew in a long breath, trying hard to remember once more. To him, it was like trying to piece together a puzzle when you knew you were missing half the pieces.

All he had to go on was the *idea* that he went to law school. It was very possible, he surmised, that he was just crazy and had made up the entire thing about college. But he focused on college anyhow. Even as memories came to him, vague and foggy, the parts of them that carried his identity always seemed to be omitted.

What a tricky thing the mind is; a gray mass, coiled and powered by neurons ... capable of holding countless pieces of data. He could tell you the top ten hits of the Beatles or the combined batting average of last year's Cleveland Indians, but his own name was lost to him. A cruel twist of fate had transformed him into a Hitchcock character.

It was all too crazy an idea ... that he was some lost psyche that had somehow gotten swapped with that of Nicholas'. It was like a game of marbles with no takesy-backsies. But what did he really know? He certainly didn't know who he was, only who people told him he was.

"I don't know," he finally said, throwing his hands up, waving them in exasperation. "I just don't know." He dropped his hands to table and let them lay there as powerless as he felt.

"Maybe that's why you can't remember," Camilla said excitedly. "None of this belongs to you! It's all someone else's life ... all of *this* belongs to Nicholas."

Maybe she was right, maybe she was wrong. All he knew was that he didn't have much to lose and only everything to gain. "Just close your eyes," she said again.

"Keep them shut, but don't strain yourself."

He closed his eyes and his mind was in darkness. Black surrounded him and it felt cold. "Just breathe in," she said through the dark. "Nice and deeply." He did so. "Hold it, hold it, hold it ...... and let it out."

She repeated herself and he followed her directions. As he did ... it was as if the darkness crept over him—as if he were moving through it. He heard her talking to him, but her voice was fading away as if she were drifting off on a black sea. *Breathe*, her voice echoed from behind him. *Just breathe.*

He breathed in deeply, holding it in for a bit, then releasing it, flooding the air before him. Over and over he did this, all the while the darkness fled pass him. *What do you see?* He peered into the dark, his eyes straining to discern the blackness from the blackness.

Tell me, she called again in his mind, *what do you see?* He saw a speck, he told her, a white speck that moved slowly towards him, and wings that batted away the coming night. He didn't know what it meant, but it brought him hope, this white bird. It called to him in a female voice, calling a name he could not understand, it was muffled ... distorted.

There came another name, screamed out loud, so loud it shook the dark walls of his mind. It was his own voice calling it out, desperate and needful. His voice echoed in his mind and spilled from his waking lips.

"Lily," he whispered.

Edward never came home. Daylight quickly slipped into night and Lily was still alone. There was no way to reach him with his phone left behind, and she was no longer willing to wait. That was when she went looking for him.

She drove easily through the winter streets. There was some snow on the ground, but not much compared to Midwest standards. Mostly it was just cold air, a bitter prelude for what was to come.

Lily kept her foot light on the gas as her eyes darted around, frantically searching for Edward. She had no idea where he would be, no one she had called had heard from him; she was left with driving in circles. Her face was blotchy, all her tears had dried, leaving her with red, puffy eyes.

She needed to talk to him, try to figure out what was going on. Was she simply overreacting to small, petty things? Was Katie right? Was it all just a reaction to all the stress and trauma from the day before? She would only know if she were able to talk to him.

It had to be some sort of brain malfunction; he had been examined in an elementary school gymnasium after all. All the bizarre behavior, the howling like a maniac on the roof ... there had to be an explanation. She had to get him in to see a doctor in a real office with *real* equipment. She only wanted to see him get better ... back to normal.

She continued to drive the neighborhood streets, seeing no sign of him. The dim light of twilight was fading and she soon found herself squinting at sidewalks and alleyways. The heavy burden of worry lightened a bit when she saw a neighbor walking about alone.

"Hey, Joyce," she called from her window, pulling over abruptly. The woman turned to look at Lily slowly as if she couldn't tell if someone had called to her or if it was only the wind. She appeared to Lily as if nothing more than a specter with her pale skin, seeming unkempt with tangled hair.

"Lily?" she called back in a far off ghostly way. She leaned over and peered into the stopped car, clasping a stack of papers to her chest.

"How's it going?" she asked Joyce. The way she asked

the question was much like how any neighbor would ask another. It was asked in a manner so that it could easily be followed up by questions about the weather, local politics, sports, or any other mundane thing.

It was only after the cheerful question came out of her mouth that Lily remember that Joyce was dealing with her own crisis, the loss of her infant son. She felt stupid for forgetting such a huge thing, selfish for thinking only of her own problems. Joyce did look ragged, as if she had aged five, maybe ten years in the past two days.

Joyce fumbled with her words, her mind obviously busy—focused on other things. She was—at that time—only capable of doing the one thing she had been doing all day; which was hanging handmade posters inquiring about her son. She told Lily that things were still bad and bound to get worse.

"My dipshit husband is going to use this against me in court, I just know it," she said through a series of mild sobs. "He already called me an unfit mother ...said he should bring up my 'drinking problem' in family court! Can you believe that shit?" She was waving her arms around wildly, like a cornered animal.

Lily watched her with a vapid look on her face that went unnoticed. "Sure," Joyce continued, "there was that Fourth of July block party ... but who wasn't a little tipsy that night?"

Lily remembered the day she was talking about, a friendly celebration amongst neighbors; small fireworks and synchronized grilling, so much potato salad that the children could have swam in it. She also remembered the 'tipsy' to which Joyce referred, and the answer to her question was nobody—not to her degree at least. But, one night of debauchery didn't earn her the label of a drunk.

Joyce continued to rant a bit, but Lily cut her off with the promise that Edward would look into her situation with his legal eyes and offer any help he could. That made

Joyce's hardened face crack into an unpracticed smile. It also offered Lily the perfect segue into why she really stopped.

"Speaking of Eddie," she said softly, slowly, not wanting to upset her. "He left the house earlier on foot and didn't tell me where he was going. He left his phone at home, leaving no way to reach him. You haven't seen him, have you?"

Joyce's face became stoic again and she planted her hands on her hips. "I saw him rocking back and forth on your roof last night, hollering like a banshee," she said through clenched lips. The warm flush of embarrassment flooded Lily's face. "What the hell … was that about?"

"Eddie … he's been acting weird since the storm … I'm a little worried about him, to be honest with you."

"I would be too," Joyce said, "first, he's running around the neighborhood, barking like a nut-job, next thing you know, he's plowing a paralegal at the office." Joyce shook her head with her complacent eyes staring at her feet. "Happens all the time."

Lily doubted that any of what she said would happen. She decided to believe Joyce's judgment was hindered by her own failed marriage. Lily thanked Joyce for the chat, wished her luck in her own search before pulling back out into traffic. Joyce faded into obscurity in her rearview mirror.

She thought of Joyce and her poor lost baby for a handful of seconds more before letting them slip from her mind. Her thoughts returned to her missing Edward and his recent behavior. It festered in her mind like a bacteria, slowly eating away at her conscious thought.

The car slipped easily through the wet streets that welcomed the oncoming night with open arms. She knew her search would end soon, cut short by the darkness that slowly settled on Columbus. She found herself winding down Olentangy River road, a long street that ran beside route-315, parallel to the river it was named for.

She hadn't a clue how she happened to get there, but knew it was too far away. Edward wouldn't have wandered this far off, no matter how 'bat-shit crazy' he may be. Lily had to call off her search; if he wasn't back by morning, she would call the police. She swept pass Union Cemetery and turned east down North Broadway.

She wouldn't sleep tonight. That was the only thing she was sure of.

The baby cried from atop his large mount as Minikins stumbled about with their tiny hands clamped against their equally tiny ears. Temelephas was not too fond of the racket either, hadn't been for the near two hours or so that it had been continuing—like a broken record. He wondered if perhaps the baby was broken, a toy that was shattered and ruined.

Maybe it needed something. It needed a lot, Temelephas was just beginning to realize. Sleep was a major thing it apparently required constantly, that and food. He had been sharing his gruel with the little one, as much as it seemed to detest the mush.

It wasn't for lack of sleep—in fact—Temelephas believed it spent more time sleeping than giggling and pulling on his flapping ears. Maybe he was a little frustrated and jealous for the lack of attention from his fledgling friend. Whatever the reason, Temelephas felt compelled to right whatever wrong had occurred.

He flung his long trunk up to meet the tantrum-driven child and cradled him lightly, pulling him gently from his back and holding him out in front of himself. The baby went silent, his face puff and red, eyeing the face of the giant before him. Temelephas cradled him, swayed him back and forth, rocking him for lack of a better idea.

Franklin smiled, even giggled, as his baby palms caressed the rough hide of his new crib. Temelephas was happy to be rid of the noise and found joy in the baby's smile. Franklin slowly succumbed to the dragging weight of sleep, fighting it off as long as he could with his wobbly head and clenched fists.

Temelephas felt relief rush through him when its eyes closed for the final time, followed closely by a feeling of triumph. Knowing the child was happy again was enough for him. So, Temelephas continued on his endless stroll, baby in the crook of his trunk.

Tyriano watched it all as it happened, the tenderness the elephant used as he saw to the baby, comforting him. The pachyderm was certainly finding new ways to astound and amuse the old Watcher. Tibil stood near his companion, stern faced and ready for anything.

"Did you see that, Tibil?" he asked softly as he kept his eyes on the elephant. "Temelephas has become almost maternal towards the baby human ... treating him as only a mother would with her instinctive knowledge."

"I thought Temelephas was a male?" Tibil pondered aloud. Tyriano laughed at the innocent ignorance of his small friend, not seeing the darkness that rose behind them.

"He is," Tyriano said. "Maybe that is why it is so fascinating to see him exhibiting such care ... such gentle nature." It was then that the soft, gasping cries of their attackers came to them as the dark fog surrounded them. "It's the Gloom," Tyriano began, terror rising in his throat as the ominous cloud swept round them. "Run!"

But, it was too late to run ... too late to escape and hide. Even if they had the time, to where would they run? After all, every light *does* have its shadow.

The Gloom is a frightful enemy to face in a fight. Incorporeal beings, they cannot be touched, but they can reach out with their shadowy limbs and grab hold of their victims, tugging at their pain and sorrow, sucking the very life from them, and leaving nothing but husks behind. Even in knowing this, Tibil swung his arms back and forth, driving the mist from them.

Towering over his small defender, Tyriano himself was engulfed by the darkness. The Gloom had him, pulling him to them and their sickly embrace. The thought of fighting hadn't crossed his mind. He was filled with dread and regret which consumed him utterly. Fear of the great sleep. Regret for not seeing it all through to the end. His vision began to waiver and his head swam as he staggered to and fro.

Death ... the Gloom whispered to him, *destroy* ... Each word they uttered seethed from their lipless mouths like venom, though without even a bite, their victims would fall ... that was the way of the Gloom.

"No ... use," Tyriano muttered to Tibil, his voice as shaky as his knees had become. "Give ... up." Tyriano fell to his knees, crumpling to the ground. Tibil couldn't obey Tyriano, refused to lie down in this fight. Tibil carried on in his battle, his head burning with rage and his arms burning from weariness.

Tyriano fell to one side and lay still as his breath escaped him in long, wheezing strands as the Gloom encircled him, ready to end his life. Tibil's hands swung slower as he heard the quiet calls of doom whispered in his ears. His hands were heavier as he realized how right Tyriano was. Why fight a useless fight? That was how the Gloom always won.

Tibil fell to his side as well, a matching pair they were, curled into balls, their very lives being slowed by the black cloud around them. All they knew was fear, the only component left in their world. It wouldn't last much longer, they knew. While terrifying and painful, death in the cold embrace of the Gloom is quick. It was the only real upside.

There came a loud crash as the cavern exploded in white light. The Gloom reared up at its arrival, allowing their victims to once again steal gasps of air. Even as the initial boom of the explosion subsided, the brilliant light remained. The Gloom yowled like dying wolves, the light itself burning into the darkness of their being.

Even as the light burned into them, their black flesh breaking apart, they pushed towards the light, searching for the source of it. The cavern was wild with the sound of the dying Gloom, as all shadows die in such bright light. "BACK ... YOU VILE CREATURES!!" a voice boomed from amid the light.

The Gloom could push forward no more, and fell back, knowing the only possible source of such power. They hovered then, in the air above their victims. "BACK TO THE SHADOWS!" the voice commanded, the light in the cavern growing brighter, eating all the shadows in the area.

The Gloom cried out in a horrid chorus then flew off, finding solace in the shadows high above, along the ceilings of far off tunnels. They rested there, letting their seared bodies cool in the darkness of their shadows. They would need time to recover.

When they had gone, the air grew quiet; the cavern became as calm as a field after a storm. Tyriano and Tibil merely lay still, but breathing; they were paralyzed with fear. The light faded, revealing the white cloak of a hooded man who stood over them.

The cloak glowed softly with the light, but when old hands pulled the hood back, the light gave way. His face was old, time had speckled it with marks and wrinkles that stretched across it like a road map across the universe. The cheeks were sunken, skin sagging, but the eyes burned with youthful zest, like two emeralds in a sea of flames.

"Uncle ... Tyrimus?" Tyriano muttered as his eyes came back into focus. Tibil was able to sit up slowly as his limbs began to work again, rubbing his legs. Tyrimus knelt beside his nephew, his knees creaking as he groaned.

"It is I, Tyriano," he replied in a hushed voice that no longer seemed as strong and furious as it had a moment ago.

"You ... wear the ... robe of ... the ... High Council?" he sputtered as his uncle cradled his head, lifting him from the dirt.

"I'm sorry I could never tell you ... it is a very secretive group, the Council." Tyriano's pale face was beaded with sweat, and his uncle wiped it away as he spoke. "Even by telling you now, I break the oath I made to the Council ... an oath meant to be kept for the rest of my days."

"Why break it now?" Tyriano asked, his voice growing sturdier than before.

Tyrimus' eyes welled with tears and he did his best to smile. "I saw you from above, as I always do. I knew what would happen if I hadn't intervened."

"You saved us," Tyriano muttered.

"I couldn't let you die."

"But, you broke your promise, putting yourself in jeopardy."

"No," Tyrimus said with an easy smile and a sparkle in his eyes. "No harm will come to either of us." He stood then, helping his nephew rise as well. "We have much to discuss. If all things work out, we will change the world ... no, the universe, for the better."

"You were wrong, you know," Tyriano said with the vague shadow of a smile on his face.

"About what?"

"What you told me all those years ago," Tyriano said. "When you told me he feels nothing?"

Tyrimus smiled broadly and laughed. "You are right," he said as he turned to lead his nephew away. "I guess even a teacher can learn from his student."

They walked away, there was much to discuss, plans to be made. Tyrimus walked slowly, the young leaning on the old as they walked. Tibil hobbled after them, his legs needing a bit more time to recover from their scuffle with the Gloom.

Nicholas stepped slowly through the graveyard, weaving between the solemn tombstones. The stone markers stood in the cold, frosty air, the dark of night breeding in their shadows. He had been there for hours searching the names and watching as families gathered around their deceased loved ones. It wasn't long before their tearful sobs went off with them in their cars, taillights burning like hot coals in the night.

Some of the stones were well kept; their flowers crisp and their plots free of weeds. The fresh mourning for their deceased occupants kept the living in attendance. Other stones stood in dismay and chipping, unkempt and lonely as the living went on doing just that.

He wondered if they knew they were left alone, the dead that is; wondered if they knew anything at all. Maybe they lay beneath the dirt, idly chatting to themselves, thinking someone is listening. Perhaps they give off ghostly sighs when no response comes.

In his wandering, Nicholas came across the headstones of many young people, ripped from life just as it had started for them. How horrible that must be, burying the young, burying your children. He felt sorrow well up inside him as he thought about the children that had barely tasted the fruits of life before seeing the dim light of death.

He saw a stone for a mother that bore a poem scripted by her young daughter and the plaque for a soldier that had died at war, at what should have been the peak of his life. So many lives lay around him, telling the forgotten tales of their lives to no one. He could almost feel the glow of them ... warm, drifting around him like a pool of sunny light.

He thought he could hear the voices of the dead, muffled and slow, calling out for answers. Why were they here? Where were they going? Heaven or Hell? So many questions ... and they called for their loved ones as they lay in the ground, trapped in their boxes. The sensations overwhelmed Nicholas and he felt he had finally gone mad.

It overwhelmed him, so he ran, trying to flee the madness that engulfed him. The voices crept after him even as he dashed through the endless night, driving him further down his unseen path. The ghosts of the graveyard pleaded to him, begged for salvation. They shared their regrets with him, life-long wishes that fell short.

They shared their failures and accomplishments, they told the many stories that made up their lives. So many stories were told, so many voices ringing out at once so that it sounded like white noise. His mind ached, trying to hear them all.

He stumbled over a small vase, spilling over its fake roses, and fell to the snowy ground. The voices bombarded him, pushing his head to a point where it throbbed. He glanced up and saw a name chiseled in a gray stone that loomed over him. 'Geraldine M. Forrest'.

"Mother," he whimpered, finally finding what it was he was looking for. He could hear her then; her voice calling to him, but it was muffled, lost in the mess of his mind. He tried to clear his mind, tried to scream for the other voices to leave him. Slowly, the voices faded away ... leaving him alone.

He sat there in the quiet dark, looking around ... completely alone. There were no voices flying at him, no eerie glow in the air about him. He could hear the far off traffic as it raced past the graveyard and its forgotten tenants. "Mother," he called again into the silence.

'*Nicholas*', a voice came to him. '*Is that you? You seem different ... what have you done to yourself?*' Nicholas' eyes exploded in tears ... hot, wet tears that shot down Edward's youthful face.

"Yes," he began, "It's me ... but something has happened ... I've lost myself."

'*You can't lose yourself, sweetie,*' she said in his mind. '*You can only let yourself go*'. The words floated in his mind, seeping in and laying the eggs of thought in him. He thought of how he always lived life, never trying to do anything and only just 'being'. Existing in the world as significantly as a dust bunny tucked beneath a bed.

"You are right, mom ... you always were."

She continued to speak to him, softly in his mind; hearing about his current predicament and sharing her thoughts. Nicholas listened intently, smiling brightly in the dark. '*You're so special*', his mother whispered to him. '*More special than I ever imagined.*'

She shared her fondest memories of his childhood as he cried. He learned a lot of things about himself that he had forgotten. He lay there, curled up next to her tomb, unaware of the sky above; crowded with dark clouds, pregnant with the coming snow. She tried to tell him more, urged him to stay awake to hear it all, but he was far too weary.

The sky split open silently and the tiny flakes fell. Nicholas nodded off under Edward's overcoat as his mother sang softly, a song forgotten from his boyhood. His mind continued to run, plotting his newfound path as he dreamed of a brighter tomorrow.

13

Tyrimus stood before his nephew and the tiny Tibil, his white robe's luminescence had faded to a dull glow. They occupied Tyriano's old office, huddled around his desk, hunched over—plotting quietly. Tyrimus looked down at the Minikin with a wary eye. "I think we should speak alone, nephew," he said, looking at Tyriano once more.

Tibil felt the urge churning his feet, the need to dash away obediently—as all Minikins knew their place in this world. He had never been one to stay where he was not wanted. He shuffled towards the great round door of the office, but was caught suddenly by Tyriano's firm grip.

"Tibil is my friend," Tyriano explained. "Whatever needs to be said ... can be said in his presence."

"As you wish," Tyrimus said slowly, carefully emphasizing his every word. "But, what I say to you *now* ... will bring a great burden upon *both* of your shoulders. You may face a gauntlet filled with peril, doom could be awaiting you around every corner."

"We will make do," Tyriano said calmly. "Nothing could be more trying than facing the Gloom, and you have already handled them for us ..."

"Do not count the Gloom out, it is a very fierce enemy

and does not like to be handled like a tool. The Watchers have been foolish, in my opinion—treated the Gloom with disrespect. All the shadows have is darkness and time. They will wait … wait for their time to strike again, and when they do, I promise you … you will *not* be ready for it."

Tyrimus' words did nothing to ease the minds of Tibil and Tyriano, but they had to know what it was they faced. They remained quiet, unable to come up with anything to say. "What a horrible creation … the Gloom. Hopefully, though, I bought you time. Hopefully, you won't encounter them on the surface."

"The surface," Tyriano asked. He rubbed his feathery chin, confused as to why they would be required to go to the surface.

"I will do all I can to help you, Tyriano … but I cannot accompany you to the surface, my attention is needed here. Besides, my days of gallivanting about the globe are over. I cannot guarantee your safety there."

"But, why must we go to the surface?"

"Because that is where your adventure begins …" Tyrimus smiled at his nephew.

There came a knock on the door. Nicholas stood on the other side of it when Lily pulled it open, but what she saw was her Edward. His face was pale and hung low, the stubble on his chin and cheeks speaking volumes on the wear he felt. His eyes were down and Lily was glad for it, not sure she truly wanted to see them. She felt that if he were to peer at her with those gray eyes that she might just fall apart.

"Where have you been?" she asked in a weak, fragile voice. His gaze stayed clear of her, as if even it knew how wrong he had been. "I looked for you *all* night." He shifted his weight from foot to foot and his eyes moved to the railing of the porch.

Could he not bring himself to look at her at all? Was it shame or pain he felt? She cried then, silent sobs that spun tiny tears down her red cheeks.

"How could you?" her voice cracked. "You don't do that to someone you love ... someone you *claim* to love, anyways." He looked up, his eyes red and wet, seemingly the victim of unspeakable tortures. Lily gasped, having seen those eyes; holding it in, fearful the next breath would be her last.

"You don't understand," he said softly. He seemed older in front of her, as if months, years had swept over him on that porch in just a moment. In a blink of an eye, the young man she loved had been somehow replaced by an older, shadowy version of himself.

"You're right," she said, a quick laugh at the back of her throat. "I don't ... I don't understand how you could be ... you've been so weird ... so elusive, distant even. You want space? ... I get it. You sat on a roof, howling like a maniac and I looked past it." She had to halt ... couldn't even begin to finish.

"Lily," he said.

"No," she cut in. "I need to finish, need to try to ... but, for you to ... to *leave* and *stay* out all night? How can you do that? ... You don't get to do that to me ... Not you ... You don't get to leave me."

"Lily, I'm not the man you think I am," he said quickly.

"I'm beginning to realize that."

"No," he said, trying to be clearer with what he meant. "I'm not the man you are supposed to marry ..."

Like water flowing over the lip of a bathtub, Lily felt her life slipping away from her. *This isn't my life*, she thought. *This wasn't supposed to happen.* Was she even breathing anymore? ... She couldn't tell. He called her name, but Lily couldn't hear him. She fell to her knees and wept inconsolably, melting into a human puddle.

The life she once saw ahead of herself, the life she dreamed of, was no longer hers. The face she once pictured in those dreams was no longer her own; it blurred and shifted into the face of a woman that one day Edward would love more than her. Their home—speckled in joyous Christmas lights—would be decorated by another woman; the children that would one day be theirs, could now only be strangers to her.

"Lily," he called again, this time she looked at him. He was kneeling beside her, looking at her with loving, worry stricken eyes. She wanted to beg him not to look at her that way. How dare he pity her?

"Lily," he almost shouted. She stopped her wild train of thought and peered at him with teary eyes. His hands were on her, one at her check, the other gripping her shoulder. She felt her breath coming back and the tunnel vision she felt before began to fade away.

"What?" she whimpered.

"I meant … I'm *not* Edward," he admitted with a cool, confidant gaze. He said it with a straight face and steady hands. If he had been lying it would have been impressive. "I'm not your fiancé."

She breathed slower then, the haste gone from her now settling heart. Her eyes began to dry and she felt the warm flush of her face dissolving. "You're *not* Edward?" she asked, confused and worried at once.

"I met Edward on the morning of the storm," he began slowly, watching as her face contorted. "He was standing there in his nice coat and shoes … carrying orange juice." Lily put her hands to her face, allowing them to collect the tears that flowed freely once more.

"He smiled at me," he continued. "I was sitting there … asking for change, but he had none to give. All he had was a scratch off ticket. He apologized even as he gave it to me, saying 'all he could offer me was a little hope'."

"I'm confused … so, you're saying you're someone else?"

"Yes. That was when the storm erupted above us … the wind pulling things into the sky … It tried to pull Eddie, tried to suck him up into the sky … but I grabbed his hand and held on to him tightly.

"He screamed as any person would, his feet dangling over his head. I promised I wouldn't let go. I held on to him *so* tightly. The storm grew stronger and I swore to myself that I wouldn't let go.

"I felt my fingers weaken, the sweat of our hands slipping between us. I thought that I would let go, prayed that I wouldn't. Instead, I let go of the one thing that tied us to the ground, so I could keep my grip with both hands, but then we both were sucked up into that black sky."

Lily stared at him with uncertainty, lost somewhere between pain and disbelief. She no longer cried, only listened to the unbelievable tale that was being spun. The man she always knew as Edward was staring out into the street, a dangerous, sorrowful gaze that could move mountains if not men.

"When I woke, I was lying in that gym, surrounded by all those lost souls, and then I saw you," he began to softly cry. "I saw you and you were a beauty. I thought I could continue in his life, pick up where he left off, but I can't. It wasn't right to even try."

There was only the sounds of the day then, the wind blowing … the errant barking of a far off dog. Nicholas' hair was blown—messier than usual—toppling over his face as he gazed at her with such confidant eyes. If he had been lying it would have been impressive … but only if someone believed.

"What am I *supposed* to think?" was all she said.

🐘

Camilla's old car puttered around the busy streets of downtown, Nicholas' face was pressed to the cold glass of the passenger side. He watched the steam from the bundled bodies as they shuffled from bus stops and crosswalks, all heading off to begin another mindless day of paper pushing. He looked at them all closely, hoping to recognize one of them. Maybe something he saw would trigger a memory or something.

But nothing came to him. "Are you sure this is the best way to go about this?" Camilla asked as they were finishing up their third pass through downtown. "Sure, *maybe* you work over here, but do you remember anything? Or am I just wasting gas?"

Edward thought about it and figured she might be right. The name Lily had been settled in his mind for a good long time now. They had searched the internet for Lilies living in Columbus, Ohio, but there were none that they could find. With all the social networking in the world, they pulled up diddlysquat.

The only fact they truly had to go on was that he was some kind of lawyer and—as Camilla pointed out— you can't throw a rock downtown without hitting one. If only he had called out Lily's last name as well, that would have been helpful. But all he could do now—apparently— was throw rocks. "It's all we can go on for now," he said.

The more he looked, the more confused he became. All of the tall buildings were too similar—with their dark glass and gray blocks. They had driven around so many times, that even the names on the buildings seemed the same to him. They seemed to run into one another, jumbled up letters which no longer made sense, nothing more than a giant game of Boggle. His head began to hurt.

He rubbed his forehead, wincing painfully through his teeth. It was the sort of pain that throbbed deep within his skull. "You okay?" she asked, shifting her eyes from the road to him and back again. He looked at her and meekly smiled, stretching his neck out as he did so.

"Yeah," he said quickly, "just realizing how hard this is going to be." *What an idiot*, he thought. He remembered reading stacks of mystery books as a kid, the sort with trouble-sniffing children that were always being trapped in wells and caves. He had always thought that they were entertaining, but secretly hoped that his consumption of them would have left him endowed with powers of deduction.

There were no fingerprints to collect though. No shadows to follow or smoking gun to uncover. This was— after all—real life, and even the supposed education of a lawyer couldn't help him solve this mystery. It wasn't as if this was an everyday occurrence, two souls switching bodies. It reminded him more him of the plot of some lame, family comedy, a premise done too often to ever truly be entertaining anymore.

"It's no use," he finally said. "This is all just too plain, nothing is triggering anything."

Camilla felt his frustration radiating off his body and slowly encompassing her. She knew he wasn't her brother, but she knew she had to help, especially if she wanted to get *her brother* back. She wanted things to work out for him. Who wouldn't? There had to be a happy ending somewhere—buried beneath this mess.

Her car slowly crept out of the bustle of downtown and puttered down Broad Street, heading into one of the many smaller boroughs that surrounded the tall buildings like an angry mob. Camilla's tummy grumbled, begging her brain to remember that they had skipped breakfast that morning. "We should probably stop for some grub," she offered up.

"I'm not hungry," he grumbled, staring out the window at the emptying streets and lonely vendors, huddled around their warm hotdog carts.

"Of course you're not," she said with a smile. "But I

am, and believe it or not, this whole day *isn't* about you." She smiled at the stranger beside her, poking his ribs with a jeering finger. He smiled back at her, even laughing a bit.

"Here's a nice place," she said after a bit, pointing to a black and red sign that only said *Tommy's*. "Some nice, greasy food sounds like just what we need." They pulled into the small lot beside it, parking amongst a scattering of cars. Camilla was busy, unbuckling her belt and talking about the different breakfast food she hoped they served. Edward just stared at the sign. It pushed at his subconscious, prodding it much as Camilla's finger had his ribs. But, instead of a smile or laugh, it freed a memory. "Wait ..." he said quickly. "This place seems familiar."

14

Once there was a School for the Deaf, cradled right in the heart of Columbus' downtown. Originally built in 1826, it was known as the "Asylum for the Education of the Deaf and Dumb". It only took a year for them to see the callousness of the name, changing it to the "Institution for the Education of the Deaf and Dumb". Opening such a school was a political ploy to keep the parents of deaf and dumb kids from taking their money to schools similar to it in neighboring states.

It started as a small house, teaching sign language and simple trades to the deaf and mute children of Ohio. It took over a hundred years before the grounds it sat upon became too small for their needs. They then moved it north to a larger lot with newer facilities.

For years, the remains of the original school were useless, dilapidated buildings that had gone overlooked as the world around it grew and changed. They just sat there like sleeping giants, waiting for a stiff breeze to knock them over. That breeze never came, but it wasn't horribly necessary either as a mysterious fire sprouted up in its dry bones, laying waste to the majority of the eyesore.

The city built a park amongst its ashes. It was a relatively well visited park where people could go to eat their lunches, couples could take a stroll, and people could read in the shadows of trees—being nestled up against the Library. The park paths remain bare—however—during the short, cold days of winter. That was why it was there that they chose to appear.

First there was nothing there but the snow covered, sculpted bushes—paying tribute to a George Seurat painting—and the cold, winter wind. And in a blink of an eye, they were standing there. Only the squirrels and birds were witnesses to their arrival.

Tyriano stood, a long black coat draping from his tall frame, the fur lining crawling up his neck. He hid his feathery hair beneath a black fedora and his eerie eyes behind purple tinted sunglasses. Even under the heavy coat, Tyriano shivered slightly from the cold air.

Tibil stood beside him, barely visible in his fluffy, bunny coat, made of soft terry with a hood that sprouted ears playfully from its crown. Its short arms ended in little paws that were sewn right in to the sleeves. Although the bunny coat was indeed warm and comfy, Tibil also found it quite embarrassing. Sadly, it was the only coat small enough, that Tyrimus had been able to provide.

Tyriano looked around at the white landscape, scattered with bushes trimmed to look like people silently gazing out onto a frozen pond. There were small children sitting with faceless adults and dogs which sat in eternal obedience. The wind howled overhead, barely masking the sounds of traffic beyond the park's walls.

"Quite a magnificent place," the Watcher said, looking down to his small, rabbit friend. Tibil nodded, scratching at his head through the woolen hood. "If only we had more time to explore, but we have an appointment to keep."

They walked through the snow to a small walkway and made their way, slowly, to the street. Tyriano held a hand out for his friend and Tibil took it with his little paw.

He then stuck out his other hand, in its black glove, waving it madly to hail a 'cab', just as he once read it was done.

It turned out to be a lot harder than he originally believed it would be, but after a while a cab pulled over. Tyriano read the address of their first destination to the hairy man behind the wheel, who merely nodded. The driver took one long look at the small child in his backseat before pulling away. He thought the child seemed odd, dressed in his bunny coat, but nobody paid him for his opinions ... those he gave away for free.

The driver slipped the yellow cab into drive and eased it back into the steady flow of traffic. The cab's steamy exhaust merged with that of the cars around it before rising collectively into the equally gray sky.

🐘

"She always had the salad," he told Camilla as he looked down at the ketchup bottle he cradled in his hand. "We always sat by the window ... over there," he said, unabashedly pointing to where a couple sat. "I purposely chose that spot ... just so I could watch the sunlight play in her hair." Nicholas' old face stretched into a wide, frantic smile. "Lily."

"What's your name then?" she asked anxiously, leaning over the linoleum table; her scarf dipping into her coffee. "It must be rattling around in that noggin of yours somewhere."

He squeezed his eyes shut and tried to call back the stray memories. At first, all that came was the sound of muted laughter ... her laugh, as if it leaked through the walls. It made his heart leap in his throat—the sound of her.

He squeezed them tighter still and could hear her talking to him, but the voice was faint and far off. He couldn't discern the words she spoke. It sounded to him as if the voice was drifting further off and it scared him more than he thought a trailing voice ever could.

He got up quickly and moved to their table by the window, which had just been vacated—the previous diners leaving behind bits of uneaten toast. He sat there—anxiously—just as another couple approached, antsy after waiting for a table. The place was so busy that any table, dirty or otherwise, was a treat.

"Hey, buddy," the man said with a frustrated, guttural cough as a prelude—doing his best to seem imposing. The woman with him simply scoffed, obviously affronted by a man taking a seat. Edward didn't hear them; he was busy looking across the table to the empty seat where he knew that once before, many times before, she sat.

He could see her, but only faintly. She was nothing more than a shimmering mirage, with her dazzling smile peeking through her penny-colored hair. And those eyes sparkling like bright gems, looking at him with more love than any man would need, breaking his heart every time she blinked.

Camilla came over and did her best to calm the man down—even offering their table to them—but the man wouldn't back down. "It's the principle," he squawked as if he stood up for all those that have ever been wronged. All the other diners sat around, watching it all as it unfolded, except Edward.

When we're married, the voice spoke, softly from the misty form, *promise me ... we'll come here every week? ... Never lose this tradition?* Edward nodded slowly, tears creeping down his pinched smile. "Of course," he muttered.

"What did he say?" the irate man spat, confused and getting angrier by the second.

I want to always be the same people we are today, this very second. I want you to stay the man I fell in love with. Edward's face shifted, became serious and dark. "Who am I?" he asked of the wispy woman. *Ooh, I better visit the little girl's room before our food gets here.* The vision of Lily rose, her form getting shaky with her movement.

"Wait," he called to the hallucination, "What's my name?" Lily couldn't hear him and he stood to follow, but she moved too quickly through the crowded diner. Edward encountered too many obstacles, like people, bags, and strollers. "Just ... say my name!" he shouted over the gradually quieting restaurant.

You better not eat my croutons, Eddie, she called out with a phantom laugh before dissolving into the awkward ambience of the crowded diner. He was left alone again, all the eyes of the patrons were pasted upon him. "My name is Eddie!" he announced to the room. "She called me Eddie!"

So busy was he in celebration that he failed to notice the girl at the register, phone to her ear, whispering into the mouth piece. *Eddie,* he thought, *she said my name was Eddie.* It was only a few minutes before a cruiser quietly pulled up to the front of Tommy's diner with its red and blue lights igniting the snow covered sidewalks.

Temelephas saw the old man standing over him on the ledge that overlooked his wheel. He wore a long, white robe and his face was wrinkled, far more wrinkled that that of Tyriano; his head covered with fine, white feathers. He knew who the old Watcher was. How could he ever forget him? He was the one that watched over him many centuries ago.

And there he stood, silently watching over him as he always did before—more a statue than a man. Each time Temelephas made his pass, those stern eyes of the Watcher fell upon him. Temelephas couldn't help but wonder about his sudden appearance.

Is he here for the child, he wondered to himself. It still bothered him that Tyriano had been missing for quite some time, but at least that younger one was gone too. There was so much hate in that younger one, he knew. He never would have cared for Temelephas as much as the other two had.

This older one had never spent the time Tyriano had, talking to Temelephas; but then again, he never tried to attack him either—like the younger had, with fire in his eyes and trembling fists. The young one would have harmed the elephant if he had the chance and he definitely meant harm to his young friend.

"What are you thinking?" the old man finally asked from his perch above. It was obvious in his voice that the old Watcher felt reluctant, perhaps foolish, speaking to him. Temelephas just looked up at him with his large, dark eyes … an absent stare. "Is it true? … Can you understand me? … Can you possibly remember?"

Temelephas wished he could answer him, but he never quite figured out how to. He understood what was said—more than any would guess—and would remember those words forever, so practiced was his mind. But each time he ever tried to form words in the past, tried to call out … all that would come were wild howls and moans.

He tried again, tried to say anything … and again it was only a shrill warble that came firing down his trunk. He felt the baby trembling atop him and knew that he had woken him. He was sorry for that, since the baby seemed to need more sleep than any creature had a right to demand. He himself never slept, so Temelephas figured *someone* should claim his unused portion.

He lifted his trunk to the baby and patted him softly, coaxing him back into slumber. The baby didn't fight it long, just laying his head back into the pillow of wiry, gray hair. With his thumb firmly inserted between budding teeth, he fell back under the Sandman's spell.

The old Watcher smiled, knowing his nephew had to be right. He just wished it was something the Council would celebrate—something they would accept—rather than something they would scorn. But he knew that would require a miracle.

The High Council was set in their ways, driven by their lust for power. That was why his plan had to work ... why it couldn't fail. *It can't fail,* he reminded himself. The idea that he was too old for such scheming entered his head. The fate of the world and its trillions of souls rested on the hasty plan of a man past his prime.

He couldn't trust the High Council any longer, couldn't even attempt to steer them in the direction his plan was pointing. Doing so would only give himself away and surely lead Tyrimus to his Great Sleep. He just prayed that the High Council had yet to figure out that he couldn't be trusted either.

🐘

The cab pulled to a stop in front of a string of brown duplexes. They all looked alike—like puppies from the same litter—spread up and down streets that all looked the same. Tyriano and Tibil stepped out from the cab after passing the driver a handful of green paper—which Tyriano was glad to see pleased him. They watched the car speed off, standing along the frozen curb.

"Impressive way to travel," Tyriano said. "These humans surely come up with some amazing contraptions."

"I prefer walking," Tibil spat quickly, a disgruntled looked upon his face.

"You say that only because you could not see out the windows," the Watcher said, smiling. Tibil just huffed and followed his friend up to the houses crossing stairs that seemed to be crumbling, falling to ruin. The steps led to a creaking porch, cluttered with smelly trash bags and uncollected newspapers.

"Is this the right place?"

"It is, my friend," Tyriano assured him as he knocked

on the door—a loud, hollow knock. Tibil stared about at the collected filth that took over the porch, his face scrunched up in disgust. "Grief can do funny things to people ... no matter how sane they may seem."

There came a rustling from behind the door and Tyriano could see shadowy movement through the fogged glass. The door opened slowly and a thin faced woman peered cautiously through the gap, brown hair in greasy strands before her face. "Yes?" she asked softly.

"Joyce?" Tyriano asked calmly. Tibil darted behind his tall friend, afraid of the look on her face, in fear of what her grief may make her do.

"Yeah ... who are you?" she asked, opening the door an inch or two more. She wore a sullied sweatshirt and faded blue jeans.

"I am Tyriano," he said with a cheerful tone, "And this little fellow hiding behind me is my associate, Tibil."

"Get lost," she spat out suddenly. "I don't have the patience today for a lesson in Mormonism." she began to shut the heavy door, but the surprising quickness of Tyriano allowed his boot to jam it open.

"You may want to hear me out," he continued in his calm timbre. "We only bring good tidings." Tyriano removed his black hat; his gray, feathered hair spilling out—a shocking site for Joyce. It was then that she noticed the strange, slightly purplish hue of his skin. "Might we come it?"

"Wait," she said, looking down at the strange creature that she had only moments ago mistaken for a child. She could see the bright red curls peeking out from under his bunny hood and those impossibly light blue eyes. "Who are you?"

"We're friends of both you and your son ... Franklin." She fell back, hearing his name spoken. Hope filled her and she realized that she was feeling it for the first time in days.

"You found him?" she asked in a new, softer tone

that quaked through her tight lips. "Please tell me you found him, if not, I'm sure my heart will shatter in my chest ... I'm sure that I'll die." She was weeping, her hands shook terribly as they tried to catch her falling tears.

Tibil stepped out from behind his friend and stepped up to her; his hand patted her elbow as she gazed down at him. "It's more that he found us," he said in his soft, high voice. She cried harder and begged to see him, begged that he be brought to her.

"It's not that simple," Tyriano continued. "But, you will see him soon enough, today most likely. We just have to tell you a story first; you have to know this story before we continue." She laughed nervously and stepped aside.

"Then come in," she said, stepping aside. She fed them a hot lunch of macaroni and cheese and to Tibil's delight, hot dogs. She sat patiently listening, just waiting for the story to end so that she could see her child.

It all sounded like utter bullshit to her, this story of the center of the earth and this Temelephas. But she couldn't find a hint of a lie on either of their faces. She examined them as closely as she ever had her ex-husband's face, but found nothing. Besides—she thought—what did it matter? She would have gone to the end of the world for her baby ... why not only to the middle of it?

She was nothing more than a
shimmering mirage, with her
dazzling smile peeking through her
penny-colored hair. And those
eyes sparkling like bright gems,
looking at him with more love
than any man would need,
breaking his heart
every time he blinked.

15

"So, what do we do now?" Joyce asked, leaning anxiously from the ledge of the couch. She'd heard their story, most of which she didn't understand. All that she focused on was the idea of her little baby and seeing him again, holding him once more.

Tyriano sat across from her, still donning his black coat and hat. She had offered to take them for him, but he politely refused. He found that even the warm home he sat in was still a bit too cold for his liking, paling in comparison to the center of the Earth.

"We must find another man ... it's imperative that we bring him with us," Tyriano said as he took a sip from a festive mug of coffee displaying a cartoon-ish Santa Claus.

"Why do we need this other man? Why can't we just go?"

"He is *too* important; we need him to fix it all, to restore order to the world," he said, leaning forward; his wrinkled hand running through his flowing beard. "He is the key to it, without him, we could lose it all." He took another sip from his mug. "Mmmm, this is rather tasty."

"I don't like it," Tibil said, he too still trapped in his bunny coat for warmth. His face was as bitter as the coffee must have tasted to him.

"Forget the coffee," Joyce barked. "Let's just go get this man."

"Well, funnily enough," Tyriano began again with a wry smile. "To get him, we need to get yet another man … they are intertwined, as it were."

"How is that possible?"

"I'm really not quite sure," Tyriano said honestly, stirring his coffee with a spoon. "I know only what I need to know … and at this moment that is only very little … for the moment at least. My uncle will tell us more once we return to the core."

"Fine," she said loud, unable to mask her anxiety. "Then let's get them both … where do we start?"

"Ironically enough, one of them lives just across the way." Tyriano again was smiling and choking a bit on a chuckle. These little twists of fate always tickled his funny bone.

Joyce wasn't laughing and she was seriously beginning to doubt the sophistication of humor at the center of the earth. *Maybe they don't quite understand it.* "Great," she said, trying to regain her composure. "Let me get my keys."

She awoke suddenly to a noise. She was alone on the large, plush couch that sat under the living room window. Her face was red and swollen; her tears had dried, only the memory of them remained. At first she thought the noise she heard was only a thing of her dreams, even though she could not remember what it was she dreamt of. She continued to lull there, unwilling to move.

Bang, bang, bang, again came from the door. Lily sat up slowly and walked to the door with about as much enthusiasm as a tortoise. She wasn't expecting anyone, especially after that morning's meltdown. She was surprised to see her neighbor, Joyce, standing on the other side of the door.

"Hey," Lily said in a dry, cracked voice. "What are you doing here? Is everything okay?"

"Better than okay," Joyce began with a frantic smile. "I know where Franklin is!"

Lily smiled the best she could, finding it hard to fake joy at that moment. *Why should it be fake? Am I that bad of a person*, she wondered as she forced her smile wider and let herself laugh lightly. "Wow, where was he?"

Joyce's face quickly went from jovial to perplexed, as if the slight breeze that blew down their street carried away her joy. "That's the weird part," she said carefully. "And trust me Lily, this is going to sound crazy, Lord knows I was …" Joyce was cut off as a tall man in a long black coat and matching hat stepped beside her.

"Might we have a moment of your time in private?" he asked, his eyes hidden by the purple lenses of his glasses.

"I'm sorry, who are you? A detective?"

"My name is Tyriano," he said with a slight nod, "and it's quite important that we have a word with you in private."

"I'm sorry, I mean no offense to you," she said sternly, "and I'm thrilled that you found your son, Joyce … But now is not the best time, could we do this tomorrow?" Lily began to shut the door, slowly, not wanting to be rude.

"It involves your soon to be husband, Lily," Tyriano sputtered.

"Eddie?" Lily asked shakily, pulling the door open once more.

"Yes," he answered. "Is he at home?"

Dezriak was miserable. His legs were hurting and his belly grumbled. In his mind he cursed Tyriano and his meddlesome fool of an uncle. Now the Gloom wouldn't respond to his calls. He had mastered them, been able to command them with only a mere thought. They had nearly killed Tyriano before the old man had intervened.

Now they wouldn't hear him, wouldn't come to his aid. They were there—lining the ceiling in silent misery—but they wouldn't even acknowledge him. He had to get free, take back the reigns of the underworld, even if it cost him everything.

"It is a shame to find you cooped up here, Dezriak," a voice called from behind the hanging cage. Dezriak was surprised by the voice and moved about in his cage, sending it spinning and rocking.

"Who's there?" he called, not able to move around quickly enough to ease his curiosity.

"We expected you to have had the run of this place by now," a different voice called. Dezriak settled himself in his rocking aviary and it slowly spun about, exposing the High Council as they stood on the ledge opposite his cage. There were four of them, all in their long, white robes—their faces hidden by the luminescence of their garb.

"I am in this cage due to your colleague's betrayal … he interfered and yet you mock *me*?"

"We do not mock you, Dezriak," a third one said. "We came here to offer guidance and assistance."

"Just a key would suffice," he said with a vexed overtone, his teeth were gnashed like a wild animal that was backed in to a corner.

"In due time," the first said again. "First, we must make sure that your goals are aligned with ours. If we find that they are … we will free you."

"And if they aren't?"

"Then you will rot in your birdcage, or perhaps the Gloom could do you the favor of escorting you into your Great Sleep."

"What could they possibly do?" he asked haughtily. "They're nothing more than shadows, so easily defeated by

Tyrimus, simply pathetic."

"I wouldn't be so dismissive of the Gloom if I were you." the first Councilman said. "It is far older than you know, much stronger than it is given credit for."

"Some powerful force they are, scared off by a little light."

"You know nothing of it," the second Councilman said. "The Gloom is older than any of us ... even the Maker."

"How can that be?" Dezriak said with a haughty laugh.

"As far as we know, it has always existed," the third began. "Contrary to popular belief, the Maker didn't make *everything*. Something was there when the Maker stumbled into existence ... he perceived it as nothing more than darkness around him."

"But it wasn't merely darkness that surrounded the Maker," the Second continued in the story. "It was something alive ... he could feel its cold breath on the nape of his neck ... its growl in his ear."

"And in that darkness came the first spark," the second continued on, "a light to balance the ever-present darkness. The Maker saw the Gloom reel back from it, howling like a cat with singed whiskers. It was then that he filled the void with stars; burning balls of gas that left no refuge for the Gloom."

"However, the Gloom never submitted to the Maker," the third said, "never deigned to respect or obey him. Nor could the Maker rid himself of the Gloom entirely, lest he flood the universe with unbearable light and heat. They found themselves at a stalemate, only able to find an unspoken balance. And with that balance came night and day, an understanding that the Gloom would have its own role in the Maker's game."

"The Gloom has been patient for an eternity," the fourth said, "biding its time. And now, knowing the Maker is gone, it can lash out. It feels as if we have invaded its home—which in a sense we have—and it is not too happy about that."

Dezriak glanced to the ceiling from within his cage. The black, inky mass of the Gloom bubbled and rolled in the dark. It did appear to Dezriak as if it was growing, little strands of black gathering to it from unseen cracks in the ceiling of the cavern.

"It boils with the hatred it feels for the Maker; it dreams of its long sought revenge upon him," said the first. The sea of black growled and rippled at the mere mention of its nemesis. It seemed to pulsate, growing ever bigger.

Dezriak silently eyed the shadows overhead, swearing he could see the shadowy specters leering at him. He could faintly hear the whispered calls of it, hungry and miserable. "It is your choice," the councilman said. "You can either be an asset to us … or die in that cage."

"I will do anything to get free from this cage," he seethed.

"Without any query of our reasoning? Why would you promise such a thing without knowing the path on which you will walk?" another asked.

"If only to exact my revenge on Tyriano," he said with a dull look in his eyes, as if daydreaming of his mentor's demise. "It is the only thing the Gloom and I have in common, it seems."

"And how would you go about doing that?"

"The only reasonable way to deal with traitors," he said coolly, staring with confidence at the remaining four members of the High Council, "by tossing him, headlong into his *own* Great Sleep."

The High Council was silent, watching him as he slowly rocked in his cage, never saying anything. They just stood there as if ingesting his words, deciphering how they could make use of him. They couldn't rule as they wanted to—not without his assistance. No, they needed Dezriak, and he knew it.

"And after you have ended Tyriano's time ..." the third Council member began, "would you do the same to the elephant?"

"I would. Once we had a mechanism in place to carry on his duty, I would gladly end his life as well."

"Oh, there's no need for any mechanism," the first said.

Dezriak shifted his head, gazing steadily at them as his cage gently swayed. Was it a trick question? Did they know what they were asking of him?

"Why wouldn't there be?" he asked. "Without a means to turn this world ... well, it would undoubtedly end it, killing off all life on Earth."

"That it would," the fourth Council member proclaimed. There was silence then, except for the far off drumming of Temelephas' feet.

"But why would you *want* to do that?"

"The universe is vast, Dezriak," the first said. "There are numerous planets, some even with life upon them ... Earth is just one of many."

"It's not an important planet in the long run," the third began. "It's the runt of the litter and needs to be put down ... for the good of the rest of the universe, it needs to be culled. Life will go on elsewhere."

"But, what of the Maker? What would he say, knowing you purposely ended the Earth?"

"The Maker is gone."

"But what if he returned?"

"He won't return, he abandoned *all* his projects and duties," the first began once more. "This Universe is ours now; we guide it, we form it, we can end it and its planets however we see fit." Dezriak still seemed unsure ... perhaps, unwilling.

"You know what it's like," the second Council member began. "Power requires the ones who wield it to make horrible decisions sometimes, all for the greater good."

"You must understand that," the fourth began. "You, being so smart, already in a great position—for such a young Watcher." Dezriak smiled at the compliment.

"You could become the youngest member of the High Council one day," the second said. "In fact, we seem to be short a member now, isn't that so?"

"I would say that it is."

"Very true."

"You *could* be the fifth member," the first began. "If that is what you *want*. All you have to do is prove that you are with us. Are you with us, Dezriak?"

"I take it that Edward has been quite peculiar—as of late," Tyriano posed, his elbows on Lily's dining room table, fingers laced together beneath his chin. The small, childish looking half-man in the rabbit ears sat close to his side, sipping a cup of instant hot cocoa that he nearly demanded. Joyce was impatient as ever sitting across from her.

Lily didn't know how to respond to that question, the words were slippery and dangerous at the tip of her tongue. She didn't want to say anything bad about Edward, knowing how rough things had been for him and how they were only going to get rougher. She still loved him, a thing that wouldn't go away so easily.

And in Lily's silence, Joyce found her own voice and spoke—as she had time and time again—about things that were none of her business. She droned on, confessing about her neighbor's odd behavior, recounting his weird howling at the moon. Lily felt the reflux of anger climb in her throat.

"Then he just took off last night, right Lily?" she ended, looking to Lily for the first time as if *just* remembering she was there. "Gone all night without even a note or anything." She seemed excited as she spoke, not a bit of pity in her tone.

"He did come back, though," Lily said in a cold, despondent voice. "Just this morning."

"Really?" Joyce barked. "What happened? What did he say?"

"I can't even think about it … He was so apologetic, though … almost like he was before, but not nearly the same."

"I know this may sound bizarre and you may think I'm a bit crazy," Tyriano said softly, slowly choosing his words with expert precision, "but he's not your Edward anymore."

"That's what he said," she said, lifelessly eyeing the tabletop.

"He told you?"

"He said, *I'm not your fiancé,*" her eyes rolled uncontrollably as she said it. She heaved a heavy sigh as the words left her lips. It was as if she had breathed in for the first time all day; as if telling this to someone *else* had eased some of her burden.

"And did he say anything else to you?" Tyriano asked her. Lily had to smile at him, the way he leaned in with a look of desperation. It reminded her of the way her great-aunt Lucinda would sit on the edge of her plaid couch, watching the daily plot unfold on her favorite soap opera.

"Oh, yeah," she said with a forced laugh. "He gave me this whole story about how he's someone else, some unnamed man … and how he and Edward had *switched bodies.*" She laughed hysterically, tears peeking out of the corners of her eyes. "Am I supposed to believe that? As if life is nothing more than a stupid movie with a lazy screenwriter?"

Tyriano's face clouded over with worry, his eyes sank and his shoulders slouched as he realized that his mission may prove harder than he once hoped it would. Why was trust such a hard thing for humankind? He had read many books on Earth's history and knew of the many horrors that mankind had to endure, the terrors they thrust upon one another, like wars and diseases and such.

But in the end, Tyriano was finally realizing that he may not know humanity as well as he thought. This trust thing was by far the hardest thing to comprehend. People seemed to grow it slowly, like a well pruned rose bush. But when it was broken it was destroyed and hard to put back together again.

"I gave him the chance to just be a man," she resumed. "I said, 'if you want out, just tell me'." Lily felt more at ease as she told her side of things, even surprised at how open she could be with strangers. "I didn't *need* that story ... he didn't *need* to lie to me. I told him, 'walk away ... don't just push me away'."

"Where is Edward, Lily?" Tyriano asked.

Joyce was quiet with a stoic look upon her face—as if she knew who spilt the milk.

"What does it matter?" she asked calmly.

"He was not lying to you, Lily," he said, soothingly, his eyes firmly fixed on hers through his purple lenses, gazing confidently at her.

"Sure," Lily laughed, it wasn't a jovial laugh, but one that was more on the side of manic. "Even when the story's totally unbelievable, all men will stick together. You were right, Joyce."

"It's not a lie," Joyce said, slow and clearly. Lily looked questioningly at her neighbor, with a hint of betrayal.

"Each has a body and a mind," Tyriano said, leaning further across the table. "First there is your Edward," he said, raising two fingers of one hand. "He is complete with both his mind and body. Then you have the other man," he lifted two fingers on the other hand. "And, for some reason, when the storm came, the two of them collided ...

and when it passed, they had swapped their souls, if you will."

Tyriano crashed his two hands together and then pulled them away. In his mind he felt he had more a clear cut case as to what had happened. "That man is not your Edward."

"You need to leave," Lily spat suddenly, pushing herself up from the table.

"It's not a lie, Lily," Joyce said once more, her voice getting louder as she tried to reason with her, needing her to go along with them for the sake of her son.

"You are unbelievable, Joyce. I thought you of all people would side with me, not this lunatic." Lily stood there, firmly pointing towards the door. "Out!"

"Look at me," Tyriano said as he rose from his own chair and slowly stepped towards her. She repeated her demand yet no one moved. She only wanted to be alone again.

"Look at me," Tyriano repeated, pulling his hat from his head and his shades from the bridge of his nose. She looked at him, the stranger she found on her doorstep. He seemed different to her now.

His face was a pale purple—she didn't remember it being so purple—blue veins visible along his wrinkled brow. His hair was still gray though it turned out not to be hair at all, but fine, silk-like feathers that fell down the sides of his face. And his eyes, red hot, like two coals thrown from a hearth.

"What are you?" This *man* had sat across from her at her own table, in her own house, yet it was as if she was only looking at him now—for the first time. As if his appearance had morphed before her very eyes.

"That is not important at the moment," Tyriano said urgently. "All that matters is getting Edward back and fixing this whole mess … or we will *all* suffer from it."

Lily felt the room spin about her and the blood

running from her face. She felt her stomach tighten into a small knot. She felt sick. She felt sorrow. She felt angry. Most of all, though, she felt guilty. Was there any truth to what he said to her?

"Lily, for the sake of all," Tyriano spoke easily, gripping her shoulders—pleading with her. "Where is Edward?"

16

Edward was sitting in a small room, its yellow walls plastered with posters meant to boost self-esteem and encourage happy, positive thoughts. They portrayed images of people accomplishing great feats and kittens dangling from tree branches, all with printed messages of endurance and compassion. Where there were no posters, paintings hung—vividly colored and wonderfully imaginative pieces of art. They were the finger paintings of the mentally unstable.

I don't belong here, he thought. *What happened at the diner was all a misunderstanding.* He tried to explain it to the officers that had arrived, but they merely shrugged it off as 'just another madman'. He couldn't blame them, though, he never would have believed the ramblings of a man screaming about being in the wrong body and seeing the ghosts of the living.

Living? Was she even alive? He realized then that it was quite possible that this Lily was in fact dead. How would he even know? Part of him knew she was something special to him, a girlfriend or a wife. He wanted her to be *something* special to him, something to leverage himself in this upturned reality.

Maybe it was nothing at all. Maybe he was as crazy

as everyone had been telling him these last couple of hours. Maybe he was just Nicholas—a man at the end of his thread of lucidity—a man whose brain had snapped, spiraling him into a wonderful world of delusion. The idea became more and more plausible to him as he sat between those yellow walls.

In this den of insanity with him were a handful of other men, all supposedly as loony as they perceived him to be. Some looked clean cut and put together, pleading to all around them that they were in fact 'totally sane'. Others were disheveled—mumbling—nothing more than sentient messes of men.

They all sat in a circle composed of green, plastic chairs. No one seemed comfortable here, he decided as he eyed his company. They all shuffled about, as restless as lit bottle rockets—ready to shoot, whirling through the sky.

The door to this sad room pushed in and a man strolled through. He was tall, with a horseshoe of gray hair and a thin mouth hidden beneath a slightly darker mustache. He held a yellow pad—the object of his constant attention. He flipped through it hastily with long fingers, his small eyes peering through the bifocals that sat haphazardly upon the tip of his nose.

He was more than likely a medical specialist that worked for the state, Edward assumed. More than likely an underpaid one as well—foreseeable by the old, worn, brown slacks and pink dress shirt he wore. Edward was willing to bet that the shirt had originally been white— once upon a time—but had met its pink fate in the washing machine, at the hands of a villain that looked suspiciously like a red sock.

"Good Afternoon," he said cheerily, his eyes never leaving the pad. "My name is Dr. Baltrix and I will be heading up your evaluations." He sat in a chair similar to theirs, and looked around at them for the first time. He gave them a look of compassion, one that he most likely had practiced and perfected while gazing into a mirror.

"I have yet to read your files," he continued. "But they will be read by the time we meet for our morning session."

"Morning session?" one of the more put together men asked in an irate tone. He was clean cut and just on the bad side of thirty, wearing clothing that would convince you that he was successful in life. Certainly not the guise of a 'mad man'. "But I shouldn't even be here!"

"I'm sure that most of you feel that way, and we will discuss those feelings in the morning," Baltrix explained with his thin, wry smile.

"But, I'm not crazy," the man shouted, his arms shooting into the air.

"Mr. Loggins, right?" the doctor asked, flipping through his pad. "It says here that you set your house on fire after you learned of your wife's infidelity with your brother?"

"False," Mr. Loggins retorted. "I set my *wife* on fire … she just happened to be asleep in *bed* when I did it, the rest was poetic justice." He looked around, shrugging off his culpability and nodding as if to find affirmation from those who sat around him.

"You killed your wife?" Edward asked.

He got no answer, but found it all disheartening nonetheless. If someone as put together as Mr. Loggins appeared turned out to be a crazy, jealous arsonist, what could be said about himself?

Maybe he was crazy; maybe he belonged here with the arsonist, the guy that smelled like last week, the man in a dress, and that other peculiar man that was consistently staring at him. The staring man stared at Edward with a determined intensity, in a way that would normally be unsettling, but was only more so in this little room.

"For now," Baltrix resumed, "You will wait here for an attendant to show you to your rooms. You'll have to share rooms, seeing how it's our busy season," he said with a chuckle, "you know … the holidays?" No one laughed, though, perfect proof in Baltrix's mind of their insanity. The doctor stood then, clicking his pen and tapping it against his yellow pad.

"Dinner's at six. In your room by eight. Lights out by nine." He rambled it all off so smoothly, giving them all a reassuring smile as if promising them each that 'it was all going to be *just* fine'. Then he was out the door as quickly as humanly possible.

Edward was alone again … with them, the crazies. His only real fear now was that Loggins would set fire to them all for some nonsensical reason or another. Perhaps that would be for the best for all of them, to simply just perish in an unexplainable bliss, at least Edward thought so in that moment.

He felt naked, after all—striped of dignity, freedom, and mental security. Even his own identity had escaped him, everything but his first name gone in the night like a burglar. It was all ripped from him in one smooth motion, like a Band-Aid.

All of the patients began to disperse, walking about and examining the art and posters as they waited to be shown to their rooms. Edward thought it best to stay in his seat—better not to attract unwanted attention. *Let them move around all they want*, he would stay put.

And yet, staying put was not as safe a route as he had hoped it would have been. That weird man just continued to stare at him with a warm smile as if they were old friends that had run into one another on the street. Edward tried not to make eye contact, but that proved impossible.

He found himself locking eyes with him, not knowing why his mind was so drawn to him. The strange man cocked his head and scratched at his stubbly chin, and a satisfied smile spread across his face. Before Edward could figure him out, the man stood and crossed the precious distance of floor that lay between them.

He sauntered over, his hands planted on his hips, his eyes looking Edward up and down. Edward just kept looking down—regretting the momentary eye contact. The tall man then sat beside him and stretched out his long legs, leaning in close to Edward. "I know you," he quietly said.

"I'm sure that you don't," Edward assured him. But maybe he did know Nicholas; Camilla had said that he had kept some rough company and led a life of questionable practice. The man just laughed softly and shook his head.

"We have a mutual friend," he responded.

"Who?" he asked softly, "Dorothy, the Tin Man, or the Cowardly Lion?" That drew another laugh from the strange man.

"Lily," the man whispered, causing Edward's throat to seize up. His face tightened—blood flowing away from it—like that of a mouse caught in a trap. He took another look at the stranger—a nice, hard look. The man's face seemed eerily familiar, but it was hard to place.

"You know Lily ... right, Eddie? ... Has that part come back, yet?"

"Who are you," he asked, his mind racing. "How do you know my real name?"

"I know your real name, because ..." the man began in a hushed voice as he leaned closer, "you're in my body." Nicholas leaned back, smiling broadly.

Tyrimus stood above the cavern, gazing down as the elephant continued marching around his wheel. He found it all fascinating. He had been here—years before—doing the same thing, watching; only now, he saw things in a different light.

The Council had always told him that the beast was

more of a tool than an animal, to never confuse the two. It was his mistake, taking them on their word. If what his nephew theorized turned out to be true—the thoughts and emotions of this beast—he suspected that the High Council would be less than thrilled to hear of it.

Tyrimus should have known better, should have seen through the veil of lies. But it wasn't he that saw the truth; it wasn't even his fellow Council members. It had been Tyriano.

"Such a smelly old thing, isn't it?" a voice said from beside Tyrimus. The old Watcher looked to his side and saw the luminous forms of his colleagues.

"Brothers," Tyrimus addressed them, shocked at their sudden appearance. "I guess you could say that, but I assure you that you get used to it after a while."

"What are you doing here, Tyrimus?" the first member asked.

"I came here to visit my nephew," Tyrimus said nervously. "It had been far too long since I had seen his face. I barely recognized it for all the wrinkles." He chuckled.

"I think you mean to do more by being here," the second said.

"Why else would I be here?"

"We've been over this before," the first said again.

"I don't see how we can overlook this," Tyrimus said, taking a step back. "It's wrong, what you intend to do … ignoring Temelephas."

"We never should have named it," the second said. "We should have known it was only a matter of time before someone thought of it as something more than a tool. A pet or an equal—and not a thing."

"But it isn't a tool," Tyrimus said. "It's more than … *He's* more than that, now. Besides, this has nothing to do with Temelephas." He eyed the Council members cautiously, like a man surrounded by snakes. "I know what you're really up to, and I won't stand idly by."

"It is no longer your concern," said the first member. Tyrimus could only look at them, gazing at them one by one in confusion.

"We've stripped you of your title and powers," said a fourth.

"You can do no such thing," Tyrimus said, the anger climbing in his throat.

"It is our right and privilege," the first said. "You no longer agree with the Council."

"You mean, I refuse to follow blindly ... like an old dog."

"I see no difference between the two," the second responded.

"All of your deeds will catch up to you," Tyrimus swore, his fists clenched and shaking as the remaining members of the High Council circled around him. "Nothing you do can change that. The secret you wish to bury will surface in its own time. The truth has a way of coming out."

"Are you finished preaching, Tyrimus?" the first asked.

"Obviously," Tyrimus quietly said, feeling an odd sorrow fill him. "Obviously, I'm finished doing a lot of things."

"Quite right," the second said. Then the five remaining members of the High Council looked upward and Tyrimus followed their gaze. He gave out a cry as the inky form of the Gloom came down upon him, choking him in their smoky fog.

There wasn't much of a struggle, how could there have been with Tyrimus' powers taken from him. The gloom growled softly as they fed on the energy drawn from its victim. It wasn't long before Tyrimus' cries fell to silence and his lifeless form lie still.

"Go easy, Tyrimus, into your Great Sleep," the second Councilman said.

The dark cloud crawled away from the corpse and

rose up before the remaining members of the High Council. It was timid to them, bowing low before them; its voice pleading with them in a low, humble tone. It begged for more to feed upon … for the revenge it had been waiting for … it always wanted more.

"In due time," the first pacified it, "You will have your revenge and more than enough to feed upon. Then you will have this space of the Universe as your own, once more."

"Till then," the second said. "It wouldn't hurt for you to feed on Minikins."

"But not all of them," the third said. "We still need them, for the time being."

The Gloom slunk back, its billowing form slithering away and into a crack in the wall. It slithered further on—a dark, silent hunter—off to prey upon the Minikins like an ethereal viper.

The High Council remained there, silently looking upon the dried husk that was once Tyrimus. They had never seen anything like it before. Perhaps they even feared what they may have unleashed, seeing what it could do to their own kind. But, what was done was done.

The Gloom was already getting stronger, but they needed it to be. They could only hope that it would stick to its end of the bargain. If it went against them, they could always lock it away.

There was so much to prepare for and the High Council went to do just that. The Universe soon would be changed forever and then there would be no turning back. Far off in the darkness came the chilling cries of Minikins— one by one—as they fell to their unseen attacker.

"I was told my brother was brought here," Camilla huffed, having just run in from the parking lot. The woman who sat behind the protective glass looked blankly at her, chewing her gum as a cow would grass. She moved her heavy hand slowly, pushing a black button on an ancient, tan box.

The speaker cracked and hissed in Camilla's face before it settled into the gentle hum of dead air. The receptionist huffed impatiently, then spoke. "... Name?"

"Camilla Forrest."

The receptionist looked disdainfully at her, the lids of her eyes blinking slowly. The button was pushed again. *CRACK, BUZZ* ... "I meant your brother."

"Oh, Nicholas Forrest." Camilla was flushed both from exertion and embarrassment.

The woman quickly assaulted the keyboard of her computer as if taking out frustrations that had piled up over the years. She lazily eyed the green text on the screen, reading as slow as she probably could. *CRACK, POP, FIZZ* ... "Yeah ... we got him."

Wanda—as her nameplate sitting on the desk identified her—had become lethargic. When she first began this job she embraced it with vigor and compassion. Now— twelve years down the line—those emotions had mutated into indifference and bigotry. Camilla just thought of her as a bitch.

"Well, can I get him back?"

BUZZ, CRACKLE, POP ... "Of course you can."

"When?" Camilla asked, her voice saturated with aggravation.

POP, FIZZLE ... "in about seventy-two hours," *POP, FIZZLE-CRACK*. Camilla tried to focus her mind, trying not to succumb to the woman's blasé attitude or sink to her peevish manner. Then the better part of her—the more animal part—slammed its fist on the counter.

"Let me see my brother!" she demanded.

POP, CRACK, FIZZLE ... "Oh, you'll be seeing him *real* soon if you don't calm down!"

"But, he's not crazy!"

CRACKLE-CRACKLE, BUZZ ... "According to Franklin County ... the Columbus Police Department ... and thirteen very disturbing police reports ... he is," she spat through the speaker. "... for the next seventy-two hours!" *ZZZZ, POP-POP.* Wanda smiled smugly.

Only two words came to Camilla's fragile, rattled mind. Two words as tall as skyscrapers and lit in brilliant lights as if in celebration.

Oh, Crap.

Joyce drove in a frantic manner that bordered on road-rage, tearing through the snow laden streets. The tires swooshed and bobbled over the ice and salt, spinning madly like wheeled mice. It was a horrible site to see. People that strolled the sidewalks were forced to run for cover. Other cars turned down side streets in hopes that she wouldn't follow.

The ride was equally—if not more so—frightening for the car's occupants. Lily prayed silently from the passenger seat as she watched Joyce whip the steering wheel back and forth as if playing the villain in a film noire. She could feel the contents of her stomach swishing back and forth.

Lily looked over her shoulder and saw that Tyriano's face had grown blue—or a more bluer shade of purple—with hollow cheeks and drool slowly dripping from his gaping mouth. He looked like a sick dog as he steadied himself against Joyce's headrest. Lily found a bit of comfort in knowing that if he *did* get sick, Joyce's shoulder would bare most of the burden of it.

Tibil didn't fare as well, sadly. He was being tossed to and fro in the backseat, tumbling around like a loose stuffed animal. Lily found it ironic considering the coat he wore. He screamed in a shrill cry with each toss.

"Must you drive so fast?" Tyriano cried loudly, barely breaching the crescendo of car noises as if it were slowly falling apart.

"Slow down, Joyce!" Lily cried.

"Not until I get my baby!" she screamed over the wailing tires as the car skittered around a corner. Lily didn't try again, knowing there would be no different outcome. She prayed, instead, to survive the ride.

The Gloom was already

getting stronger,

but they needed it to be.

17

It turned out to be a rather productive trip to the nuthouse for Edward. In a pleasant turn of events, he found himself rooming with, well ... *himself.* He sat on a squeaky bed that seemed to have been bought secondhand from an old summer camp for wayward youths. Edward barely noticed the tiny squeaks as he sat there, watching himself.

It was *his* body—filled with Nicholas' mind and soul—that stood by the window, gazing peacefully out. He watched as the snow fell and gathered on the once green field just outside his window, tiny blades of grass protruding through as remnants of warmer days gone. They had been that way for quite some time—silent, neither sure how best proceed.

For Edward it meant verification of his sanity. He could breathe easier now knowing he was just as sane as the next man. For Nicholas it was an opportunity to make things right, or in the least, make an attempt.

"When did you figure it out?" Edward finally asked. He had let it fester in his mind enough, deep in the back where it grew like a football dog pile on a Sunday afternoon.

"I knew the whole time," Nicholas said with quiet confidence, his eyes still taking in the wintry scene.

"The whole time?" Edward felt betrayed, he felt the

anger from it building inside him like a furnace. His face became rigid then, his jaw jutting out. He could feel his fists clenching into tight balls beside him.

"Yeah, sorry," Nicholas said with little remorse as he turned to face him with a humbled smile. "I wasn't thinking too much about you, honestly. I only thought of it as a new beginning, a fresh start with a beautiful woman that loved me."

"But she never loved you," Edward said aloud. "It was me she loved."

"Still," Nicholas said in a hushed voice. "It was nice … if even for a while." Nicholas dropped his eyes to the floor, trying to hide possible tears or maybe just shame. "You have a wonderful life, Eddie."

Edward felt guilty then—oddly—about his own good fortunes, whatever they may be. He was so furious in that moment. But then that anger sizzled out and he was left with a sense of pity for the man that stood before him.

Edward looked sadly at him as Nicholas walked to his own bed, stretching out across it with his hands tucked behind his head. "But I always remembered that … that it was your life … never mine; her love belonged to you." Nicholas gave a soft chuckle, as if laughing at his own misfortune. "It would always be yours … and I, nothing more than a thief."

It was quiet then, both of them left with their thoughts. Nicholas' admission hung in the space between them, taking on a life of its own. It breathed in the same air as them.

"*Your* face she smiled at," Nicholas continued. "*Your* name she whispered … just *you*. Besides … she had her suspicions."

"Is that how you ended up here?"

Nicholas smiled with Edward's smile as he rolled to his side, chuckling lightly. "No … she called the monkey wagon right after I told her the truth." It was Edward's turn to laugh; it was all so crazy. "It was time, though. I didn't know where you were, but I knew that wherever you were you didn't belong there anymore than I belonged here."

"Well, as you can guess, I've been with your sister," Edward said. Nicholas' face sagged as he thought about his sister, guiltily realizing for the first time that he had abandoned here. "You know … she's probably out there right now, raising hell to get me out."

"Does she know?"

"Yeah," Edward said. "She knows all about us getting Freaky Friday-ed. She's anxious to get you back where *you* belong."

Belong … the word hung in Nicholas' mind like a solitary bat in a cave steeped in darkness. It was a word that had followed him around his whole life, a part of a larger question he fought to answer.

He never felt he belonged anywhere. Always on the outside looking in … that was how he was. He felt more like a cosmic misfit or a celestial vagabond, dispersed and bouncing throughout the universe.

Nicholas had dreamed of belonging just the night before as he slept atop his mother's grave. But now, he couldn't remember any of it, except for the sound of her voice as she sang to him. It felt important to him, this dream; but no matter how hard he tried, it evaded him. He didn't even belong in his own dreams.

Edward could tell Nicholas was deep in thought, so he decided to leave him to it. So he went about devising a plan, or at least the framing of one. He knew it would be hard, anything worth doing is.

First, he would have to get back into his own body, which was far too absurd to even fathom. Then he would have to find Lily and try to convince her that all was well again. Even that seemed like a farfetched idea. *'I was crazy before, but I'm all better now, tee-hee!'* he imagined saying, then groaned aloud at his own absurdity.

Switching bodies … convincing Lily; they both seemed like hard roads he would have to endure. The only remaining question was which would be harder.

🐘

Camilla continued to sit quietly in the pale green Hell that was the waiting room. She had been there for over an hour and had vowed to keep her cool. She just passed the time, reading back issues of *Highlights* over and over again. She had found all the hidden items and read all the comics. All the children's jokes were laughed at, forgotten for a moment and laughed at again.

Every so often she would glance up at Wanda; the vile woman not only kept her from Edward, but did so purely for her own amusement. She wondered why she hadn't moved on to the BMV yet, or any of the other jobs that required a comfortable acquaintance with sadism. Wanda—in turn—would shoot her a mock smile with a little wave.

Camilla did her best to smile back, grinding her teeth—invisible steam flowing from her ears. In her mind she imagined things she never thought she would, wished things upon Wanda that hours before she never would have thought possible. She envisioned slamming Wanda's wide face into the glass of her gorilla cage, then planting her head deep into the computer monitor—sparks flying out in triumph.

No, she thought, *don't go down that road. Don't let her get the best of you.* She closed her eyes and breathed in—deep, cool gulps of air. She would never call herself a 'full' Christian, one reason being that she believed in Karma. She knew that one day Wanda would meet her Maker. Camilla only hoped he would see fit to smash her face against the glass of her cubicle.

She finally laid the magazines aside, determining

it was best to meditate. She began to breathe in and out, clearing her mind of all negative thoughts. Camilla kept at it until not a single thought remained in her mind … not even a glimmer of that hideous woman that continuously taunted her from behind her protective glass. *Stupid Wanda!*

In and out she breathed, pulling her mind into focus, imagining herself as nothing more than a vessel through which power flows. And in her mind she felt it … a stirring. It was as if something was moving towards her, something powerful and strange to this realm.

She had read enough books to know that it could only be a witch, or a ghost, or a dimensional creature, or a demon, or a many number of other things. She felt foolish realizing that she couldn't be certain as to what it was. *Damn those books!* All she knew for sure was that whatever it was, it was coming towards her and it was coming fast.

In a dark alcove of the core—in the deepest of chasms—lurked the Gloom. It basked in the darkness, resting after feeding on so many Minikins. It could feel itself growing stronger.

Soon … it told itself. It called for its tendrils and they all came, tiny wisps of blackness from all over the Universe. They came, slinking through the black of space—creeping out from far off shadows.

Most thought of the Gloom as if it were many. *But they would be wrong*, it whispered to itself with a mirthful laugh. *The darkness is whole, as is the Gloom … we were only spread too thinly.* Now—however—it reeled itself in.

It had to be lured back, like a wandering mind back to the task at hand. It took time … it took promises. Promises of plenty to feed on, promises of a safe dark place to lay—promises of revenge. Like a trickle of black ink, it seeped into its abyss, pooling in the cool dark; rejoining itself.

It grew stronger as they came—all the splintered bits of it. It hadn't felt this strong in many eons. Once it was the most powerful being ... until He came. *The Maker,* it seethed, enraging each growing ounce of it. But, the Maker was gone now, the High Council said it was so.

He wouldn't be there this time, unable to push it back—splintering it into tiny, useless fractions. It had been weakened so greatly then, but now there was no stopping it. It would feed, it would devour ... but, it wouldn't stop with this small part of creation. Its revenge would be complete; its home all its own again.

The Gloom's dark laughter boiled over as it dreamed its ebony dreams. *Not long,* it swore to its tendrils, calling them back from far off corners of existence. *Come ... take part.* And they came—like good drones, home to the hive queen.

Joyce's car came to a screeching halt, one that should have shot the tires off the frame. People that saw the car skittering towards them as they walked in front of Harding Hospital immediately fled. They darted away, screaming unintelligibly to no one in particular. The engine cut off, but it would have been understandable if it simply fell out after such a trip.

One rear door swung open, spilling Tibil from his seat—bunny ears and all. He fell into the slush along the curb, turning his once white bunny coat the same dingy gray as the wintry sky. Tyriano poked his head out, checking on his tiny friend.

Lily heaved as she hopped out of the passenger seat. She stumbled a bit; one leg snagging on the seat belt, the other still wobbly after the ride. She felt all of the food in her stomach trying to break out, but instead spewed curses at Joyce. In response, Joyce merely shrugged it off.

A heavyset security guard—as alarmed by the car as anyone else—came waddling over, armed only with a flashlight and a smirk. It was days like this that he pined for, filled with excitement and danger, a day he rarely saw. He tugged at his belt as he approached, his mind trying to come up with the perfect line.

"What in Sam Hell's going on 'round here!" was all he could muster. The two ladies he confronted seemed to be nervous, which meant it worked decently. They mumbled and blurted out nonsense as if waiting to be saved. The guard took that moment to dream up another line, in case he should need it.

Tyriano stepped out from the car, stretching his long back and legs as he went. He did his best to shake the experience of the ride out of his mind as he watched the calamity unfold. There seemed to be no end in sight, so Tyriano did the only thing he could think of.

"Sorry," he muttered to the guard as he walked up to him. The guard turned in time to see Tyriano's hand; it's bluish, glowing palm reaching out to him. He saw nothing after, save for the flash that sent him flying backwards. The girls screamed loudly, curses flying more freely about than if it were a seedy bar.

"He will be fine," Tyriano assured them. "He may have a headache upon waking, but even that will pass." Tyriano did the only kind thing that remained—given the circumstance—dragging him from the sidewalk and in to the snow, in effort to prevent him from being trampled. "We must continue on."

Tyriano lead them in to the hospital. They followed signs that were conveniently posted, moving quickly through the hospital, but not so fast as to draw attention. The hallways all looked the same—one after another—all green, with furniture from the seventies, and tables piled high with magazines.

People were all around, but none took too much notice of them. They all figured you would see that kind of weird behavior in a place like this. The troupe then turned down another hall and Tyriano pointed out, "This is it!"

🐘

The door burst inward, which is considered poor conduct by the staff of a psychiatric hospital. Camilla was shook from her meditative state and gave off a regretted 'yip'. Everyone shot up in their seats, their heads shifting to see the source of the commotion.

A strange man stood there, his skin paler and more purple in hue than one would expect. With him were two women, both of which looked disturbed, and a small child in a bunny suit with a sour look on his face. Fear ran through Camilla like an icicle, but she couldn't shake the feeling that they were what she sensed coming.

She would have asked them what they wanted, but they were too quick to move through the room. The man pushed his way through, sending people flopping to the floor, giving off varied cries. He headed straight towards the Witch's glass box, waving his hands around like a stage magician.

"You must let us by!" he screamed tumultuously at the troll. His hands waved before him, the fingers twitching as if by magic or psychotic energy.

"You must be out your fucking mind!" Wanda screamed, her face beyond any description of bewilderment. She seemed so cool in the moment, so prepared for anything. Only later would she admit to the police, that this was the "craziest shit she'd ever seen".

The man seemed to wait for clarification, as if he hadn't heard her at all. One of the women with him then told him that she meant 'no'. The man shrugged then, seemingly disappointed. "Oh, well," he said as he placed his hands on the glass.

Wanda's window exploded in a shower of flying shards, bits of glass soared through air that rippled in crackling, blue light. Wanda emitted a train of obscenities. Her eyes were wide and her hands trembled, even as she reached for the phone. She never made it; her hand was intercepted by those strange blue hands, and she shot back with an electric crackling.

Wanda's unconscious body slumped against the wall of her cubicle, silenced by the will of another for the first time in her life. By then, most of those who had been in the waiting room had already dashed out, running for safety. Only Camilla remained, watching intently with a smile on her face. *Karma.*

The little child looked back at her and she realized then that he wasn't a child at all. His face was far too old for anyone to call youthful. She had no way of knowing how much aging that face had done the last few days. "Who are you people?" she asked as she stood there.

No answer came to her, they merely started down a hallway that lay behind the protected door. She didn't think they would mind if she followed them, they didn't seem to be too secretive. So off Camilla went, trailing behind the small group that had silenced the beast known as Wanda.

A few rooms down the hall, however, a second receptionist was busy calling the police. She wasn't quite sure what was going on, but a lot of people had dashed into her waiting area, screaming about blue lights and exploding glass.

The Gloom's dark
laughter boiled over as
it dreamed its ebony dreams.
Not long, it swore to its tendrils,
calling them back from
far of corners of existence.
Come ... take part.
And they came—like
good drones, home to
the hive queen.

18

Noise came tumbling down the hallway. At first it seemed far off, something that they could easily overlook. But as it grew so did their anxious curiosity. Edward and Nicholas had their ears pressed to the door, trying to make out what was happening.

All they heard were cautionary commands and loud pops, followed by noisy crashes. After each crash came a curt yet sincere apology. The ruckus grew louder and closer, and the two of them began a slow retreat from the door.

Step by step they gave ground until they both stood with their backs pressed safely against the window. They could hear voices calling out through the madness, although none seemed familiar through the din. But the words were clear.

Voices were calling out for Edward, a name that while not truly his own, drew Nicholas close to the door once more. He pressed his ear hard against the door, trying to pick the voices out, focusing on them. One of the voices was Lily.

"I'm here," Nicholas cried through the door, both fists banging on the thick door. Edward protested behind him, begging that Nicholas stop calling the trouble to them.

"I'm here," he cried louder, his fists banging as hard as he could.

The noise came right to the door, voices excitedly calling out. One voice, which belonged to a man, cried for them to stand back from the door. There was the smell of electricity in the air as Nicholas did as he was told.

There was a loud crack as the door blew in, shredded by an unseen force, splinters showering them both. A man in black stood quietly there in his purple shades, both of his hands still humming as they softly glowed. Lily stood behind him, next to an odd child in a bunny suit.

"You really *aren't* Edward," she said reproachfully. She was whimpering, a bit of her injured soul bleeding through. Nicholas did his best to smile. He shook his head. "No, but he is." Nicholas looked back at Edward, who seemed a bit flustered.

Edward crept up behind Nicholas, "Lily?" he asked, his voice weak. He peeked around Nicholas' shoulder, trying to catch a glimpse of the woman who had haunted his memories.

Lily stepped through the door way, stepping beyond Tyriano and slowly towards the old man. His face was loose and hung in wrinkles. His hair was gray—for the most part—and thin in places, any sign of youth gone. The older man looked away, as if in shame.

She reached out with an unsure hand, catching his chin as it dipped away, pulling it towards her. His eyes didn't seem to fit. They were softer, unlike the face that held them. They were wet, ready to sprout tears that would bathe the rough skin.

Could it be true, she asked herself. *Is this really possible, or am I just losing my mind?*

Those green eyes, Edward thought, *they are impossibly bright*. It would be hard to mistake them. He had seen those eyes far too many times to be wrong, they were Lily's. He wanted to pull away from her hand, finding it hard to look at her with this face.

All he knew was her name. And now he knew her touch, the gentleness she showed him; proof that they were lovers—once upon a time. But it was his real body that she knew, not this old one he wore. He tried to remember her—more than her name or what she ate for lunch—but nothing came to him.

She was looking at him, almost as if peering through him. The gaze she had was so intense, so convinced.

"Is it you?" she asked softly, her sweet breath against his face.

"I wish I could be sure," he answered. Her face drooped, her eyes shaded by her sadness. Edward thought they seemed sadder than any two eyes should ever have to be.

"Don't you know me?" she asked weakly, slight tears ripping pathways down her freckled cheeks.

"You're Lily," he said, his voice hushed as if it brought gain pain to even say the word.

"So you do know me?" her voice cracked. "You recognize me?"

"Always," he said, looking over her eyes and freckles. She wept harder then, her eyes almost as red as they were green. "Your face … it haunts me."

"Edward gave me a gift," she said with a sniffle. "It was just before the storm. He said it was something I should always remember … what I should never forget."

She looked hard at him, searching. "Do you know what it was?"

Edward closed his eyes; his lids dropping, decapitating his tears. He peered into his mind, trying to call forth any memories. *What should Lily remember,* he asked himself. *What should she never forget?* There was nothing there but cold blackness.

He pleaded with his subconscious, *let this one thing loose … please … just this one thing.* In the dark came a faint shimmer, far off lights dancing in his mind. He focused on those lights till they became more solid. He recognized that they were words, but only faint words that seemed fuzzy. It was like reading a street sign through a blustery storm.

He focused all of his mind on those words, drew them nearer to him in his mind. Then the words caught fire in his memories, blazing hot from a silvery sea. He mumbled them, but it didn't seem right, his words dying in the still room.

"What was that?" Lily asked, choking back her sobs.

"You are loved," he said slowly. "You should never forget it."

Lily smiled broadly, her eyes squinting, popping out tears. She laughed lightly before pulling his mouth to hers. Her tongue parted his lips and it all came back to him, then. The mornings, the kisses, the shampoo that smelled like a strawberry patch … the orange juice she never got. It was as if a bus came out of nowhere and ran him down with his own memories.

Lily pulled back from their kiss and found that Edward's eyes were still clamped shut. He smiled when he opened them and somehow he seemed more familiar to her. "I knew it was you," she laughed, cradling his wrinkly face.

"How could you?" he asked, "I didn't even know it was me until that kiss." Lily laughed, pushing her wet face against his. She sighed deeply, he wept softly. She shushed him quietly—comforting him as the others watched unobtrusively.

"I'm sorry for all of this," he said suddenly, hushed. "I'm sorry for this face."

"The face doesn't bother me," she said in a frantic tone. "I don't care about the face. As long as it's you behind it," she said with a smile. "That's all that matters." They clung to one another then, like binary stars, the empty mass between them pulling them together as they burn with their love.

Tyriano coughed, clearing his throat. "I'm sorry to cut this reunion short, but we must get going." Edward looked at them for what might as well have been the first time.

"Who's this guy?"

"I'll explain later," Lily said.

"And, why's Joyce here?"

"I said later," she laughed.

Edward, saw Camilla then, standing shyly behind them all. "Camilla?" he called to her, but she looked pass him, to the younger face behind him. She gave off a loud laugh, seeing a familiar expression on a stranger's face.

"Eddie, you are a lot better looking than I would have guessed," she said.

"Hey, sis," was all Nick could get out before being ensnared by her thick arms. She smothered him with all the love she had.

"We really must be going," Tyriano reiterated. Joyce jabbed the old watcher in his side, calling his attention.

"Does this mean we have both the guys we need?" Joyce asked hopefully.

"It would appear so," is all he said, rubbing his sore ribs. The wailing sound of sirens erupted in the distance. "Now we must truly be going!"

All he knew was her name.

And now he knew her touch,

the gentleness she showed

him; proof that they were

lovers—once upon a time.

19

The cold air hit them like a wall when they fell through the door. They were standing in a small—and apparently rarely used—parking lot, far from where they had started. Going back to the main entrance was useless, police were undoubtedly swarming it. Joyce's car was pretty well shot, anyhow.

Edward huffed and puffed, the old body he was in was spent from the running. Lily gently rubbed his back. "I think I'm going to be sick," he said between breathes.

Tyriano eyed the snowy street and found it empty, not a single sign of life. It was as if it was early on Christmas morning and all the children were still fast asleep, dreaming of the presents they would soon open. There wasn't even a parked car for them to hide behind. Even the cars were nestled safely in their warm garages.

"We may have come as far as we can," Tyriano said solemnly as he looked back at the hospital, bathed in red and blue light. No one raised an argument against him, their hope drained away by the empty street.

It was then that a rusty, blue minivan tore around an icy corner a couple of blocks away. It carelessly barreled down the road, thick black smoke billowing from its exhaust. They collectively sighed at the sight of it. Edward was more excited about sitting down than anything else.

Tyriano stepped out into the street, paying no regard to the speeding ton of steel bearing down on him. The van kept coming, showing no change in its velocity. He stood in its path and held his palm up to it, and commanded loudly for it to stop. Everyone looked away, unable to watch what was guaranteed to be a bloody demise.

There was a horrible screech—as if the road was being tore up—and the horrible, hot, skunky smell or tires in the air. When they looked again, they saw Tyriano as he stood—unharmed yet shaken—before the halted vehicle. "Hurry," he cried to them.

They all ran towards the minivan as Tyriano meandered up to the driver side door. The driver was a young girl, so young that she seemed too young to be driving at all. "My dear," Tyriano said calmly. "We need to borrow your vehicle."

She whimpered and moaned, her teeth tripping up the words in her mouth. She was frazzled by the near accident—so discombobulated that it seemed it would take her an eternity to understand. All she could mutter was a questioning, "mwaaah?"

"Get out!" Joyce screamed from the backseat of the minivan, which she had already slid into. The girl jumped at the sound of the command, quickly unbuckling herself and hopping out. She backed away slowly as the rest piled in. It would have been an utterly horrifying incident if it hadn't have been for the little fellow in the bunny suit.

It wasn't enough to make her smile, though. The sliding door of the van closed loudly as the tires spun on the ice. She sat—defeated—on the cold, wet sidewalk. It wasn't but a few days ago that she had wrecked her own car in that storm. Now she was to blame for the family minivan being stolen.

The van quickly disappeared around the nearest corner, its fragile transmission hiccupping in to a higher gear, black smoke spilling out from behind it. It wasn't long before the sound of its tortured engine was out of earshot, leaving her only with the quiet rhythm of her weeping.

Temelephas had noticed the absence of Tyrimus; not having the old Watcher around had laid a heavy burden on his heart. *Where is he,* he wondered, *and what could be keeping him away?* He had grown accustomed to being watched; the absence of eyes upon him felt eerie to him. Even the tiny Minikins were gone, perhaps called away on some task.

Even with the small baby sleeping on his back, Temelephas couldn't shake the presence of loneliness that now hung over him like a lone, black cloud. All he had was the heavy, deep notes of his own footsteps and the vibration in his chest from his beating heart. His eyes sagged greater than ever, their lids heavy with worry.

All he could do now was wait, but for what, he couldn't know. Until then he would just continue in his walk; because, even though he hated it, he had this *urge* to continue on. In his heart he felt it was his duty to go on, pulling his heavy wheel with him.

"Welcome back, Columbus," a woman said from the studio of a news station. She was in her late twenties and had honey-hair, molded and perfect. She was well made-up, smiling with blood red lips.

"Be sure to stick around, at the bottom of the hour Chef Francis will be here and attempt to teach me how to make my favorite Spanish dish, paella!" she said with a giggle. "It's bound to get messy. But for now, we welcome— via satellite—Dr. Joseph Reisinger of MIT, a professor of geology. Welcome, Doctor."

The screen split and was shared then by a pale, skeletal man with dark hair; his eyes staring wildly into the camera. He kept licking his lips—perhaps from nervousness—as he sat there in an ill-fitting blue suit. "Thank you, Denise ... it's a pleasure to be here."

"Now, Dr. Reisinger ... I've been told that you have a theory on the global storm that occurred earlier this week."

"That is both correct and incorrect, Denise," he said with a hesitant chuckle. "I do have a theory, but it has nothing to do with a supposed global storm."

"Please explain."

"It would be nearly impossible for a single storm to cover all of Earth, Denise. Even the tumultuous surface of Jupiter is plagued by not one, but many storms."

"Then what happened the other day?" she asked, trying her best to appear interested. She tried to convey it on her face—engrossment—but couldn't pull it off. Instead, she had the face of someone who took a sip of sour milk, and though not finding the taste pleasant, continued to drink it.

"I offer up that perhaps the Earth stopped spinning, but for only a moment. If the Earth *were* to stop, the atmosphere that surrounds our planet would continue on its original path, at its normal speed of over sixteen-hundred miles per hour."

"That is some *fast wind*," Denise chimed in.

"Yes it is, Denise," Dr. Reisinger seemed more nervous than ever, his face had gone a bit green as if he might get sick right then.

"So, could this *event* happen again?"

"It is more than likely that it will. I have some friends, Denise, superstitious friends that believe it's the first sign of the apocalypse . . ."

There was silence on Denise's end as she nodded, staring blankly into the camera as she listened to someone off camera. "I'm sorry, Dr., but we have some breaking news and we'll have to cut away."

The screen returned to normal and focused on Denise. "This just in, there appears to be a police chase at this very moment—right here in Columbus. It apparently began on the North Side and is quickly heading southbound.

"If you had any plans to go out, we recommend that you steer clear of High street. We have no further details for you, but we are working on getting them. From what I've been told, it appears that a soccer mom is suffering from a severe case of road rage," she said with her bloody smile.

🐘

Lily—as it turned out—was no better a driver than Joyce, at least when it boiled down to caution. She used the van with its shaky frame to slice through the rush hour traffic. The tires shimmied and squeaked as she switched lanes—accelerated, and braked, seemingly at random.

The sound of sirens followed them, but the red and blue lights were far behind; like flashing dance club lights. The van was filled with screams of terror, some shouting out commands and directions, others as a way to bleed off the fear that grew in them.

"Lily?" Edward called from the backseat.

"I'm driving Eddie," she said, dismissively. She whipped the wheel to the left to get around a dump truck right in front of them, swerving back in front of a car whose driver exploded with creative profanity.

"But do you have to go so fast?" he begged, his face becoming green from the motion.

"It's a police chase, babe … and we're on the wrong end of it."

"RED LIGHT, RED LIGHT!" Joyce cried from her seat. Lily slammed her foot on the gas and wove the van through the intersection, narrowly missing a pair of cars that stopped suddenly.

There was a patch of open road in front of them and Lily kept her foot planted. Camilla was looking back, watching as the police lights fell further behind in the dimming light of twilight. "We're losing them!"

"Better make some more room between us," Lily said, excitedly weaving between cars.

"Maybe we should get off High street ... use the side roads?" Edward asked, hoping she would agree with him. But there was a glare in Lily's eye—a far off look of adventure.

"Nah," she said with a tremble. On the outside, she seemed terrified; but inside Lily screamed for joy. Flooded with exhilaration, her blood pumped with dopamine. She felt guilty for how she scolded Joyce for her driving, only now knowing how thrilling it could be.

Eat your heart out, Vin Diesel, she thought to herself. "Hold on to your lunch!" she yelped as she tried her best to push the gas pedal through the floorboard.

Dezriak loomed over Temelephas' cavern—hidden in shadow—watching as he continued his march. The High Council had left him burdened with his task. He had always wanted to *change* the world, how it spun and operated—wanting to streamline it. But, now they asked for him to simply end it all.

It would happen, regardless, he mused. With or without him, the High Council would put a fork in this world. At least by going with them he would stay gainfully employed, rather than *dead*. He just couldn't wait to see the look on Tyriano's face when he unleashed the Gloom upon him and his outdated pet.

There was something in him ... a kind of yearning to see the old Watcher crumble, turned into nothing more than a dried out husk. He hungered for it, more than he dare say aloud. He craved it. *Strange*, he thought ... not expecting to feel so at home with his own villainy, his newfound appetite for death and destruction.

The peace of oblivion ... the idea of it filled his mind ... sweet, sweet freedom from all the Maker held dear—and that too was odd. Why should those thoughts enter his mind? *No matter*, he thought, it would be over shortly. He only prayed Tyriano would be here to see it ... the undoing of this world.

Yessss, the Gloom hissed, out from its dark portal. *We hear your prayers ... we long for it too.* They had tapped into Dezriak, feeding off of his anxiety, feeding its own wishes into him, manipulating him and his own thoughts. It was so powerful now, nearly strong enough. *So strong*, it relished.

He was theirs to control, now—like a puppet, he would dance for them. He would continue to *think* he was in control, oh yes, they wouldn't let that slip. *He must call us down*, it spoke to itself. *We will rain down upon that gray beast ... fill the cavern like a black sea. We will devour all we set eyes upon.*

It grew ever bigger, stronger as the seconds strolled by. Soon it would be too strong even for the council to stop. *Home*, it seethed, *we will be home in our dark universe once more.* It became gleeful thinking of it ... *sweet, sweet freedom.*

There was something in him ...
a kind of yearning to see
the old Watcher crumble,
turned into nothing more than
a dried out husk. He hungered
for it, more than he dare
say aloud. He craved it.
Strange, he thought ... not
expecting to feel so at home
with his own villainy, his
newfound appetite for
death and destruction.

20

The tires nearly jumped from the van as it slid across an especially icy patch of road, skipping like a rock into a parking lot. The engine bellowed and boomed from under the hood, competing with the angry shouts of its occupants. Library Park was nearly vacant, those few that walked beside the park were quick to run away.

The sliding door of the van fell open and its riders tumbled out onto the cold lot, heaving with relief. One after the other, they stumbled out, seemingly afraid the van would lurch at them like some starving monster. Tyriano stood on tall, shaky legs and thanked the Maker that he would never have to ride in another of those *infernal contraptions*.

Lily smiled broadly as she exited the driver's seat. Camilla was shouting at her, but the words were lost in the sea of exhilaration that Lily exuded. She just continued to smile as Camilla got redder and redder, ready to snap like a hidden viper.

"We have no time for bickering," Tyriano called out in his booming voice. "We must hurry!"

For all their complaints, Lily's reckless driving had been quite good for them. At one point in the nightmarish road trip she had—what 80's television criminals would call—*shaken the fuzz*. It happened suddenly after she had run what would have been her fourth red light. It would forever be a highlight in Lily's life.

Tyriano was off, hoofing it through the snow to the entrance of the park and the others followed as best they could. They found the park void of life—except of course for the dumb birds that thought it was best to stay put for the winter and the gray squirrels that heckled them. All else was still in the park and the noise from the city streets seemed to be muted by the park's tall hedges and trees.

All they could clearly hear were the sounds of their own breathing and the crunch of snow beneath their feet. Night was setting in and the field of snow about them caught the moon's mystical glow, illuminating the landscape around them.

They looked upon the scene—the lonely, frozen arboreal figures that gazed for an eternity onto a frozen pond. The clean beauty of fresh, fallen snow in an untouched park struck each one of them as they walked. "This is amazing," Edward said. "I can't believe I've never been here before."

"I've never even heard of it," Lily said, running her hand down a snow covered hedge that was shaped like a dog. The branches snapped back to place, tossing snow into her face. She laughed, wiping the flakes from her jacket.

"I've lived my whole life in Columbus and never once came here," Camilla said, flexing the small of her back with her balled up hands.

"You humans do a lot of that," Tyriano said, "overlooking things and underestimating the things you *do* see."

"It's easy to do, though," Joyce said with her aggravated tone. "People lead such hectic lives nowadays."

"You people have always led hectic lives," Tyriano shot back. "Since the dawning of your kind, you've been busy: hunting, gathering, building, migrating, and spreading to the end of this world and outward. You've *always* been so busy," his voice got softer as he went, the excitement leaving his voice until it was nothing more than a whisper. "Warring and destroying.

"Some would even argue that the technology you now wield frees up more time so you can sit back and enjoy your lives, but all you do is keep pushing, on and on through eternity ... such busybodies." The others were silent as lectured schoolchildren.

"You know what the worst part of humanity is?" Tyriano asked, though found no answers. "Your inability to simply except things as they are. You always have to know 'how' and 'why', it's a curse. There's no magic left in the world for mankind.

"Why is the sky blue? ... What causes a rainbow? ... Nothing's ever a miracle for your kind. I've seen your science and history books, I've seen how you took this world apart in search of *unnecessary* truths!"

The wind kicked northward, carrying Tyriano's loud words off to the world as he knelt down. He pulled the glove from his hand and cautiously ran a slim finger across the untouched snow. He chuckled, pulling his hand back, "Feels colder than I thought it would," he said, scooping some into his hand.

He stood, holding his hand out for them to examine its fluffy contents, hoping they would show any sign of joy. The crystallized water in his hand glittered like tiny diamonds catching the moonlight. "It's such a shame that you are *so* quick to tell your children that *this* isn't magic. This ... fragile, frozen fluff from the sky."

The snowflakes began to fall apart—like a sandcastle caught at high tide—melting in his warm hand. Tyriano watched it as it ebbed—slowly turning into a cool, little pool in his palm. "Such a shame," he said to the silence.

Tyriano pulled his glove back on and walked; they followed him—tip-toeing through the snow. They meandered through the topiary art and walked behind a large tree. There on the ground before them lie a slab of concrete with a metal lid in the middle of it. Tyriano knelt down and began to brush the windblown snow away from it.

"We're going down a manhole?" Joyce asked with a laugh. They stood around the large metal portal, it's once shiny color now aged with rust.

"And why not?" Tyriano asked.

"Well, after that whole lecture about magic around us, I expected to find a glimmering portal in the side of a tree or something."

"Well, as plain as it is, it's our only way to the center," Tyriano said with a smirk as he tugged on one of the lid's rungs. It barely budged, so Nicholas began to tug on the other end. It wasn't long until the warm air of the underground came up to meet them with all its horrendous smells.

"Ladies first," Tyriano offered, smiling at Joyce. Joyce recognized a challenge better than most and wasn't one to back away from any. So she positioned her feet on the ladder and started down, trying to hide the look of disgust on her face.

She went down slowly, the sound of her clanging shoes echoing down the pit. One by one, the others followed. Nicholas came down last, pulling the lid tightly over them, closing out the moonlight. Darkness engulfed them and Tibil gave out a cry, thinking he heard something in the dark.

Now what?" Joyce asked. "We can't see a fucking thing."

"LUX!" Tyriano shouted, his voice boomed, reverberating all around them. His hand glowed like a hot, white ember, bathing the oubliette in its eerie light. "How's that for magic?" Tyriano asked smugly.

They looked around themselves and discovered that

they were definitely in a tight spot. The walls were made of dirty blocks, mold beginning to spread across them. The only other visible way out of the pit was a small drain pipe that ran off into the wall. "Where do we go now?" Edward asked.

Tyriano didn't answer, his attention was kept on the opposite wall. He walked towards it and slowly ran his hand over its surface, shining its light upon it. The others watched quietly, waiting to see if he would unleash Hell itself. He moved his hand faster as he found a thin line that seemed to glow back at him in its own light.

He followed that line with his hand, slowly it met with other lines and soon became an intricate spiral. Then he found what he sought, a glowing hand on the wall itself. He held his hand over the glowing one on the wall and it became obvious to all that the spiral originated there, blossoming outward like a golden spiral.

Tyriano placed his palm to the hand on the wall and the room shook. The others mumbled in fear, afraid of an unknown doom that may appear before them. The blocks of the wall began to glow, as brightly as Tyriano's hand, and separated, showering the floor with pebbles. They shifted and slid—like a complex puzzle box—until a tunnel lay before them.

It seemed manmade, with a beautifully shaped frame and smooth walls. If they hadn't seen it appear before them, none would have doubted it had been there the whole while. Tyriano leaned forward, his glowing hand crossing the magical threshold. It was easy then to see the slope that fell away into the darkness.

"We must hurry, the opening will only remain open for a moment or two," Tyriano said. "You must slide down to the main hall of the Underworld. Wait for me there." They lined up, and one by one, they went, spiraling downward, crying out in the dark.

Tyriano went last, wrapping his coat tight around

him. The ground rumbled once more and the passageway was gone. It was dark again, moist and empty, just as it was supposed to be.

🐘

The ride down was different for each of them. Some found it not easy to be swooshed along in the darkness, their bodies being shuffled around. Tibil wept and yelped like a puppy locked in a bathroom during a holiday party. Lily, on the other hand, was thrilled with it, hooting and hollering. It was nothing more than a rollercoaster for her.

Nicholas almost napped along the way … that's all. The slide just sort of lulled him to sleep. The others shared the same silent horror; their teeth gritted, their breath taking a quicker pace, trying to keep up with their heartbeats. Their minds cluttered with the same repetitive mantra; *ohgodohgodohgodohgodohgodohgodOHGOD!!*

They all spilled out of the slide at the bottom, becoming a pile of a nauseated rag dolls. Tibil came first, followed by Lily, who pounded down onto him, then all the rest. It was a surprise that none had vomited at any point.

They slowly stood in the faint light of torches that lined the curving walls. They seemed to be in a cobble-stoned hall that went on forever, always turning inward. All along the outside wall were holes similar to the one they had tumbled out from.

Tyriano stood amidst them, lifting his hand once more, reactivating the bright glow. He held his arm up and its light fell on a large oak door—impressive in size, but not design. "That is the door we must take," he slowly said. "But, before we do, I have to ask, are any of you Irish?"

"Why?" Joyce asked softly.

"No matter, *really*," Tyriano decided, "as long as none of you start speaking Gaelic."

They approached the door and it began to swing open on its own, slowly though, reluctantly giving way to the light of his passing hand. Dust escaped from the inside, tumbling up and out. With the dust came the strong stench of sweat and sulfur. It was a sufferable smell for only Tyriano, as he had been many times before.

They slowly stepped in; the light there was red and upon looking up they saw that the ceiling was made of rock. The rocks above were large, individual slabs that fit together like an archaic puzzle. They shifted and swayed above their strange pillars, as if they would tumble down.

Then one of the pillars moved slightly, and they saw that it was actually a man there—not rock—a giant of a man as well. His back was to the ceiling and he held his slab there, pushing against it, causing it to slightly shift back and forth. His face winced from pain and exertion, sweat flowing down his brow.

He wasn't alone either; each slab had its own giant doing the same. Each wore a furred toga, matted with dirt and sweat. They wore tattered sandals on their smelly feet.

"Who are they?" Joyce asked, in hushed terror.

"They are the Fir Bolg," Tyriano said, "They once made their home on the surface, just as the rest of you. Long ago they lived on a plush, green island, but they were fought and chased into the earth itself by the Irish."

"IRISH?!?" the nearest Fir Bolg cried, roused by the mere utterance of their foe.

"IRISH?" another called, starting off the others around them in a childish game of telephone.

"We hates the Irish," the first giant mumbled.

"THE FILTHY CREATURES!" Tyriano shouted theatrically, shaking a balled up fist.

"That they is," he said, agreeing with the Watcher. "None of you's Irish, is ya?" he asked of his company. They were all quick to shake their heads. The Fir Bolg left his rock hanging in the air, pinched between three others, and strode closer to them. He was easily fifteen feet tall.

He knelt before Lily, examining her closer. "You's gots hair like 'em," he said, a large finger touching her red locks. "Is you's sure you's ain't Irish?" He peered at her even closer with a large, accusatory eye and a toothy grin.

Lily shook her head furiously. "German," she quickly lied, "Guten tag." The giant seemed confused, scratching his head, showering the poor girl with its dander. Then he went back to doing his job—which was literally back-breaking labor.

"What are they doing?" Edward asked, watching the Fir Bolgs pushing their rock slabs towards heaven.

"They are holding up the plates of your world," Tyriano said, leading them through the Fir Bolg. "Literally holding the weight of the world on their shoulders. It's a horribly tough job, but someone must do it," he said with a laugh.

"When they first came down here, it was the only job for them. They pleaded, saying there was no place left for them on the surface, so the Maker said they could stay."

"The Maker?" Edward spat with excitement. "Do you mean God? … He's real?"

"Of course he's real," Tyriano said with a bewildered glance. "Do you think we—the Watchers—could have made all of this? No, it was the Maker … or, 'God' as you call him. He is truly a great and powerful being."

"Is he nice?" Lily innocently asked.

"How should I know," he huffed, walking faster.

"What, haven't you met him?"

"No, in fact, I don't know any who have."

"How's that possible?" Camilla chimed in as she stepped around a particularly stout Fir Bolg.

"He has been gone for quite some time," Tyriano said, shocking everyone that listened. They all seemed plagued by old doubts born from late night conversations held long ago. Conversations infested with arguments about evolution, creationism, and the old idea of a God that didn't care.

"Gone how?" Lily asked. She was saddened by it all, but Edward could not comfort her; the idea of touching her with Nicholas' hand was too much for him. Nicholas watched awkwardly as Edward let his hand fall to his side.

"I had hoped not to go into all of this," Tyriano said, halting. "But, seeing how you all are so inquisitive, I might as well take this moment to have a rest." Tyriano looked around and found a fairly beefy Fir Bolg calf to sit upon.

"The Maker made this world and all others. It was over two thousand years ago that he grew bored, watching you all down here, futzing about. By that time, most of the work was being done by the Watchers, all that was left for him to do was continue creating animals, which we all can agree there are enough of them already.

"The lethargy soon turned into sadness. The life he had created was so enthralling, with all the births and deaths and everything in between, all things he would never experience. He had a grand plan, but it all changed with you people. You broke his mold … began to change it all on your own, and he became obsessed with you.

"So, he went to the Watchers—those like myself— and said he wanted to be with *you*, to experience life for himself. He enlisted the wisest of us, at the time, to oversee everything in his absence. But, the High Council protested against this *experiment*; they didn't feel it was right for him to go down and mingle with you humans.

"But, he was the Maker! Who could say no to him? He took off on his sabbatical, but was only supposed to be gone for a short while. He was to live one life here on Earth, then straight back. That was the plan."

"You mean Jesus?" Lily asked.

"Yes, that was the Maker," Tyriano smiled. "But in the end, one life was not enough for him. He had to live more … live longer, do great things, and see the beautiful world he built. From death to another birth … over and over again. He became an addict."

"He never came back?"

"Not yet," Tyriano said with a wink. "Not yet … but, we have more pressing things. We need to make sure all is put right. My Uncle Tyrimus is afraid the elephant may stop again and never start."

"What happens then?" asked Edward.

"Well, the world will end, of course," Tyriano said matter-of-factly. "But fear not, we have it all under control." Tyriano stood then and brushed his coat off, looking up to thank the Fir Bolg for the rest as he did so.

They began to walk on, none of Tyriano's companions seemed relaxed by his story. But there was nothing else for them to do but follow. The ground shook as they went and there was a loud rumble.

"Is it happening now!?!?" Nicholas asked as he grabbed hold of a Fir Bolg's knee to steady himself.

"No," Tyriano said easily, "It's just a lazy Fir Bolg."

"Sorry," a nearby Fir Bolg said in a deep, sorrowful tone.

"But we must hurry or else it may happen again," Tyriano said, moving onward.

"Well, how will we stop it from happening again?" Edward asked, quickly following.

"All we need to do is get there," Tyriano said with confidence. "Uncle Tyrimus will know what to do."

21

Dezriak sat in his office with the dried lifeless corpse of Tyrimus sitting in the chair across from him. He marveled at it, the way it looked more like a poorly crafted clay doll than a thing that had once lived and breathed. The Gloom were efficient, that he was sure of, efficient and crafty.

They would soon do the same to Temelephas and Tyriano, Dezriak was anxious for it. *The power ...* he mused, *such power, in the Gloom.* He coveted it, wanted to be as powerful himself. *Yes,* he heard in his head. *You could be as powerful as we.*

I ... he corrected in his own mind, *I could be as powerful as* them. He shook his head; he was tired and anxious, a horrible combination. He almost believed the old corpse had been talking with him.

All you need ... is the hunger, the voice said, creeping through his mind, making him drowsy. *We know the* hunger, *it consumes us.* Dezriak tried to sit up further, but he found his body slumping further in his chair.

Let us fill you with it. Feed with us, and be just as powerful. The voice melded with Dezriak's mind, he could no longer tell if it was himself talking, or the voice. *All you need do ... is say yes.*

"I'm so tired," Dezriak mumbled, flopping his head to the table. He was so overwhelmed by it that he could not see the black sludge that seeped through the cracked walls.

Say yes, the voice pled *... say yes, then you can sleep ... then we will be one ... say yes ... then we will be more powerful than ever.*

Dezriak was fighting the sleep, not sure what the subconscious voice meant by any of it. *Damn you waking dream,* he said to himself. He couldn't feel the thin, black tendrils as they slowly crept up his leg, wrapping about it like hundreds of worms.

But we are *a dream ... a great, dark dream of ultimate power ... say yes ... be a part of that dream ... feel our strength ... our fury ... stand with us, in our greatest hour ... just ... say ... yes.*

"Yes," Dezriak finally said, able to fight no more. "A million times yes, just let me sleep." He mumbled the last bit, his head wavering as the black strands climbed higher, wrapping around his chest.

You are wise to join us, the voice said, comfortingly. *We chose the right vessel ... sleep,* it mumbled in his head. *Sleep ... we will do the rest ... sleep.*

Dezriak's head fell forward, thumping against the desk. The inky snakes continued on, covering his body, seeping in through his pores. The Gloom was very crafty, indeed, able to go and prosper anywhere that is dark and shadowy. Dezriak had been nothing more than that, a dark and shadowy place.

The Gloom poured into him, pushing his organs around to make room for its hefty, black mass. Dezriak slept, though found no rest; he became the plaything for the Gloom. It tortured him—using his own desires, fears, and frustrations; he belonged to *it* now.

No matter how loud he cried, his voice never poured from his lips. And silently he screamed and yelled in pain and fear. The Gloom traveled down all of his limbs, wrapping around his bones and muscles. It seeped into his brain and learned how it worked.

Slowly, the body of Dezriak rose from the desk chair, but not by his will, merely a vessel. Step by step, it walked, much like a baby learns its first steps. Dezriak screamed within himself and the Gloom laughed back at him, feeding more and more on his terror. The puppet had become the puppet master.

Temelephas grew used to being alone in his cavern, no longer minding the absence of the Watchers. The small human was awake once more. He could hear him cooing atop his head. Luckily, the child wasn't hungry—not yet at least—as there were no Minikins around to feed it.

But, how long could that last? He wondered. It was only a matter of time before that little mouth opened as wide as any cave and bellowed out. Temelephas lifted his trunk in the air and blew a long blast, trying to draw a Minikin out from hiding.

None came of course and he only wondered more why they would be gone. He felt a grumbling in his stomach, a pain that he knew could only be cured by his gruel. Oh, the misery … it always seemed to find Temelephas.

He felt weird then, a feeling as if being watched. But he could see no one there and heard nothing. Though when he turned his wheel, he was standing there, that miserable little Watcher, Dezriak.

He looked different than before, his face seemed darker, his grin more devilish. Temelephas felt fear, strong and sudden, like a vise around his heart. The feeling was new to him, like most emotions were, and the reason for this fear was unknown to him.

"Soon," the Watcher murmured to him through his wicked grin. "Soon, we will feed on you." He laughed, a long and gruesome one, a type of laugh that penetrates bone and flesh. "You …," he continued, "the Watchers … the world … then the universe. We consume all and leave nothing behind, but the Gloom."

Temelephas had no idea what he was talking about, but he knew he didn't like it. It sounded more nefarious than anything he had said before. The world? The universe? The Gloom? *What were those things?*

"In the beginning … there was *only* the Gloom. And in the end … there will be nothing more."

They crept, slowly down an ancient stairway, the kind that clings to the wall, descending down a chasm. The rock of these walls were a deep crimson, with deep crevices of black. The whole pit was humid, warm air coming up from far below. It carried with it rising ash, much like snow falling in reverse.

"Keep your eyes on the stairs," Tyriano called from the front of the company. "Don't peer down into the chasm, it will only dishearten you."

Edward certainly wasn't going to look. He just stepped carefully down—one foot at a time—his sweaty hand against the wall. His knees shook, just from thinking of the fall he would take if he were to slip. *What is with all the ash*, he wondered.

He knew he wouldn't like the answer. It was best *not* to know. *Just keep walking,* he reminded his legs, *pay no attention to the brain.*

They walked on and on, an endless trudge with no end in sight. As they went, the air got thicker, warmer; sweat began to drip down their faces. The only one who seemed comfortable was Tyriano, who at one point shed his coat and hat, flinging them into the red glow coming from below.

"How much farther?" Camilla called, her own face streaming with sweat.

"Not much," Tyriano said dismissively, continuing in his oddly strong, confident strides down the stairs. But it quickly became apparent to the others that Tyriano's idea of 'not much' varied greatly from their own. Further down they went; the air became so thick and hot it was like sitting in a steam box on a beach along the equator, dressed in wool.

The current of air got stronger and smelled more of sulfur as they went, blowing their hair upward. The ash cloud became thicker, too, its little flecks clinging to their clothing—getting into their mouths and nostrils when possible. It was close to unbearable for the surface dwellers who were used to cool, breezy air.

Tyriano halted, calling back for them to stop. The ash made it hard to see too far, but they could tell Tyriano was examining a wall. Finally, he seemed to find what he was looking for. He reached out with his hand and turned a small bit of stone that jutted out, no different looking than any other stone.

The wall swung in and Tyriano directed them in. They were quick to follow, wanting to get out of the oven. It didn't matter to them what they would find beyond that wall.

The door closed behind them when they all had passed through, leaving them in a dark, narrow cavern. All had to hunch down, except for Tibil, who was glad to finally be home in the tunnels of the core.

"You can lead here better than I," Tyriano said to his smallest companion, giving way to him. The little one took the lead, moving smartly through the dark. The others followed as best they could, each grasping hold of the one before them.

Lily was reminded of the haunted houses of her youth—the part where you were forced into a black maze.

It was a pretty scary thing back then—being stuck in the dark—unknown hands touching you in the deep black. It was pretty scary even now.

But they all found it to be a bit more comfortable. It was just as warm, but the humid air was gone and there was no drop to fear. All they had to worry about was getting cricks in their necks.

Tibil proved a very deft guide. He knew his way well and could see far in the dark of the caverns. It helped that he didn't move all that fast, either. It thrilled him, knowing that for once he had to slow his pace so the others could keep up.

They walked on and on, but each step brought them into a little bit more of an open tunnel, allowing them to lift their heads more and more. The further they went, the more light there was as well. At first it was firelight that bounced off of far off walls, curving through the moist tunnels. Then it was torches, spitting off magical flames.

They were able to walk normally by then, no longer needing to grab at each other. "Good work, Tibil," Tyriano said, and the rest of the company echoed his gratitude. But, Tibil's face seemed low, confused and worry struck. "What's wrong, my little friend?"

"We are so close to the Great Cavern," he said slowly.

"And that should be a reason to smile," the Watcher responded.

"But where are all the Minikins?" he asked. "Where are my friends and family? We shouldn't have gotten this far without seeing at *least* one of them." Tyriano hadn't thought of that before, but now the idea nested in his head.

"Odd," he murmured. He turned to the others and whispered. "Stay clear of shadows," he warned. "And tell me if you hear any voices that should not be there."

"Why?" Camilla asked.

"The Gloom," Tibil shuddered, knowing exactly to which Tyriano referred. The others asked about the Gloom, wanting to know what exactly they meant.

"It does no good to tell you about them," Tyriano said solemnly. "If we do meet them, you most likely will not survive. Nothing I tell you would help stave them off, and only scare you further."

They continued to walk in silence, no more questions were asked. It was for the best—their minds were already filled with terrible ideas as to how the world was going to end. Would it explode into dust, fall in on itself, or just ignite in a blaze of hellfire?

They tried their best to remain hopeful and it was easier to do as the tunnel became brighter and larger. There were more tunnels now, shooting off from either side of the one they walked, delving deeper into the black nooks aside them. They all peered down the tunnels, looking for any sign of Minikins so they could pass good news on to Tibil.

But they found none, and no matter how far and long they walked they wouldn't. Minikins—being small and clever beings—knew how to hide very well, when hiding was in need. *But, why would they need to hide at all?* Tibil wondered, *especially so close to the protection of the Core.*

The further they went, a loud and steady drumming began. The more they walked the thudding beat grew in volume. It set the others on guard, but was a welcome noise to Tyriano and Tibil. "What is that?" Edward called out.

"It's Temelephas!" Tyriano shouted. "It means we are nearly there." Tyriano was definitely set at ease by the sound of the beast's footsteps. He hadn't failed his uncle after all. *Things will be fine,* he thought.

That feeling of security was not long for his heart and mind. They reached the Great Cavern and his eyes immediately fell on Temelephas, the big gray elephant that dwelled so harmlessly in the Earth's core. Atop him sat the little baby, cooing happily. Tyriano could feel Joyce's anxiety building up behind him. But he held her back, much to her confusion.

Tyriano's face went sour quickly, and none knew why, save Tibil. There, against a far wall stood Dezriak ... eyeing Temelephas with his strange and vicious eye, free from his cage.

22

"How did you get free?" Tyriano bellowed as he charged into the cavern. Dezriak swung his head and looked at him quizzically, not a trace of surprise or fear on his face. He seemed to be thinking, devising the perfect answer.

"Free?" he muttered in an odd, harsh and deep voice. "It was a matter of patience." he spoke slowly, looking away from Tyriano, up into the shadows of the vast caverns above. "Anything is possible, given time ... it only takes patience."

"Where is Tyrimus?!?" he demanded. There was a slick, evil grin from Dezriak. It looked more vile than Tyriano dreamed Dezriak could manage, like a ghastly jack-o'-lantern.

"He ... is gone," Dezriak managed, his face slightly twitching. Tyriano was only then seeing the incongruities of Dezriak. There was the twitching, which first caught his attention; even his eyes twitched uncontrollably. Then there was the darker skin, just barely noticeable, as if a cloud hung over him. It made Tyriano feel ill at ease. "We ... saw to it."

"What do you mean by *we*?" Tyriano asked carefully, even though his heart already knew what was meant.

"Hello ... Tyriano," came a voice from the Watcher's right. He turned and saw the High Council standing there in their dimly glowing robes. "We are sorry to have had to sick the Gloom upon him."

"You ... monsters," Tyriano uttered, his body shuddering in anger. "Why would you do such a thing?"

"He stood in our way," one said.

"He betrayed his vow of secrecy," said another.

"I know there's more to it ... you mean more harm than you do good, my uncle told me as much."

"Your uncle," another began. "Was too afraid to handle the power that was laid before him. He was scared to make the choices that were necessary."

Dezriak remained quiet, watching the Council as they spoke. He smiled at them in a sick way. None of the High Council paid any attention as he slowly moved closer, creeping up next to them. Still, he eyed them.

"Only when you mean to end the world," Tyriano seethed. "That is against everything we stand for ... it's our duty to protect this world!"

"*We* must overlook the *whole* universe," the first said again. "Not only one, small planet. Why does it bother you so greatly? Why did it your uncle? These people are on track to destroy their world, anyway, why not jump forward in this short tale of humanity and euthanize them?"

"If they destroy themselves, well ... that would be on them. But they can change, they can be better. Trust me ... I know all too well how naïve and arrogant man can be ... But to end it for them... by choice? That is a monstrous act!"

"Well," the fourth Councilman began. "As you already pointed out ... we *are* monsters, Tyriano." The High Council laughed, even as Tyriano lifted a hand, trying to call on his abilities. But nothing happened. "You are powerless now, Tyriano, ever since you stepped foot in this cavern."

Tyriano looked at his hand as if his gaze might ignite his powers. He could hear the soft whimpering of his companions behind him and felt more sorrow. How could he have led them down here?

"You waltzed right into a trap," the second said. "He's no smarter than his uncle." They laughed again—a low, ominous thunder that rolled through the cavern.

"Dezriak," the first said, turning to their aide. "As soon as we leave, call the Gloom down. Make sure they're all dead, especially the elephant, then we will call you up before this world falls apart." Dezriak said nothing, only twitched and smiled.

"Dezriak?" the first repeated. "What's wrong with you … aren't you listening?"

"There's no need," he said, quiet and slow.

"No need for what?"

"To call the Gloom down," he was salivating, black little dribbles coming from his open mouth as he smiled.

"And why not?"

"Because," he muttered, his eyes tired and lazy; his voice on the verge of a maniacal laugh. "We … are here." Dezriak's mouth fell open then, and a thick dark cloud fled out of it, engulfing the Council like a swarm of locusts. Their cries were quickly drowned out by the explosive noise of the murky cloud bursting forth.

"The Gloom!" Tyriano shouted. He had never seen anything like it, never even thought something like it was possible. He watched as the massive cloud made easy work of the remaining members of the High Council. *How can this be?*

The black cloud slowly slipped away from the pile of bodies, slow and lethargic, like overfed pigs. Its miserable voices could be heard in all their heads … sounding satisfied, licking their fingers. All that remained were the shriveled up husks of the Council, cloaked in white robes. Not a drop of blood was spilled.

The cloud slinked back into the body of Dezriak and he glared at Tyriano. "Dezriak?" Tyriano asked.

"You speak to the Gloom," he said, his voice slightly different, darker and thick, as if many spoke.

"So, I take it Dezriak is dead?"

"No, he is in here with us, he is alive," the Gloom said with that same twisted smile. "Though, he wishes he were not."

"Get the baby," Tyriano said, turning to the shaky people he had brought along. He had no idea what they could do, but he wanted to be prepared for whatever may happen.

"What are *they* doing?" the Gloom asked, its voice like a grumbling stomach. Its eyes followed the group of humans as they walked slowly towards the chained elephant.

"The baby that sits upon the elephant ... he belongs to the woman, here," Tyriano said, drawing the attention of the Gloom, his arms wide open and shaking. "All she wants is to have him back." Tyriano's voice quaked, breaking and tearful.

The Gloom swelled with joy. Here ... a Watcher was groveling before the Gloom. *Should have always been this way*, it thought. *Certainly, it should have been.* "She can have him for the remainder," it said softly.

"Remainder?" Tyriano asked.

"Of their lives." *Not long*, the words bounced into Tyriano's head. *Soon ... not soon enough ... be patient ... we've been patient long enough.*

"And how long will that last?" Tyriano asked, calmly. "Please ... tell me."

"Not long," it sneered. It watched as the woman stood beside the elephant's path. Temelephas seemed to acknowledge them and the baby that cried for its mama. *We can do it now ... silence ... but it would be so easy ... we must wait, need to grow stronger ... we are strong enough.*

"You can't last long in that body," Tyriano said, watching it twitch and sweat with a black fever.

"You know nothing of the Gloom," it growled. *Take him now ... no ... Tear him to shreds, let this cavern fill with his painful howl ... be still.* "We ... we are stronger than ... than you know." *Then why wait? ... Be quiet.*

"It looks like that body can't hold you much longer," Tyriano said, glancing at the elephant's wheel. "It looks like a tattered coat, falling apart at the seams."

"It doesn't have to last much longer," *do it ... do it ... we have waited long enough!* Temelephas scooped the baby up from his back, handing him to his mother with his trunk.

"What do you hope to gain?" Tyriano asked, watching as the tearful mother carried her baby away, holding him close to her. "What do you get for destroying this world?"

"We get *our* home back," *home ... we are so close ...* "We will get the cold, cold dark." *give it to us ... enough with the talking ...* "We will feed and grow stronger ... fill the void left by the Maker ... We will take this universe back." *do it ... do it, now ... do it ... DO IT!!*

Dezriak's body began to crack, like a porcelain doll. The face still held that grizzly grin, even as pieces of it fell away. Tyriano backed away from him, knowing all too well that this would not lead to anything desirable. There was a loud crash as the body exploded, a black, thick mass rising in its place.

It rose—looming over head—taking on the form of a giant made of black ink, more solid than smoke. It was slimy, dripping big globs of itself to the cavern floor, only to have the drippings slowly creep back to it. "Oh, by the Maker," Tyriano whispered in prayer.

"*FEED*," it howled. "*DESTROY!!*" Its mouth was a black abyss, sticky strands of black straining across the opening. Tyriano raised his hand, but was reminded that he was powerless when nothing happened.

236 / M. P. McVey

The Gloom moved towards Temelephas, but only slowly, not used to moving in such a way. "Don't let him near the elephant," Tyriano cried out.

"How are we supposed to stop it?" Edward asked in a bewildered shriek.

"Any way you can," Tyriano shouted. "Try torches … it hates the flames … light of any kind." Edward and Lily ran down a small cavern, seeking the torches they had passed earlier. It took some doing but they were able to wrench them from the wall.

When they made it back to the main Cavern, they found Nicholas and Camilla there, both holding their own torches. "Get Joyce," Edward shouted, "You four find a safe corner and stay there … keep the baby safe."

"But we can help fight it off, four flames are better than one," Camilla said.

"Just go, keep Lily with you."

"I'm not leaving you here," Lily said, tears streaming down her face. She paid no attention to the Gloom as it stumbled forward.

"It's not up to you," he said firmly, tears in his own eyes. "I love you." Lily wept, struggling as Nicholas dragged her away, trying to comfort her. But Nicholas' words had little effect when they came with the sound of Edward's voice. Camilla handed her torch to the real Edward, smiling at him.

Edward turned to the Gloom as it moved forward. It laughed as he swung his torches back and forth. "*You mean to harm us?*" it asked as it got closer. Edward swung harder, lunging dangerously close to the darkness. He could hear voices in his head, evil voices … telling him things he never wanted to hear.

The torches seemed to do nothing, it was like flicking match heads at the dark monster. The Gloom laughed harder, even as Tyriano was doing the same from behind it. "*Hope is so funny,*" it laughed. "*So delicious.*"

The Gloom turned suddenly ... its hollow eyes peering down on Tyriano. The Watcher stood there defiantly, his shoulders back and chest out. He waved his torch back and forth, screaming into the face of the Gloom. Then the black sea crashed down upon him.

There was no cry from Tyriano as the Gloom came down, just the slight whimpering of him as it fed. Edward felt his stomach turn and his knees shake. He could hear the cries of Lily from behind him, hear his own voice as Nicholas tried to hush her.

The Gloom rose once more and turned to him. Edward could not bear to look at the old Watcher, not even to steal a glance. Instead, he focused his eyes on the black beast before him, tried to be as brave as Tyriano had been.

"Why don't you go away?" Edward asked, his voice saturated with fear. The Gloom only laughed back at him, its tendrils stretching towards him along the ground. "Why do this at all?" Edward wept.

"Why not?" it seethed—snagging Edward by the leg. Edward was ripped from the ground and swung in the air like an abused stuffed animal. He hit the wall of the cavern hard and slid to the ground.

The Gloom then eyed the elephant, drooling as it stared. Temelephas lifted his trunk and blew a powerful blast, but continued his walk. The Gloom fell on Temelephas and he gave off a great cry as the black mass slammed him to the ground.

"Stop him!" Camilla cried out, shaking her brother.

"How?" Nicholas howled, fear strewn across his face.

Temelephas shrilled in pain, the black beast holding him down, his wheel shattered. The earth shook around them and Joyce wept, clutching at her baby. Lily ran to Edward's side and held his head in her lap, crying for him to wake up.

"Throughout all of your life," Camilla wept, "You've

done nothing ... absolutely nothing ... you just sat by and watched life go on around you." She grabbed her brother and held him close to her, whispering to him, "Don't let me believe you would do the same as it ended."

Nicholas looked over his shoulder and watched as the dark monster fed on Temelephas, draining his life away. The ancient elephant writhed as the blackness pinned him to the ground, his tusks wrenching back and forth. The walls began to crumble ... first pebbles ... then rocks slid down the cavern walls. *The world is ending*, he thought to himself as he stood, hoisting his torch.

He walked towards the monster, calling out to it. *The world is ending*, he reminded himself. *What harm can it do?* "Over here!" he cried as he began to run at it. He swung madly with his torch, the dark fleeing from wherever its fiery light touched it.

The Gloom reeled up, leaving the elephant heaving for breathe beneath it. It eyed him carefully, pulling away, the noise of the earth shuddered around them all. *"Wait,"* it called, backing from Nicholas.

"Get back!" Nicholas howled. Camilla ran to Temelephas' side, placing her hand on his large chest. Temelephas looked at her—fear and tears in his eyes; he stroked her arm with his weary trunk.

"He's dying!" she shouted, crying at the gentle touch of such a large beast. "He's dying, Nicky!!"

"Stay back!!" Nicholas howled at the black beast. The walls in the cavern began to crack, large gaping cracks that crept down them.

"We know you ..." the Gloom seethed. *Could it be ... no, it's impossible ... but it is, it is, just look at him ... he's only human ... no, look again—look closer.* Nicholas' head ached from the voice of it, confused by its words.

"It is you ... you thought you could fool us?" the Gloom asked.

"What?" Nicholas asked. *He doesn't know ... quiet ...*

he's powerless to us in this form ... I said shut up. Then through the voices, Nicholas could hear other voices ... millions upon millions of voices. All crying out for help ... all calling for him.

"*You can do nothing to us, Maker,*" the Gloom chuckled. "*You are trapped in that frail ... weak body.*"

"Maker?" he asked. *We told you ... he doesn't know ... quiet ... it makes no difference now.* "I'm not the Maker!"

The Gloom crept closer to Nicholas, laughing as it went. Nicholas could only wave his torch at it, still unsure what he could do. The walls began to fall away ... empty silence of space coming in, flinging the rocks and pebbles around.

"*It is over ... Maker ... and you have finally lost to the Gloom.*" The Gloom engulfed the man that stood before it. Nicholas cried out in pain, feeling the black cloud grabbing at him, seeping into him.

Nicky ... the voice called in his mind. *Fight it, Nicky ...* Mom, he thought. *What it says is true.* But, it couldn't be ... there's no way. *But it is, Nicky ... you've always known it ... somewhere deep down ...* no ... *you knew you were different.*

But not like this, he said to himself ... *don't be afraid ... the power is in you ... you just have to tap into it ...* no, I can't ... *you can, you must ... the world depends on it ... don't be afraid ... all you have to do, is just ...*

"Fight it, Nicky!!" Camilla cried, calling him back out of his mind, the vacuum of space pulling at her hair and clothing. He could feel the Gloom forcing its way into him, prodding at his insides. *Fight it ... give in, go easy ...*

He could feel his own life, slipping away. He felt weary. He felt crushed ... Then he felt something else ... *fight, Nicky.* He felt a tiny spark inside him ... something that had lay dormant for more years than he could count ... *you are too weak ... FIGHT IT!!*

Nicholas gave off a loud cry, a wail that shook what remained of the Earth's core, even as it fell away into

nothing. There came a bright, deafening explosion of light, erupting from within him and the Gloom cried in horror and disbelief. The light filled all, engulfing everything.
Then it was gone ... all was gone.

.... all was quiet and darkness, then.

23

There was nothing. The murky blackness of it was everywhere and silence dwelled within it. That was all there was. Everything else had fallen out of existence in the blink of an eye, even the Gloom. And none had seen it coming.

Once, there was life ... on Earth and throughout the Universe. It bloomed and changed, evolved and fluttered, then it was gone. Like a light switch had been turned off.

It was all empty and useless space. Not a speck of light was shining in all of existence—all stars had been extinguished. All was nothing more than a great, black canvas waiting for the painter's brush stroke.

...... Then, Temelephas was there. He floated, alone—in the darkness.

All he remembered was being in unbelievable pain before and now it was gone. Confusion swept over him. He was tired ... he was scared. Loneliness filled him. The darkness around him was so vast that he feared becoming a part of it.

Then, as if summoned by his own, silent pleading ... a soft light appeared before him—piercing the darkness. The light was a small, flickering kind—like that of a dying candle—playing against his rough, gray face. As tiny as that light was, it somehow brought Temelephas comfort.

He could see now that he was no longer bound to his wheel, no chains dug into his flesh. Odder than that was the fact that he stood on no ground at all, just empty darkness beneath his feet. Save for the soft, flickering light, everything around him was dark and empty.

"Temelephas ... my poor friend," a voice called to him from out of the darkness. It was a familiar voice, but he could not place it. So he waited ... not afraid ... not eager ... just, waited.

"All of this is my fault," the figure said, stepping into the soft light. "I should never have bound you to that awful wheel." Temelephas frowned, feeling the guilt rush from the speaker's words.

Nicholas—once again in his old, worn body—stepped closer to the elephant, laying his gentle hands on the cracked skin of his face. "In the beginning, it was easy ... I thought I knew it all. Making land, water, and sky ... it's always easy in the beginning ... I never knew the pain that could come from it."

Temelephas looked at his Maker, watched as the tears slipped from his eyes. "I never meant to hurt you. Never meant to *hurt* at all. For that, I am sorry ... but, it's all over now, anyway."

Temelephas cried. *Over,* he thought, *how can that be?*

"You can speak," Nicholas whispered to him, "Go on ... let me hear your voice."

"How ... can it ... be ... over?" his voice boomed, raspy and soft and new. He liked the sound of it, his voice.

"Things end, my friend."

"But ... what I did ... my walk?" Temelephas said anxiously. "It had purpose ... no?"

"It had great purpose," Nicholas said with a tearful smile. "Life ... life grew on the rock you spun ... Life happened because of the sacrifices you made."

"And ... life is good, yes?"

"Life is great."

"But … if life is great … why let it end?" he asked, wrapping his trunk around Nicholas, holding him close. Temelephas wept, thinking of his home—unwanted or not. Remembering how life had touched him, even momentarily through the hand of Camilla.

"Life isn't over," Nicholas said with a gentle laugh. "Life can never end. I don't think even *I* could end *all* of life … It's too strong … too runs too deeply inside of everything. I meant the part of you suffering is over … you will never have to push your wheel again."

"Then what will become of me?"

"You, sweet Temelephas … all that is left for you to do, is live." Temelephas laughed, a strong, sturdy belly chuckle. "Now, to find a place for you in the universe … I don't think Earth will do."

"Why not?"

"I think a giant, immortal elephant—walking around and chatting—might just be too much for those humans, don't you think?" he asked with a smile. Temelephas shrugged his ears, trying to mirror the smile back as best he could. "So, where would you like to call home?"

"Hmmmm," the great elephant mumbled. "I don't *really* know anything more than my wheel."

"Good point," Nicholas said with a wink. "How about you leave it to me then … creating things is my specialty." Temelephas gave him a clumsy nod and Nicholas snapped his fingers.

🐘

They stood in a great, rolling field with a cotton candy hued sky swirling overhead—a bright sun falling over the hills in the distance. Surrounding them were acacia trees and peanut plants, all bearing sweet treats. The wind blew and Temelephas felt it against his face and in his long, gray hair—it thrilled him.

"It's so beautiful," the elephant said.

"It's all yours," Nicholas smiled. "I hope you don't mind that I brought the Minikins here, as well. They needed a place to live as much as you did, and I thought you could use the company."

Temelephas looked around again, his eyes growing accustomed to the light, and saw that they were there. They moved between little huts that sat upon a hill, confused and excited all at once. Tibil was there—running wildly as he pushed a hotdog cart—screaming to his kin to come and sample them.

"Thank you," Temelephas said as he watched the little ones run and play.

"No problem," Nicholas said. "And if you ever need anything, be sure to just ask." He gave the elephant a gentle pat on his head. "Oh, but you must promise me one thing."

"What's that?"

"Enjoy your life," and with that Nicholas was gone. Temelephas stood alone, but only for a moment. Then he was greeted by the Minikins as they ran up to him.

They embraced him warmly and laughed when they heard his voice for the first time. Temelephas smiled again, slowly getting used to doing so. The Minikins were anxious to explore and begged for him to follow. Temelephas was more than happy to oblige them.

They began to walk and Tibil tugged on his trunk. "Wait until you see the stars," he whispered. Temelephas laughed for the first time, finding he couldn't wait to see them, regardless of what stars might be.

The old elephant walked in a straight line ... for the first time in his existence. He thought that too was funny, so he laughed. It felt good, this laughing ... the way his chest tightened around his heart and his breath burst out of him in a joyous eruption. He planned to do it as often as he could, and he would have plenty of opportunities.

Epilogue

The organ music echoed through the church, shaking the stained glass even as it splattered dim, colorful light around. The priest stood quietly before them all, waiting for that one pesky cougher to have his way before beginning.

Cough.

"Dearly beloved," he called out loudly over the couple's heads, reaching out over a sea of faces. "We are gathered here today to share in the celebration of the union of Lily and Edward."

Lily was nothing more than a smile with legs and arms, and Edward looked as if he could have sweated through three sticks of antiperspirant. He smiled back, if only a bit nervously.

"We are here, *not* to witness the beginning of a relationship," the priest continued. "But, to *recognize* a bond that has already existed ... Love *lives* within this bond. The world is a place filled with joy and despair. We traverse it ... searching for a higher meaning."

"Excuse me," Lily butted in with a whisper. The priest looked aghast at the intrusion, but hey ... it was her day after all.

"Yes?" he whispered back.

"Can we have a moment?"

"By all means," he said with a forced smile.

"I just want to make sure," she whispered to Edward.

"Again?" he asked, nervously eyeing all of his family and friends; they watched the halted ceremony with morbid fascination. "How many times do we have to do this?"

"Last time," she whispered.

"Promise?" She nodded with a smile. Edward couldn't resist Lily or her many smiles. "Ok ... shoot."

"What do I say is the scariest movie I've ever seen?"

Edward smiled, snorting. "*White Chicks*, starring the Wayans brothers," he said and she lightly laughed. "Why is that again?"

"Because they remind me of Jeremy Irons in *The Time Machine* and he was super creepy in that," she said hastily.

"Then why isn't *The Time Machine* the scariest?"

"*Hello* ... because there's two of them in *White Chicks!*" She smiled at him once more, then turned to the priest, "Sorry ... you can continue." The priest straightened his back and cleared his throat, trying to remember where he left off.

Camilla sat alone at the rear of the church. She wore a pretty dress that she felt made her look more like a flower than a person. It was odd to be there alone, though. Sure, she saw Joyce and Franklin—smiling and waving from across the aisle—but in truth ... she was alone.

It was nice of them to have invited her—given the strange way they had met. She looked forward to meeting all of their friends and families. They were certain to be happy and at ease, seeing how none of them remembered the earth dying.

One second, they had all been crying at the center of the earth, watching the walls of the great cavern fall away, the next they were sitting in the park. Nothing had changed ... everything was the way it was meant to be. It was as if none of it had happened.

Joyce had gotten her son back and Lily had gotten her Edward back in body *and* mind. It seemed unfair to Camilla, seeing how it was her alone that had lost anything. She found it hard to live on knowing her brother was gone. The worst was that no one seemed to care. It was as if *he* never happened, either.

He's not dead, she thought, finding comfort in that alone. *Gods never die ... they just continue to live on in the back of our minds and in our hearts, lingering there until we need them to come again. Then they always come.*

"And, I always will," Nicholas said from beside her. She turned towards his voice and gasped, never expecting to see his face again ... or in a suit.

"Like it?" he asked, seeing her eye his white suit, so bright it seemed to glimmer.

"Seems a bit gaudy," she quietly said, brushing tears from her eyes. "Only the bride is supposed to wear white."

"I don't think anyone will object," he said with that same, Nicholas smile. "You're the only one that can see me."

She grabbed him and felt his warmness against her, crying into his shoulder like a lost child. She held him so tight, afraid that if she loosened her grip on him that he would slip away.

"I can't stay," he whispered to her. "You know that."

"Then how cruel of you to come at all," she sobbed into his shoulder. Her mind flashed over their lives together, pictures of them as children, even grainy in her mind. "Don't leave me," she quietly begged.

"There's too much to do," he said, gently patting her back as he always had. "I have neglected far too much for far too long."

"I need you," she whimpered. "I can't let you go."

"Shhhh," he said. "Don't say that."

"I can't help it … you're my brother and I love you."

"I know," he said, looking guiltily at her. "I love you, too." *You can't do this*, he told himself. *It isn't right.* "You'll always be my sister … that will never change." *But it should, if only for her sake.*

"Will I see you again?"

"Of course," he said, tears peeking out the corners of his eyes … *be careful not to make promises you cannot keep.* "I just can't say when or how. But … I'll always be watching you." He kissed her cheek, letting his lips linger there … savoring the moment, trying to make the memory last.

"Will you miss it?" she asked, sniffling.

"What?"

"You know … life?" she asked with a sniffle.

Nicholas thought on the question, looking around at the church filled with people. Family, friends … all of them strangers to one another, here celebrating love.

"Yes," he said. "I'll miss *being* alive … I'll miss the smell of everything, even those things that smell bad." She chuckled. "I'll miss the sound of laughter, such a wild and strange thing … I'll miss the people and all the chaos they create and endure."

"And what will you miss most of all?"

Nicholas smiled at her, knowing there was only one possible answer. "You," was all he said. She smiled and he knew she wanted him to stay and knew too well that he couldn't. *You never should have let them remember,* he scolded himself. *None of them.*

He knew she would live the rest of her life crying, wanting to have him near, but never being able to. She would always be sad for him. He could see it in her future, simply by looking into her eye—a sad woman that can't move on. *That's no way to live,* he told himself. *That's no way at all.*

He stood, wordlessly, brushing his jacket. *It needs to be done*, he told himself. "Oops," he said as something fell from his pocket. Camilla bent over, grasping a silver pen with her hand, feeling the coolness of it ... dazzled by the light that reflected off of it.

So strange, she thought, *to pay so much attention to such a thing as a pen*. She shook her head. "You dropped this," she said, sitting back up. The man that stood there smiled as she handed it to him.

"I would lose my head if it wasn't sewn on," he said with an odd smile. Camilla smiled back, but only out of politeness. "Thank you," he said again. "For everything." Then the man walked away, heading for the church doors.

What a strange man, Camilla thought as she watched him go. *First to leave a wedding early, then to wear white ... only the bride is supposed to wear white*. The stranger was gone then and Camilla was fine with that and smiled. She went back to watching the ceremony, and being happy.

Winter beat against the front of the church, its cold wind having no effect on the warmth that hummed within. All of Columbus still bustled with Christmas cheer; people raced about to visit friends and family, running errands. But none saw the strange man that stood on those church steps in his gaudy, white suit.

Nicholas stood there for a moment, breathing in the frosty air with a goofy grin. He looked around as if trying to cement the image in his mind, so he might remember this moment for all time. It would be hard, he admitted to himself ... leaving all of this behind, though he knew it wouldn't be forever.

He walked down the frozen steps of the church as he began to hum the tune to his favorite song. The sun broke through the clouds as God stepped into the street. The ice and snow retreated from his path as if spring itself sprung from the soles of his feet—and he sang.

But we are a dream ...

a great, dark dream of

ultimate power ... say yes ...

be a part of that dream ...

feel our strength ...

our fury ...

stand with us, in our

greatest hour ...

just ...

say...

yes.

M.P. McVey lives in Columbus, Ohio with his supportive and patient girlfriend, Laura, and a one-eyed cat named Stanley. He creates worlds filled with magic and intrigue, drawing upon the city and people that surround him for inspiration.

All that he accomplishes in his life is due to the support from friends, and family.

Like him. Follow him.

www.facebook.com/mpmcvey

@mpmcvey

Check out other works and essays by M.P. McVey over at his blog!

www.mpmcvey.wordpress.com